D0458730

The
Adventures
of a
Girl Called
BICYCLE

The Adventures of a Girl Called BICYCLE

Christina Uss

Margaret Ferguson Books

Holiday House • New York

Margaret Ferguson Books

Copyright © 2018 by Christina Uss

Map art copyright © 2018 by Jonathan Bean

Printed and Bound in March 2018 at Maple Press, York, PA USA

First Edition

1 3 5 7 9 10 8 6 4 2

Library of Congress Cataloging-in-Publication Data

Names: Uss, Christina, author.

Title: The adventures of a girl called Bicycle / Christina Uss.

Description: First edition. | New York : Margaret Ferguson Books, Holiday
House, [2018] | Summary: Left at the Mostly Silent Monastery as a toddler
and home-schooled by a retired nun, twelve-year-old Bicycle rides
cross-country to meet a famous cyclist who she hopes will be her first friend.

Identifiers: LCCN 2017028847 | ISBN 9780823440078 (hardcover)

Subjects: | CYAC: Bicycles and bicycling—Fiction. | Voyages and
travels—Fiction. | Friendship—Fiction. | Nuns—Fiction.
Monasteries—Fiction. | Foundlings—Fiction.

Classification: LCC PZ7.1.U98 Adv 2018 | DDC [Fic]—dc23 LC
record available at https://lccn.loc.gov/2017028847

To Jack and Susannah, who cheer me on

CONTENTS

The
Adventures
of a
Girl Called
BICYCLE

THE MOSTLY
SILENT MONASTERY

The front door to the Mostly Silent Monastery was missing.

Sister Wanda Magdalena walked up the front steps and started to reach for the doorknob that wasn't there. She stopped, pursed her lips, and put her doorknob-reaching hand on her hip. Examining the wide door frame, she saw three stainless-steel hinges attached to nothing. Luckily, Sister Wanda had chosen to retire years ago from being a Nearly Silent Nun. She could use her voice to say anything she wanted to, and she had something to say right now.

"Big Al!" she yelled. "Where are you? Please hang the front door immediately! This place can't be mostly silent without a door to keep out the noise!"

When Big Al, the construction worker in charge of finishing the brand-new building, didn't answer or appear, Sister Wanda sighed. Move-in day for the Mostly Silent Monks at 65 Monastery Lane in Washington, D.C., had officially happened yesterday, but the building still had a lot of odds and ends that were not quite right. Some of the light switches didn't switch. The hot-water faucets squeaked. And the pesky front door had needed to be taken down and rehung in order to close properly. Sister Wanda never settled for not-quite-right and had presented Big Al with a list of problems and strict instructions that every item on it would need to be completed and shipshape by six o'clock today—or else. It looked as though one of the workers had gotten as far as taking the door down but not as far as putting it back up.

Sister Wanda went into the front hallway, zigzagging around heaps of empty cardboard boxes. She could see the door leaning against a wall with its shiny new nameplate MOSTLY SILENT MONASTERY—OPEN TO THE PUBLIC. A little girl crouched next to it. Her scruffy black hair stuck up every which way. She was dressed in a faded pink T-shirt decorated with a drawing of a bike and the word BICYCLE printed in block letters. She blinked up at Sister Wanda and clutched the bottom of the shirt, which was two sizes too large.

"Goodness me, leave the front door off its hinges and look what finds its way inside!" Sister Wanda said, wading through the boxes. "Come with me," she ordered, taking the girl's hand and guiding her toward the office.

Sister Wanda and the little girl sat on opposite sides of Sister Wanda's big desk. "All right, my child," the nun said, pulling out a yellow pad and a sharp pencil. Sister Wanda had plenty of yellow pads and sharp pencils. Since all the monks of the monastery had vowed to be Mostly Silent, the monastery had hired Sister Wanda when she retired to do the sorts of things that require a lot more talking than silence, like answering phones, making sure deliveries got where they were supposed to go, scheduling washing-machine repairmen, and supervising the construction of the new monastery building. She was the kind of person who relished getting a job done, and she rarely missed her days of following the Nearly Silent Nuns' vows. But she did continue wearing the Nearly Silent Nuns' black robe because she found it to be nicely intimidating to those who questioned her authority. The plain black garment resembled a traditional nun's habit, although the Nearly Silent order had never bothered with any elaborate head coverings and simply went without them.

"We need to figure out who you are and where you ought to be. What can you tell me about yourself? Name? Address? How you came to be hiding in our hallway?" she said.

The girl didn't say a word.

"Not talking, hmmm? Is that because you haven't learned how, or because you haven't got anything to say?" Sister Wanda peered into the girl's face. "How many years old are you? This many?" Sister Wanda held up three fingers. The little girl just stared back. Sister Wanda leaned forward in her chair, tapping the pencil against her short silver hair. "Silent as can be. Well, you'll fit in perfectly around here," she said.

Big Al jogged into the office. "Excuse me, Sister," he said. "Something slipped my mind with the long list of items you gave me, but I've remembered now, and it's quite import—" He broke off suddenly when he saw the girl in the pink shirt sitting in Sister Wanda's office. "Oh, you've found her yourself. Okay, then, I'm off to check on the light switches."

"Big Al," Sister Wanda said in her no-nonsense tone.

Big Al stopped in his tracks.

"What do you know about this little girl?" Sister Wanda demanded, her frosty blue eyes fixed on the workman.

"I'm sorry, Sister—I spotted her sitting on the front steps at the same time the replacement faucets were delivered. When I asked her why she was there, she wouldn't answer. Because you were very, very clear that things needed to be 'shipshape by six o'clock or else' and I didn't want to find out what the 'or else' meant, I tucked her away safe and told her to stay put until I could drop the faucets off upstairs and get the boys started on replacing them." Big Al looked sheepish. "I guess I should have dropped *her* off first."

"Yes," Sister Wanda agreed. "Now, details. Did you see anyone nearby who may have left her?"

"I didn't see anyone, Sister. But," Big Al continued, "there used to be a public lost-and-found office on this very spot before we built the monastery. Maybe someone thought

6

this was still a place to drop off lost items . . . and maybe lost children." He shrugged.

"That's it?"

"Well, the faucets are done."

"How about the front door?" Sister Wanda said.

Big Al raised his hands. "I'm on it."

Another worker in the hallway shouted for him, asking how to tell if light switches were installed upside down or right side up.

Big Al rubbed his forehead. "Please excuse me," he said as he jogged off.

After that, Sister Wanda found she didn't have much to say, so the girl and the nun eyed each other in silence for some time.

If you don't live near a Mostly Silent Monastery, you may wonder what they are. The Mostly Silent Monasteries are part of an old and venerated order, founded centuries ago by a monk named Bob. One day, Bob observed that the human body is made with two ears but only one mouth. He felt this meant that we humans are supposed to listen more than we speak, and so he vowed to be Mostly Silent and dedicated his life to listening to others.

Bob decided on being *Mostly* Silent because he knew if he took vows of total silence he wouldn't be able to call for help in an emergency or politely agree if someone said it was a nice day or ask for a sandwich, so he cut down his vocabulary to what he called the Sacred Eight Words: "yes," "no," "maybe," "help," "now," "later," "sleep," and "sandwich." It turned out with eight words plus a few hand gestures, a person can get across a lot of meaning.

People went to visit Bob if their friends or family didn't pay enough attention to them. Each person would talk as much as he or she wanted while Bob listened. It seems very simple, but it was brilliant, too—centuries ago, just like today, people really liked to be listened to. Soon more monks joined Bob in taking vows of Mostly Silence and dedicating their lives to listening to others, and the order was begun. Bob's cousin Euphemia started a branch of Nearly Silent Nunneries, which proved to be equally popular and were staffed entirely by women who also used the Sacred Eight Words. Eventually, there were Mostly Silent Monasteries and Nearly Silent Nunneries in most U.S. states and around the globe. They were open to the public, so anyone could go to one any day of the week and talk about anything they wanted, for as long as they wanted, and a monk or a nun would sit there and listen, guaranteed.

Over the years, the Mostly and Nearly Silent orders had debated adding some new words to the Sacred Eight Words, but the debates hadn't come to anything. One word the monks and nuns had pondered was "Duck!" (A young monk had proposed this new word after a painful incident with a flying Frisbee.)

The Mostly Silent Monastery where Sister Wanda and the little girl now sat had replaced a decrepit old building on the other side of the city. In addition to public listening, this new monastery also served as a home for monks-in-training. Construction had taken longer than expected, so the monks were ready to move in before the building was entirely ready for them. That explained the cardboard boxes and the front door in the hallway. It did not, however, explain why the little girl was there, too.

Sister Wanda spent the rest of the day on the phone, calling hospitals, police stations, schools, hotels, and even the zoo, trying to figure out where this quiet child belonged. No one knew who she was. No one appeared to be missing a girl in a pink T-shirt. So Sister Wanda proposed to the Top Monk and the older head monks that it would be best if the girl stayed with them until someone showed up to claim her.

The Top Monk said, "Sandwich," by which he meant, "Of course, let's make her feel right at home here." (The Top Monk was the oldest and most silent of the monks, and had managed to cut down his vocabulary to one word: sandwich. It was amazing what he could communicate by saying "sandwich" with different inflections in his voice.)

The other monks replied, "Yes," and that was that.

During her first evening at the monastery, the little girl poked her head inside a cavernous room and saw rows upon rows of monks of all sizes, shapes, and nationalities dressed in pale blue robes, kneeling on square pillows, eyes closed. This was an Advanced Listening class. Quiet as a piece of cotton blowing across the floor, she padded into the room, perched on a pillow, and closed her eyes as well. Despite the fact that the monks were listening very intently, no one heard her come in. She sat, still and peaceful, throughout the class. When the monks finally opened their eyes, they goggled at the little girl who had appeared in their midst without a sound. The child broke the room's stillness by giggling at their pop-eyed expressions.

Over the next few days, Sister Wanda brought the little girl with her while running errands around the neighborhood, hoping someone would recognize her and know where she belonged. Because the girl insisted upon always wearing her pink T-shirt with the word BICYCLE on it, neighbors and shopkeepers greeted her by asking, "And who is this youngster wearing a bicycle?"

The girl would either smile or stare, depending on how friendly the asker's voice sounded. On the third day, she opened up her mouth and brightly repeated, "Bicycle!" to every single question asked of her.

Sister Wanda had found that addressing her as "little girl" was becoming tiresome, so right then and there she began calling her Bicycle. Bicycle beamed so joyfully that the name stuck.

Days became weeks. Bicycle gradually demonstrated a limited vocabulary, but she still had no answers for who she was and where she came from. The monks set up a temporary room for her on the second floor of the monastery.

Weeks became months. Sister Wanda finally called the Top Monk into her office to ask if she could sew Bicycle some new clothes, hang pictures on her walls, and consider the girl their responsibility.

"Not temporarily," Sister Wanda insisted. "Permanently. For better or worse, it seems she's a part of the monastery now."

The Top Monk, of course, said, "Sandwich."

"Sandwich!" A small voice seconded the Top Monk from the doorway of Sister Wanda's office.

The monk turned, startled, but then smiled at Bicycle's I-gotcha-again face. She really seemed to enjoy sneaking up on the older monks when she could, and her tiptoeing skills were second to none.

"As I have said before, she'll fit in perfectly around here," said Sister Wanda.

CLUNK

NOW that the Mostly Silent Monastery was her permanent home, Bicycle took the Easy Listening class. She had her own comfy pillow and knelt on it alongside the blue-robed monks, listening without speaking for an hour a day. Sometimes the class members practiced listening to visiting speakers or to recordings of speeches. Sometimes they sat in complete quiet, listening to things left unsaid and things that go without saying.

Sister Wanda broke out the monastery sewing machine and whipped up some simple outfits for Bicycle to wear. Not knowing the girl's age bothered Sister Wanda, and when she was sewing some new shirts for Bicycle, she hit upon the idea of comparing the girl's measurements with pattern sizes. Bicycle was a perfect toddler's size three, so Sister Wanda went with her first instinct and entered Bicycle's age as three in the monastery records. In a fit of whimsy, she picked one newly stitched green T-shirt and mimicked the girl's original pink top by ironing on the same pattern of a bike with the word BICYCLE underneath. Bicycle's enthusiastic squeals convinced Sister Wanda to sew a new BICYCLE shirt in a new color every year to celebrate her arrival at the monastery.

Two bike-decorated T-shirts later, at the age of five, Bicycle was ready to start kindergarten. Sister Wanda decided to homeschool her. Sister Wanda had developed a great fondness for the girl; plus she suspected she would excel at teaching if given the chance. It also hadn't escaped the retired nun's notice that whenever they walked past the neighborhood public school, Bicycle pulled the neck of her T-shirt up to her eyeballs and hid behind the nun's robe, peeking anxiously at the rowdy crowd of kids running through the playground.

Bicycle was especially bright, and she learned many things under Sister Wanda's tutelage. Once they'd covered the basics of letters, numbers, colors, and shapes, they branched out into reading, arithmetic, and writing. Every day, Sister Wanda wrote the Sacred Eight Words on the blackboard and used "yes," "no," "maybe," "help," "now," "later," "sleep," and "sandwich" as the basis for many lessons. They spent months considering what defines a sandwich and comparing varieties of handheld foods around the world. Discussing "now" versus "later" led them to work on clocks and telling time. Bicycle excelled at playing word games like jumbles and anagrams. She eagerly rearranged the letters in the Sacred Eight Words to discover what other words could be constructed from them, like SEW, PLEASE, and the girl's proudest discovery so far, MAYONNAISE. Bicycle's least favorite lessons were on manners and etiquette, but Sister Wanda insisted upon them.

One morning after a Scrabble session, Bicycle, now six years old, asked, "When are the monks going to add 'duck' to the Sacred Eight Words list, Sister? Once they do that, I can spell COLESLAW to go along with MAYONNAISE." After years of consideration, the word "duck" had still not been approved.

"Change happens slowly in the Mostly Silent world," Sister Wanda said. "Probably because we have so few words with which to discuss the possibility of change. But slow and careful change is not a bad thing, in my opinion."

Bicycle agreed. Each week was much like another to her, and she had no complaints about that. Sister Wanda took her on errands and museum outings. They were regulars at the library and the park. At home at the monastery, Bicycle chipped in with chores like sweeping and tidying, and she helped the monks-in-training practice their skills by pretending to be a visitor who had come to talk at a Mostly Silent listening session. If she was feeling silly, she might also throw out a question to the monk-in-training, like "If there was a big spider on top of your head, would you want me to tell you or not?" The monk-in-training would almost always say, "Yes!" and then she'd answer, "Yes I *should* tell you, or yes I *should not* tell you?" and then he'd end up saying, "No! Maybe! Help!" until Bicycle burst out laughing and reassured him she was just goofing around. Some monks bungled their vows more than others—one young man had talked to her for ten minutes straight about his fear of spiders—but since they knew Bicycle would never report their infractions to any of the head monks, they took her teasing in good spirits.

When Bicycle was seven, Sister Wanda designed a lesson showing Bicycle how to translate the Sacred Eight Words into fourteen different languages, including French, Japanese, Urdu, Vietnamese, Swahili, and American Sign Language. Although the nun got lesson plans from a homeschooling website, she rarely consulted them. Sister Wanda, as far as anyone could tell, knew everything.

"What have we learned from this?" she asked after the words had been satisfactorily memorized and repeated. (Sister Wanda loved asking "What have we learned from this?" She believed every experience should be a learning experience.)

"Um, people can be Mostly Silent in a lot of different languages?" guessed Bicycle.

"Correct, but don't say 'um.' That's enough for today," said Sister Wanda, laying down the chalk.

Bicycle got up to leave the classroom.

Sister Wanda watched her walk toward the door. "Bicycle, wait a moment," she said. "Are you looking forward to tonight's showing of *The Good, the Bad, and the Ugly?*" A local movie theater had donated an old projector and a few movie reels to the monastery, and the monks had hung a sheet at one end of the dining hall upon which to project the movies. The monks adored the actor Clint Eastwood, whose tough-guy characters usually spoke very little while communicating a whole lot.

Bicycle shook her head. "I was going to read tonight."

Sister Wanda sighed inside. Bicycle was an excellent student, very advanced for her age in learning and listening. However, growing up in such a hushed place, she didn't play or run or shout, and didn't have any friends her age to talk to or laugh with. While Sister Wanda knew the monks were very kind and took the time to listen to anything Bicycle had to say, it was hard to become someone's friend when you could exchange no more than eight words with them. The nun often wondered if she'd made a mistake by not sending Bicycle to public school, but when she had suggested to Bicycle last month that they could enroll her in school next year, Bicycle had begged Sister Wanda to continue tutoring her. She'd pulled out her perfect spelling tests and above-grade math work, plus the awesome brand-new Sacred Eight Words anagram CHAINSAWED, and then gazed at the nun with a long, pitiful, silent look. Bicycle had advanced to an Intermediate Listening class, which included Facial Expression Control, and Sister Wanda had to admit that the girl had some skills in this area.

Sister Wanda said, "Well, I know Brother Otto and a few other monks are going to the market to buy popcorn and candy in addition to groceries for dinner. Wouldn't you like to go with them?"

Bicycle also sighed inside. She was no dummy. She knew Sister Wanda thought she needed to make some friends. The retired nun had recently begun arranging playdates with kids from the local schools and inviting children from a city orphanage to visit the monastery. However, Bicycle couldn't stand these other children. None of them wanted to sit in silence, and none of them knew how to listen. In fact, they all talked—a lot. After four years surrounded by Mostly Silence, Bicycle thought that being Mostly Silent was a pretty good way to be. However, she knew Sister Wanda meant well.

"Sure, Sister, I'll go," Bicycle said. She always enjoyed spending time with Brother Otto, who did the grocery shopping for the monastery and loved food—choosing it, cooking it, and especially eating it. With his round face, glasses, and ready smile, he looked like the Dalai Lama might if the Dalai Lama always took second helpings of dessert. It was a pleasure to go to the market with him and watch him pick out some marbled sausage or a bushel of fresh, fuzzy kiwi fruit. He often got so excited that he'd forget his vows for a short time and start describing recipes in tasty detail.

"Excellent!" Sister Wanda said. "Make sure Brother Otto gets a Snickers bar for me."

Bicycle nodded, thinking of her own plans. After the shopping trip and dinner, she'd head straight for the monastery's library. With everyone watching the movie, she could read in undisturbed quiet for the entire evening.

That afternoon, Brother Otto beamed as he pushed his little shopping cart down the sidewalk on the way home. He'd gotten a very good price on pork chops, and nothing made him happier than getting a bargain on tasty food. Bicycle walked beside the plump monk, followed by three young monks-in-training who were toting bags of groceries. Brother Otto hummed a happy little cooking song to himself, looking off into space and imagining what side dishes he'd pair with the chops.

They were passing the post office when Brother Otto's shopping cart halted with a clank, blocked by something metal that had fallen over on the sidewalk. Bicycle and the other monks hurried forward to help and saw what blocked their path. Underneath the spots of rust and clinging cobwebs, the two-wheeled machine was glaringly, screamingly, almost unbearably orange. A hand-lettered sign hung from a piece of string: FOR SALE. SEE POSTMASTER.

"Ooooh!" Bicycle said.

"Well, that's fate!" Brother Otto said. Then his eyes went wide with dismay and he clapped a hand over his mouth. Brother Otto simply wasn't cut out to be Mostly Silent.

"Is that what I think it is?" asked Bicycle.

Brother Otto looked torn for a moment, then seemed to think, *I've already broken my vows today, so a few more words can't hurt.* "Yes, my little cabbage, that is your namesake. It's a bicycle."

The three monks-in-training shushed him with disapproving looks.

Naturally, it was love at first sight.

"Brother Otto . . . do you think I can buy it?" Bicycle reached into her pocket, pulling out eighty-nine cents.

Brother Otto glanced at the orange bike and then at Bicycle's face. With no further ado, he took her coins and went into the post office. He must have thrown caution to the wind and completely ignored his Mostly Silent training to get such a bargain, because he came back outside with a big smile and said, "It's all yours."

It was of no surprise to anyone at the monastery when Brother Otto brought Bicycle home with the orange bike. With a name like Bicycle, the girl was bound to start pedaling around sooner or later.

In fact, Sister Wanda was relieved to see the young girl with the two-wheeler. She wrote *child-size bike helmet* on her shopping list and said, "It's high time she found an activity that will get her out of the monastery and engaged with the world. I've said it before, and I'll say it again: the girl needs to make friends. Surely a bicycle will help her do that."

The Top Monk said, "Sandwich."

The cobwebby bike required some tender loving care. Bicycle lost no time getting started. She found a thick bicycle repair manual in the library and wheeled the bike into the monastery's small garage. She spent the rest of the afternoon dismantling the machine piece by piece, barely looking up when Sister Wanda dropped off a plain black helmet with an admonishment to wear it whenever pedaling.

"Crankshaft, bottom bracket, pedal, rear de-rail-leur," Bicycle read aloud from the book, picking up each rusty, fiddly-shaped bit and turning it over and over in her hands. While the monks were watching the Clint Eastwood movie that evening, she scrubbed every nook and cranny with an old toothbrush, greased the parts that needed greasing, and reassembled the bike. By anyone's standards, the bike was not a pretty thing. It was a dense, heavy, clunky lump of steel. It was quite old, and had clearly been ridden many miles, but it was fundamentally sound and ready to ride with its new owner. It was a smidge too big for her, but if she stretched, she could reach the pedals. Bicycle hugged her bicycle. She named it Clunk.

For the next five years, Bicycle cycled every moment she could. She rode beside Brother Otto to the market every day. She rode around the block so many times she nearly wore a groove into the road. She slept with Clunk next to her bed, and occasionally she thunked down the wide staircase to breakfast on the bike. (Sister Wanda threatened to throw Clunk in the trash heap when Bicycle did this, so she rode down the staircase only when she was sure Sister Wanda was busy on the other side of the monastery.)

The theater that had donated the movie projector to the monastery had also donated several black-and-white films about famous bicycle races. Bicycle watched those films over and over, shouting encouragement to the racers on the screen. Most of the races took place in Europe, and Bicycle was fascinated with the wire-thin men on their elegant, nimble bikes, whizzing together through historic towns, struggling up mountains, riding in huge jostling packs usually without crashing into one another.

Bicycle's shouting at the movie screen attracted the attention of the Top Monk. He liked to watch Bicycle while she watched the screen, and to listen to her shouts of encouragement. He seemed to hear something special in her voice, because he was sometimes inspired to shout "Sandwich!" himself. He gave Bicycle a gift subscription to a popular bicycling magazine. She read each issue cover to cover, and in this way learned about the famous bike racers of the world.

The most famous, and Bicycle's favorite, was young Zbigniew Sienkiewicz. He was a tall and lanky nineteen-year-old racer from Poland with a blond mustache. He had won every major race in the world as a rookie, and he always sprinted across the finish line with a grin on his face, waving with wild enthusiasm to his cheering fans. *"Dziękuję, Dziękuję!"* he would shout, which means "Thank you!" in Polish. Polish, you should know, is not the easiest language in the world to pronounce and understand. For example, although *Dziękuję* looks like a sneeze when you write it down, it actually sounds like "Jen-COO-ya." Because Polish was so tricky, none of the racing announcers could pronounce Zbigniew Sienkiewicz's name correctly (it sounded kind of like ZBIG-nyev Shen-KEV-itch), so everyone called him Zbig.

Zbig was Bicycle's hero. She rearranged the letters in his first name to spell E-Z BIG WIN and found the words NICE and WISE in his last name. She started dreaming about winning the Tour de France and the Giro d'Italia and other famous bike races like Zbig did, riding her bike for hundreds of miles with a grin on her face, waving wildly to her own cheering fans. She thought her dream wasn't too far-fetched. She knew she was growing up to be tall and lanky just like Zbig—after all, she'd had to raise Clunk's seat post every time she had a growth spurt, and now that she was twelve years old, it was as high as it could go.

While Bicycle's dreams of winning international races grew more vivid, Sister Wanda's dreams of Bicycle making lots of new pals while biking around the neighborhood did not. In fact, riding Clunk seemed to have separated her even more from other children.

Part of the problem was that Bicycle was a very fast cyclist. If someone tried to start a conversation with her, she started pedaling hard and left them in her dust. Now when Sister Wanda set up playdates with local girls and boys, Bicycle hopped on Clunk and headed outside, passing the children in a flash of flying hair and spinning spokes, pretending she couldn't hear Sister Wanda telling her to come back and meet Betsy or Billy or Jenny or Frankie. Bicycle didn't want to meet them. She just wanted to ride Clunk and be left alone in peace and quiet.

THE FRIENDSHIP FACTORY

One unlucky Saturday morning, Bicycle heard the sound of a gaggle of girls coming in the front door and being ushered toward the main hall. Clearly, Sister Wanda was going to try another one of her friend-making get-togethers.

Bicycle hopped out of bed, threw on some clothes and shoes, and decided that if she was quick, she could ride Clunk down the staircase and out the side door near the kitchen before Sister Wanda could see her. She pedaled into the hallway and started down the staircase, but on the middle stair, she felt Clunk's heavy frame drop out from under her with a terrifying crash. The world went sideways and bits of wood flew everywhere.

"Help!" she screamed.

Every monk in the monastery came running.

Brother Otto pulled Bicycle out of the ruin of the staircase, poking and prodding at her arms and legs, pulling back her eyelids, and peering into her ears. "Are you hurt? Are you broken?" he asked in agitation. Then he clapped a hand over his mouth as the other monks gave him the Mostly Silent Shush.

"I'm . . . okay . . . I guess." Bicycle was a little scratched and banged up, but no permanent damage was done to her.

Amazingly, Clunk also came out of the pile of wood and dust with nothing more than a few scratches in the orange paint and a handful of loose screws. But the staircase? The staircase was toast.

Sister Wanda was a dark thundercloud moving toward Bicycle. Holding Bicycle by the chin, she asked in a dangerously soft voice, "What have we learned from *this*?"

"Uh . . . I will not ride my bike down the stairs ever again?"

Sister Wanda repeated after her, "You. Will. *Not*. Ride. Your. Bike. Down. The. Stairs. *Ever*. Again."

Bicycle nodded, chagrined.

Sister Wanda's eyes flashed like blue lightning. "Brother Jianyu!" she called. Brother Jianyu was the carpenter of the house. "You will go to town and buy wood to repair these stairs right now, and when you return, you will have this one"—she gave Bicycle's chin a shake that rattled the teeth in her head—"help you for as long as it takes to fix this."

This was the first time Bicycle had ever gotten into serious trouble with Sister Wanda. She meekly went to meet the giggling girls in the main hall. She pretended with all her

25

might to enjoy their company until Brother Jianyu came and set her to work yanking nails out of broken pieces of wood with a claw hammer.

A few weeks later, Sister Wanda took Bicycle out for her annual haircut at the barbershop. Bicycle rode on Clunk, and Sister Wanda jogged to keep up. They were passing a travel agency when a large poster with curly lettering caught Bicycle's eye. She pedaled over to take a look and almost banged into the side of the building. The poster announced:

ZBIGNIEW "ZBIG" SIENKIEWICZ TO
VISIT AMERICA!
His First-Ever Visit to the United States!!
Zbig Will Host the Blessing of the Bicycles
in San Francisco, California, on July 8

All bicycles are welcome to be blessed for safe, fast riding.
Zbig will choose one Lucky Cyclist at the event to tour the
country with him.

✲A Once-in-a-Lifetime Ride!✲
✲Reserve your plane ticket TODAY!✲

There was a black-and-white drawing of Zbig at the bottom of the poster. His arms were raised in his signature wave.

"Sister!" Bicycle exclaimed, and made some unintelligible gargling noises. She had so much to say, the words caught together in a jumbled rush in her throat. Sister Wanda jogged up and read the poster for herself.

"Yes, yes, I know you're a big fan of this Zbig fellow." Sister Wanda paused. For the first time in Bicycle's life, the indomitable Sister looked dismayed. "I'd like to say we could afford tickets to California. However, we used up the monastery's savings to fix the broken staircase."

Bicycle gulped.

"I'm sorry. I know you didn't intend to vaporize the staircase, but you will not be attending that event." Sister Wanda started toward the barbershop.

Bicycle followed behind, slowly pushing Clunk, dumbstruck by the bad luck she'd brought on herself. "You're sure, Sister? There's no extra money at all?" Bicycle pleaded.

Sister Wanda pressed her lips together. "Well, there is the emergency fund. And I do have a little reserve of money," she said.

Bicycle felt hope leap up inside her.

Then Sister Wanda continued. "I was going to tell you this next week, but I've been saving up to send you to sleep-away camp at the Friendship Factory."

Bicycle's hope crashed back down and went splat.

"Now, I know you'd rather go see this Zbig bicycle racer person, but you have to understand." Sister Wanda had that no-nonsense look. "You simply can't go on this way, refusing the possibility of friendship. Since you don't seem to be able to find any friends here, it's time to do something more drastic. The Friendship Factory is a very successful place. They have facilities across the country. There's one right outside D.C., and they say in their ads 'Three Guaranteed Friendships or Your Money Back.' I signed you up for their Spring Break Special, which certifies if the spring session isn't effective enough, you will automatically be enrolled into their six-week summer intensive." Sister Wanda's expression softened slightly. "Please believe me," she said. "I'm doing this for your own good. Someday you will look back on this and thank me."

Bicycle was dazed throughout her haircut and the ride home. Not only could she not meet her bike-racing hero on his trip to the United States, but she was going to be condemned to this dreadful-sounding Friendship Factory. She'd probably be trapped in some drafty cabin in the woods, forced to make friends with annoying children, and boring children, and maybe even some children who were both annoying and boring at the same time. And if it didn't go well, she'd end up back there for practically the whole summer. Three guaranteed friendships or your money back? It sounded like a guaranteed nightmare.

She was in a funk for days. She sent a long, pleading letter to Zbig, asking if he might be able to change his visit from San Francisco, California, to Washington, D.C., preferably someplace near the monastery. She also talked to the monks about her problem, and they listened with great patience and attentiveness. However, listening was not enough for Bicycle this time. She wanted someone to talk to her and say, "Wow, that's terribly unfair," and "I'll find a way to make Sister Wanda see reason," and "You don't need to make friends; you need to go see Zbig Sienkiewicz and maybe win a cross-country bike trip." Instead, they said, "Yes," and "Sandwich?" This was very unsatisfying. Bicycle moped.

In mid-April, a week before the Friendship Factory bus was scheduled to arrive, a big envelope with a Poland postmark arrived. The return address was from ZBIG S. ENTERPRISES. A reply to her letter! She held her breath as she slit it open. Inside, there was a photo of Zbig crossing some anonymous finish line on his bike, hands up in the air, smiling at the camera. Scrawled on it in thick black marker were the words *Keep riding!* and it was signed *Your Friend, Zbig Sienkiewicz.* Bicycle stared at it. As she did, an idea began to form. Once the idea formed, it grew wheels and starting spinning through her mind.

A sunny Saturday morning in April was something Bicycle usually savored. But her pale face showed no savoring when the big yellow Friendship Factory bus pulled up to the monastery. She clutched her bulky backpack to her chest while the driver got out and helped Sister Wanda attach Clunk to the luggage rack on the rear of the bus. Bicycle had insisted that the only way she could stand to go to this loathsome camp was if she could bring her bike with her, and Sister Wanda had finally given in.

Sister Wanda gave her a hug and a going-away present, a book titled *Wheel Wisdom: Great Thoughts from Great Cyclists.* "You probably won't even get a chance to read this until you return, you'll be so busy having fun with your new friends."

Bicycle didn't trust herself to talk, so she nodded silently. She squatted down to unzip her backpack and slide the paperback book inside.

As Bicycle stood back up, Sister Wanda continued, "I know you aren't completely sure about this, child, but I'm sure enough for both of us. Think of what you will learn from this experience."

Brother Otto was also there to see her off and he gave her his most sympathetic smile and a brown bag filled with snacks for the trip. When he leaned in for a hug, he whispered, "Good luck."

Bicycle nodded again.

The bus was already filled with naughty little boys throwing spit-soaked wads of paper at one another's heads and nasty little girls making fun of one another's shoes. These were the children who couldn't, or wouldn't, or even perhaps shouldn't make friends without a camp to force them to do so.

Bicycle sat down in the one available seat, her backpack in her lap with her helmet clipped onto a side strap. The boy next to her was wearing a T-shirt that said BE GLAD I'M NOT YOUR KID. He stuck a moist wad of paper in her hair.

The girl across the aisle looked down at Bicycle's sneakers and squeaked, "Ewwww, those shoes have no sparkle!"

Bicycle tried to ignore them, but it was difficult.

The bus pulled away from the curb. Sister Wanda and Brother Otto waved good-bye until it was out of sight. "She'll thank me someday," Sister Wanda declared. "I hope," she added under her breath.

The bus trundled through the traffic-clogged streets. After a few minutes, Bicycle got up and approached the driver. "Excuse me, sir, but could we stop? I really need to use a bathroom."

"Awww, why dincha go before we left?" the driver asked. "We have to stay on schedule, ya know."

"I'm sorry, but I really need to go," she replied, shifting from one foot to another.

Another girl overheard her and chimed in, "Yeah, I need to go, too." Then a chorus of voices started in the back of the bus. "Stop the bus! We need to go!"

The bus driver grumbled, "Kids!" but he pulled over at the next gas station. "Make it quick!" he yelled.

Bicycle grabbed her backpack and ran off the bus, but she didn't head for the bathrooms with the rest of the boys and girls. She went to the back of the bus and had Clunk free from the luggage rack in no time. Before anyone noticed what she was doing, she'd attached her backpack to Clunk's rack with a bungee cord, stuck her helmet on her head, and started pedaling away in the opposite direction of the bus and the Friendship Factory.

Early that evening, one of the monks went in to tidy up Bicycle's room. He found a note under the pillow when he was making the bed. After he read it, he brought it straight to Sister Wanda in the kitchen, where she and Brother Otto were baking oatmeal cookies.

Sister Wanda read the note once, then twice, and fell back into one of the kitchen chairs. "Silent Saints preserve us all, especially this little girl!"

Dear Sister Wanda,
I figure you will be hearing from the camp pretty soon that I never showed up, so I wanted to tell you not to worry. I know it's important to you that I make a friend. Maybe you are right. But the Friendship Fac-

tory is not the place I'm going to find one. There is only one friend that I want to make, and that is Zbig Sienkiewicz. Clunk and I are going to California to find him. I'll send you postcards along the way to let you know I'm okay.

Bicycle

Sister Wanda sat staring at Bicycle's note without seeing it, lost in thought. "She doesn't want to make friends with any of the nice children I bring to meet her, but now she wants to take off for California to meet this mustache-faced bike racer!" Then she demanded of the oatmeal box in frustration, "How does that foolish child expect to get across the country by herself?"

The Top Monk walked into the kitchen and read Bicycle's note over her shoulder. He squinted in thought. "Sandwich," he finally said.

Sister Wanda turned around to face him. "If you're saying we need to send the police after her, I think that will push her to do something even more foolish. No, no, she's going to come to her senses." She rubbed her eyes with both hands. "Don't a lot of children try running away from home at one point or another? They eventually cool off and come back, ready to make amends." She exhaled slowly. "She's a smart girl. She'll soon realize that bicycling across the country isn't something a person just up and does. I bet she'll be home later tonight."

"Sandwich," the Top Monk said again.

This time, Sister Wanda wasn't the least bit sure what he meant.

Bicycle didn't feel foolish. She had thought and thought about ways to get out of spending spring break at the Friendship Factory. But it wasn't until she'd gotten the photo from Zbig signed *Your Friend, Zbig Sienkiewicz* that it hit her: all that really mattered to Sister Wanda was that she make a friend, right? It shouldn't matter if she made a friend at the Friendship Factory or somewhere else—like California. And she had a perfect way to get there: Clunk would take her across the country.

She'd studied U.S. geography last year with Sister Wanda, so she knew how many states lay between her and California. After staring at the picture of Zbig for a while, pondering the best way to get from the East Coast to the West Coast, she'd headed to the public library to make her own cross-country cycling map. She went to the reference section, took a pile of atlases to a table, and spent a long afternoon with a ruler and a calculator and the photocopy machine.

Sister Wanda's rigorous instruction on how to read a map legend paid off. Bicycle knew that the thickest, straightest lines on the atlas maps were the interstate highways, where cars would roar by at high speeds and no bicyclists were allowed. Instead, she looked for the skinniest lines, the ones that meandered a more indirect way across each state—the local byways marked CR for "country route" or RR for "rural road." A few states even had trails designed solely for bicycles and pedestrians. She traced those routes in green highlighter across each photocopy and stapled them into a thick packet. Adding up the mileage for each state, Bicycle figured she had to ride almost four thousand miles to get to California. She needed to be there on July 8. That meant she'd need to average about fifty miles a day. *How hard could that be?* she asked herself. *Zbig and those other racers ride over a hundred miles every day for weeks on end. Fifty miles should be a piece of cake.*

When Sister Wanda told her that she needed to pack for camp, Bicycle had instead secretly packed supplies for a long-distance bike trip. She raided the kitchen pantry and put bags of crackers, dried fruits, chocolate, cereal, and beef jerky in a pile. She folded her favorite T-shirts, leggings, and shorts; rolled up an old wool blanket; found a washcloth and soap so she could wash herself and her clothes on the go; and added a toothbrush and toothpaste, a flashlight, a penknife, bungee cords, some postcard stamps, and a tiny yellow spiral notebook with several pens to her pile. From the monastery's library, she'd taken a pocket waterproof Polish-English dictionary so she could talk to Zbig in his native language when they met. Her photocopied maps fit nicely inside a gallon-sized Ziplock plastic bag, along with a roll of duct tape to secure the map bag to her handlebars. She put her saved-up allowance money, $154.20, into an envelope and wrapped it in several layers of underwear. For Clunk, she put in an Allen wrench set, chain lube, a bike pump, and a tire repair kit. She covered the supplies with two extra-large rain ponchos, planning to use the ponchos as a kind of make-shift tent on the road, and crammed the whole wad into her backpack. She leaned two water bottles against it to slide into Clunk's bottle cages. "Ready as I'll ever be," she judged.

The night before leaving, she went to bed and listened to the clock in the hall chime midnight. Too tense to sleep, she kept thinking about whether she ought to go through with her plan.

I showed up at the monastery in a T-shirt labeled BICY-CLE, *didn't I? Therefore, if I am going to make any friends in life, they are probably going to be bicyclists. So why not start out with the best bicyclist in the world as my first friend? He's even got the word* NICE *in his last name. When it works out perfectly and Zbig and I become great friends, Sister Wanda won't be angry. She'll see why I did what I did.*

Yet no matter how many times she went over this in her mind, Bicycle wasn't convinced that Sister Wanda wouldn't be angry forever after this. This was a big deal.

When she'd climbed on the Friendship Factory bus, though, she knew she had to do it. Right or wrong, she needed to get away from those . . . those . . . those *kids*.

Now she was on the road, moving as fast as she could. It was too late to wonder if she'd done the right thing. She focused instead on pedaling the first mile of the four thousand that lay ahead.

MR. SPIM'S SPLENDID SPONGES

Bicycle wound through city streets and biked over the Fourteenth Street Bridge. She felt a little thrill after crossing the Potomac River and realizing she'd left D.C. behind and entered Virginia, her first state. *California, here I come,* Bicycle thought, squeezing Clunk's handlebars.

She joined a paved bike path with a few other cyclists. According to her map, this path would last for about twenty miles, which would be the longest she'd ever ridden in her life. After that, she planned to pedal thirty more miles to make her goal for the day.

Pacing herself, she stopped after an hour at a water fountain and took a drink. As she started refilling her water bottle from the fountain, she heard the unmistakable whirring-whizzing noise of bicycle spokes behind her. She turned to watch three cyclists come racing up dressed in matching red jerseys with the word SPIM'S in white across the front. They gave her serious nods and one-finger waves and were gone down the path in a moment. Another, much flabbier cyclist dressed in the same uniform came wheezing up more slowly. He was pedaling a very expensive skinny racing bike that creaked and groaned under his bulk. A leather briefcase sat in a basket attached to the handlebars.

"Good morning," he panted, nodding at Bicycle and stopping his bike. "Did some other riders come by here?" Beads of sweat dripped off his nose and chin. He pulled a small dark-blue sponge from his jersey's back pocket and dabbed at his face.

Bicycle said, "Yes, sir, they just came by. You can probably catch them if you hurry."

"I certainly can," he agreed. But instead of following the other riders, he rested his haunches back on his bike seat. He lifted a water bottle from his basket and drank its last dregs.

Bicycle took the bottle from him and started refilling it from the water fountain.

"How kind," the man said. "My company, Spim's Splendid Sponges, started a program this month encouraging employees to bike to work instead of driving. As I am Mr. Spim, company president, I felt I needed to set a good example for my workers, and so forth."

Bicycle handed him back the bottle.

After a long drink, he asked, "Are you on your way to soccer practice or some such thing?"

"No, sir," said Bicycle. She thought his sponge company must be a pretty great place if they wanted employees to ride bikes to work. "I'm on my way to San Francisco to attend the Blessing of the Bicycles, and I'd better keep moving. I've got more than forty miles to go today if I'm going to stick to my schedule."

Mr. Spim let out a long whistle. "The Golden State of California? Excellent! Do you know, when I was younger, I rode my bicycle from Great Britain to Africa and back again? I pedaled in circles around the decks of the ferries, so crossing the English Channel and the Strait of Gibraltar still counted as cycling miles, you see. Those were the days!" He slapped his side, and his considerable tummy jiggled and wiggled. He looked down at it with some disbelief, as if he'd been ambushed by this unfamiliar flabby body somewhere between Africa and here. "Ahem. Well. Tell me about your journey. Do you have maps? Places to stay along the way?"

"I do have maps, and I'm going to camp out with my bicycle," Bicycle answered. "I planned it all last week."

Mr. Spim gave her a pleased look. "A single week of planning, eh? Well, what more do you need when adventure awaits? I once led an expedition to the South Pole with one night of planning. What fun!" He smiled, remembering. Then his smile faded. "But those sorts of things are best done when a person is young and has inherited lots of money.

It's amazing how quickly funds run out when adventuring. At some point, a man must accept that he must work for a living. And seek excitement and challenge wherever possible, like on the bike path to one's sponge factory, for example." Another rider wearing the same red-and-white jersey came buzzing by them. "Oh, rot! I must continue slogging onward. Can't let those employees of mine get too far ahead. I also don't want to delay you," he said. "I am not one to stand in the way of a journey. But before I go, I'm willing to share some of my traveling advice with you. I've sailed some seas and trekked some trails, let me tell you! So, if you're willing to listen . . ." He paused hopefully.

Bicycle put an expression of polite listening on her face.

Mr. Spim harrumphed and puffed out his chest. He held up one finger. "First, don't be afraid to eat strange-looking things. Strange-looking to the eye is often heaven to the tongue! Second"—he held up a second finger—"always have a sponge or two close at hand. Many's the time a sponge has saved my bacon." He clicked open his briefcase and handed her a small pack of assorted sponges. "Third"—he raised one more finger and waggled all three of them at Bicycle—"never, and I mean *never*, turn your back on a zebra. Those things may look like pretty striped horses, but they can be really ferocious when they want to be! Take it from an intrepid old traveler!"

Bicycle couldn't think of a response to this, so she relied on her training from Intermediate Listening. "Yes," she said gravely, trying to nod like an intrepid young traveler.

Mr. Spim put his foot on a pedal. "I believe wonderful things are in store for you. Best of luck, young adventurer!" With a glow of resolve in his eyes, he rode off.

Bicycle watched him go and said to Clunk, "See? Our first day and I already know to be careful around zebras. This is going to be much better than that horrible Friendship Factory ever could have been." She shoved the sponges into the top of her backpack and followed after Mr. Spim. Although she expected to catch up to him wheezing alongside the path, she didn't see him again. Maybe offering advice had given him a second wind.

When the bike path ended, she ate some dried fruit and crackers to celebrate. "This is it, partner, we've officially gone farther than we ever have before," she said to Clunk. "This isn't that hard at all. We'll be in California in no time!"

UNFINISHED BUSINESS IN VIRGINIA

Several hours and hundreds of pedal revolutions later, Bicycle reached a WELCOME sign on the outskirts of Manassas, Virginia. Bicycle knew from her American history class with Sister Wanda that Manassas was the site of a huge Civil War battle, and she followed some historic markers that pointed her down Route 29 to the battlefield itself. She looked around at the neatly mown green grass dotted with trees and decided it would be a nice spot to stop for the night.

She pulled off the road and into a stand of maple trees. "We don't want anyone noticing we're here," she said to Clunk as she unfastened her backpack from the bike's rear rack. "Sister Wanda might send someone to look for us, and we're not ready to be found."

Bicycle picked the tree most hidden from view to camp under and, using her bungee cords, fashioned a makeshift tent by securing one side of her green rain poncho to her bike and the other side to the tree. She laid the second poncho down on the ground with the blanket on top and stretched out. It felt wonderful to lie down. She chewed on a piece of jerky as the sun set and thought about getting out the *Wheel Wisdom* book to read, but her eyelids were unusually heavy. "Maybe I'll go to sleep now, Clunk, and then we'll be ready to get started early tomorrow." She yawned, the shadow of Clunk's frame lengthening over her as the sun dropped below the horizon.

"What did you say?" Bicycle asked sleepily, opening her eyes. She felt quite disoriented, expecting to see the white walls and wooden floor of her room at the monastery, but instead finding herself surrounded by nothing but dark and the smells of grass and wind and damp. Then she pushed herself up on one elbow, banged her forehead on Clunk's pedal, and recalled exactly where she was.

"Owwwww," she complained, rubbing her head.

"Ohhhhhhh," called a low whispery voice.

Bicycle's eyes went wide, and she jerked around to face whoever or whatever had made the noise. There was nothing there. She stared into the shadows. Wait—what was that? Sort of a misty movement? She kept staring and tried to remember if she had packed a flashlight in her backpack, and where exactly her backpack was at this moment, and wondered if she'd bang her forehead on Clunk again if she moved around to look for it. Before she worked any of that out, her eyes adjusted to the darkness and she made out the indistinct shape of a person sitting atop a tree root next to her blanket. The low sound came again, but this time Bicycle stayed absolutely still.

"Ohhhhh . . . lllohhhh . . . hello?" The shape had the face of a teenage boy wearing a strange-looking hat. His outline was insubstantial but lit with a faint glow. He made a throat-clearing noise and said in a soft voice, "I'm sorry if I scared you."

"Well . . . ," Bicycle said uncertainly, and then yawned. Probably this was a dream and nothing to get too worked up over. "I might be more scared if I knew what you were. Are you a ghost?"

The shadow-figure looked confused. "I'm not sure. Do I seem like a ghost to you? I seem like myself to me." He touched his chest and rubbed his tummy. "Do ghosts get hungry? I think I'm hungry."

Whatever he was, Bicycle decided she wasn't scared of him. She moved away from Clunk and felt around on her hands and knees until she found her backpack. She dug into her stash of food, pulling out some chocolate squares to offer him.

"Oh, thank you!" he said.

He reached out a hand to take the squares, but they dropped right through his palm onto the ground. He scrabbled at them with his fingers. The chocolate lay there without moving and his face fell.

"Well, ghost I am, I guess." He scratched an ear. "Last thing I remember, my best friend, Joe Branch, and I were pouring powder into our muskets behind this big tree, and then . . . then I'm sitting here with no musket and no Joe." He looked around. "Just you and the trees and the stars."

"I'm sorry I don't have anything you can eat," Bicycle said, wrapping up the chocolate. She wasn't used to having complete conversations with anyone other than Sister Wanda, and here was her second conversation of the day, although admittedly Mr. Spim had done most of the talking earlier. She racked her brain for something to say. What do ghosts talk about? Then she had an idea. "Do you have some unfinished business, anything like that? In most books I've read, ghosts usually seem to have unfinished business they need to complete. Think about it—why are you appearing now? Maybe you remembered a stash of money you needed to tell your family about? Some evil villain you want to wreak your vengeance upon?"

The ghost thought, wavering in a breeze, and finally said, "Nah. I didn't have much money, or even much of a family, and never knew any villains." He paused. "I never even really had any plans other than going along with Joe to fight with the Missouri Volunteer Infantry. Say, is the war all done? Did everybody stop fighting?"

"Yes," Bicycle said. This boy must have been a casualty on this very battlefield. She did the math in her head to figure out how long ago the Civil War had ended. "They stopped fighting more than a hundred and fifty years ago."

"Well, that's good," he said. "Turns out, war's not so great." The boy looked at Bicycle and shrugged. "So. No unfinished business I can figure. Is there some other reason your books say that ghosts appear?"

"They also haunt stuff," Bicycle said. "Maybe you've woken up because you're supposed to haunt this battlefield. To remind people that war's a bad idea or something. If someone rests near this tree, you have to appear and share your ghostly wisdom."

He placed a hand against the rough trunk of the maple tree. "Huh. That could be it—I'm here to haunt this battle-field. Since ghosts don't have to eat, that feeling in my gut might not have been hunger after all, but my ghostly wisdom rising up."

He started to fade away. Bicycle watched the spot where he sat until it was free of ghostly vapors, and then she lay back down, making sure her head wasn't close to Clunk's pedal this time. She was almost asleep when a voice whispered in her ear.

"Hey, I thought of something. Unfinished business, maybe."

Bicycle sat up and sighed, getting into her most

comfortable listening position. "Okay, tell me about it," she said to the soldier's apparition, which was gradually reappearing.

"I was thinking about my friend Joe and how he could pack away food. He was a pie-eating champ. One time, he entered this contest and chomped up his pies so fast, he grabbed a couple of extra ones that weren't even baked yet." The ghost's eyes crinkled up.

Bicycle stifled a yawn and tried to look attentive.

"Anyhow, Joe was planning on opening up a fried-pie shop in our hometown after the war. Five different types of fresh fried pies every single day. He never stopped talking about it when we were on the march with the infantry. He was gonna call it Paradise Pies. You ever had fried pie?"

Bicycle shook her head, trying to imagine it.

"No? They're these crisped-up pockets of dough and fillings. They're taaast-eee. Joe had lots of ideas for new types of fried pies. Raspberry and chocolate, roast chicken and sweet potato." If ghosts could drool, that's what the boy was doing. He swiped at his lips. "So I wanted to know if he ever did open Paradise Pies. If he did, maybe I could go there and haunt it instead of this lonesome ol' battleground. Could you find out about the pie shop for me?"

Bicycle gave it some thought. "I can try, if it's along my route. Where were you and Joe from?"

"Green Marsh, Missouri, in the Ozark Mountains."

Bicycle got our her maps and flashlight and studied the roads of Missouri.

"You're in luck—Green Marsh is on my way. I can see if there's a fried-pie shop in town." She thought she might like to try a crisped-up pie pocket or two. "Wait, though—even if I find it, how will I let you know where it is? I want to help, but I don't have time to backtrack. Can I mail you a letter or something?"

The ghost pondered that one for a while. He was starting to look less substantial again. "I've only just figured out that I'm a ghost, you know. I'm not sure how this works. Thinking too much about it makes me feel sort of weak and wobbly." His body wobbled in the night air as he spoke. "Maybe I could come along with you."

"How?"

He scratched his faint chin and glanced around. "I guess I'd have to haunt something that you're carrying with you." They both looked at Bicycle's pile of belongings. "Could I haunt your velocipede, there?" He pointed at Clunk.

"What, my bike? You want to haunt my bike?"

"Yep, I think I could haunt that and go right along with you back to Green Marsh."

He was looking very, very faint now, and rather pitiful. When he'd joined the army, he couldn't have been much more than sixteen years old, and although more than a century had passed, he still looked very young.

"What do you say?" He smiled hopefully.

Bicycle looked at Clunk, and then back at the apparition. She didn't want to ride a haunted bicycle on her first trip away from home, but lessons on helping others in need had been drilled into her by Sister Wanda. "Okay. You can haunt my bike. But you'd better not weigh anything, and whether or not there's a pie shop, I've got to drop you off to haunt something else in Green Marsh. Deal?"

All that was left of the ghost was his face. His teeth flashed in the darkness as he whispered, "Deal. Thank you, young miss." And he was gone.

Bicycle dropped back to sleep.

NINE HUNDRED COWS
AND COUNTING

Woken by the light of the rising sun on her face, Bicycle felt a gnawing hunger. She rolled over and opened up bags of dried bananas and apricots and walnuts, wolfing down mouthfuls of each. She stood to stretch and felt the muscles in her legs and back groan in protest. "Urrrrrgh," she said to Clunk. "Something tells me today isn't going to be as easy as yesterday."

She'd been in the habit of talking to Clunk for years. But for the first time ever, Clunk spoke back. "Good morning. Got any oil for the chain?"

Bicycle's eyes opened wide. She looked around, but no one was anywhere near her campsite. Leaning her head toward the bike frame, she asked, "Clunk, is that you? Are you *talking*?" She got excited. "Did riding fifty miles bring you to life?"

"It's me—Griffin. We talked last night? You said I could

come with you?" The voice of the young soldier was emanating from Clunk's handlebars.

Bicycle rubbed her head and recalled her nighttime chat. "Right, Griffin, I sort of thought that was a dream. I forgot to ask your name last night. Mine's Bicycle. Let me oil that chain."

"Pleasure to meet you, Bicycle. I'm Griffin G. Griffin, and I surely do appreciate the lift."

Bicycle took care of lubing the chain, crammed her belongings back into her pack, and tied everything to Clunk's rack. She threw one leg over the bike's saddle and sat down. Every body part that touched the bike twinged in pain, but she told herself to deal with it. "Okay, Griffin, here we go," she said to her handlebars. She pedaled slowly away from the old Manassas battlefield.

Griffin quickly settled into his mobile haunt and began chattering about the nice weather and the road's smooth surface, what an improvement it was over cobblestones or hardpacked dirt. The first car that passed them made him yell in surprise.

"That carriage is out of control—it's going too fast! And where are the horses?"

Bicycle calmed him down and explained the invention of cars and how they moved without being pulled by animals. When Griffin asked if they ran on steam like trains did, she said they ran on something called gasoline. He then asked if the gasoline made things move inside the car the way steam did inside locomotive engines, and she admitted she didn't have the faintest idea how gas made cars go.

The next car made Griffin whoop in surprise and laugh in amazement. So did the next, and the next, and the next. "How many of these things are there?" he asked. After being passed by a bunch of different vehicles, he announced that he liked pickup trucks the most. When a tractor drove by pulling a flatbed wagon stacked with straw, Griffin yelled, "Look, that machine-riding man's waving at us. Wave back, Bicycle, wave back!"

She did. Bicycle really wanted Griffin to be quiet, but she didn't say so. She felt sorry for him. After all, he'd been a ghost ten times longer than he'd been alive. Instead, she gritted her teeth and politely listened to everything he had to say and explained the modern world as best she could.

The road they were on was surrounded on both sides by green hills and fenced farms, and herd after herd of contented cows grazed in the sun. Bicycle pedaled up one green, grassy, cow-covered hill and coasted down the other side. Pedaled up another green, grassy, cow-covered hill and coasted down the other side. And so on. And so on. Griffin must have been lulled by the repetitive motion because he quieted down, and Bicycle started counting cows to keep her mind off her aching body. *Ten more cows*, she found herself bargaining with her legs to continue pedaling. *Pedal past ten more cows and you'll get a break.*

When Bicycle reached six hundred cows, she wasn't pedaling another inch. She rolled the bike toward a half-blown-down red barn and dismounted with a whimpering groan. She set up camp on a flat patch of ground on the side of the barn hidden from the road, attaching one poncho end to a worn wooden fence post and the other to Clunk.

Griffin spoke up when Bicycle sat down to eat a little meal. "You're pretty good," he said. "I've never seen a girl move so far so fast. This is much better than walking!"

"Yes, it is, but I'm going slower than I should be," Bicycle said, discouraged. "I didn't make it fifty miles today." Yesterday, leaving the Friendship Factory bus had seemed like a brave and brilliant idea. Today, a sharp sliver of doubt was beginning to poke holes in her plans to befriend Zbig Sienkiewicz. How could the world's greatest bike racer be friends with a girl who complained about cycling after only two days in a row?

She tried to shake off the aches. *Tomorrow's another day,* she thought. *Maybe the second day of a long ride is always the hardest.*

The second day, however, had been a breeze compared to the third day. When Bicycle got on Clunk after sunrise that morning, her hands, her feet, and especially her bottom did not want to be there. Her leg muscles felt like they'd probably always hurt, even if she lived another 150 years. She stopped looking at the green, grassy, cow-covered hills around her and focused on the little gray strip of road in front of her. Push the left pedal, push the right pedal, moan a little. Push the left pedal, push the right pedal, moan a little more. Push moan push moan push moan moooooooan. Was Clunk too small and too old for this? Or was she too small and too young for this?

At the first town Bicycle rode through, she wanted to stop at a convenience store for a breather, but she waited until she pedaled past a bank with a big clock outside so she knew what time it was. She wasn't sure if it was spring break week outside D.C., so she thought the best thing to do was to stop at stores before or after regular school hours so she could blend in with other local bicycling kids. The bank clock showed a couple of minutes past eight, so she pulled in at the next store she saw.

Bicycle browsed the revolving rack of flimsy ten-cent postcards. Most of them were blurry photos of churches and old brick buildings. She had just picked out one of a historic monument that said MY SISTER ATE SOUP HERE 1873 when the store's candy display caught her eye. She sternly reminded herself she had a budget of two dollars per day, then decided that she could spend her whole two dollars right now as long as she read every candy bar's nutritional information. She picked the one with the highest number of ingredients and calories she could find.

Bicycle barely waited until she was outside the store to rip open the wrapper. She bit into the candy bar and closed her eyes for a second at the wonderful comfort of chocolate, caramel, nougat, and peanuts filling her mouth. She found the wherewithal to climb back on Clunk and start pedaling again, using one hand to steady the handlebars and the other to feed herself more blessed mouthfuls of the candy. It was the best breakfast she'd ever had.

Griffin piped up. "I know a lot of good traveling songs. Would you like to hear some?"

She swallowed. "Uh . . . I don't know," she said. That wasn't true. She did know. She wanted peace and quiet instead. But she didn't want to be rude.

"Don't you worry, it's no trouble!" And he began to sing: "I come from Al-abama with a banjo on my knee, I'm going to LOU-isiana, my true love for to see . . ." Griffin's voice seemed to reverberate down from the handlebars into the rest of Clunk's steel frame, producing a twangy sort of amplification.

"I know that one." Bicycle smiled in spite of herself, surprised to have something in common with a ghost soldier. After she finished her candy bar, she joined in, panting between words. "Oh! Susanna, Oh don't you cry for meeeeee, for I come from Alabama with a banjo on my knee . . ." The song seemed to help convince her muscles to persevere. As Griffin kept singing, Bicycle got into a rhythm, moving her pedal strokes in time to the sound of the lyrics.

She finally hit fifty miles near dusk and stopped with a great sigh of relief. She pushed Clunk up a grassy slope to set up camp under a tall oak tree, noticing some flickering lights out along the darkening horizon. She watched them for a while until she recognized she was looking at a distant drive-in movie screen. Bicycle felt a moment of homesickness sweep over her. She wondered if the Mostly Silent Monks were watching a Clint Eastwood movie back at the monastery. She also wondered if Sister Wanda and the monks missed her. She began to unpack with a pang of self-pity. This was nothing like riding around the block in her neighborhood. Who knew 130 miles would be 130 times harder than one mile?

Griffin started humming, and she looked over at the bike frame and realized she was grateful to have some cheerful company. She arranged her rain ponchos and blanket, and pulled out her pen to write a postcard to the monastery.

Somewhere in Virginia, Under a Tree

Dear Sister Wanda and Mostly Silent Monks,

I am well. Please do not worry about me. Clunk is doing a good job of moving me along the roads. Did you know Virginia has at least 947 cows? I've been counting.

Bicycle

She considered adding a line about meeting a Civil War ghost named Griffin and bringing him along with her to find a Missouri fried-pie shop, but then she thought better of it. Mentioning ghosts might push Sister Wanda to call the Virginia State Police to come find her and drag her back home. Instead, she added a P.S. that she thought would set Sister Wanda's mind at ease:

P.S. I'm using everything you taught me, from good manners to geography, and promise I will think to myself every single night, "What have I learned from this?"

She would drop this postcard in the first mailbox she saw.

Bicycle spent her fourth morning struggling up a steep and sunny stretch of road. At home she didn't think about her speed much, but on these long country roads, her mind started to mutter, *Am I going fast enough to get to California in time? How much farther? Are we there yet? When can we stop for a snack?* She wanted to reassure her muttering mind that she could average ten miles per hour because it made the math of how-much-farther easy, but right now her pace seemed to be somewhere between Unhurried Tortoise and Elderly Sloth.

She watched a black-and-yellow butterfly fluttering along next to her head. She admired it until she noticed it was fluttering faster than she was biking. It soon outdistanced her and flittered away up the road. "Slow down, you . . . you . . . insect!" she yelled. "Why does this have to be so hard?"

Griffin asked, "Is it harder than it should be? Maybe this old bike isn't working right. We did drop a couple of screws a while back, but I can't figure where they came loose from." Since he'd starting haunting Clunk, he had been pretty good at checking for problems with the bike from the inside out, like spotting if the tires were low on air or if a brake was rubbing on the wheel.

"It feels like I'm dragging a dead hippopotamus up this mountain!" Bicycle huffed. The fact that she was feeling upset made her feel even more upset. "What is happening? I've ridden this bike for years and years and *years*. I thought I was prepared for this. It looks so easy in the bike-racing films." She knew she was whining, but she couldn't seem to stop. "My maps are flat, why aren't the roads flat? Why can't the roads just go around the hills and stay flat? This is not fair!"

"Well, there's fair and there's fair," mused Griffin. "In my opinion, this day is as fair and fine as can be. I don't know what your maps say, but a person doesn't need a map to tell 'em it's beautiful out here, or to know that we're lucky. We get to go along as free as we please, the wind in our spokes, the sun on our backs—"

"*You* get to go along as free as *you* please, because *my* legs are carrying you along! And *my* legs are tired of these hills!" Bicycle shouted. With her outburst, she swerved and crashed into a sign framed by tree branches at the side of the road. She fell off the bike and lay in the grass for a moment, dazed.

A white-haired woman wearing a sweatshirt proclaiming I NEVER MET A COOKIE I DIDN'T LIKE peered down at her with great concern. "Are you okay? You took a nasty tumble there!" She held out a paper cup of something. "Here, drink this—it might help."

Bicycle took the cup with mumbled thanks, and sipped. After the first taste, she drained the cup dry. Cold lemonade was a welcome change from the plastic-tasting water in her water bottles. "Thank you very much," she said. "I'm sorry I hit your sign." The sign that Bicycle had hit read: HOME OF THE COOKIE LADY. "Are you the Cookie Lady?"

"I sure am, and don't worry about the sign. You certainly aren't the first bicyclist to fall over in my front yard. It's a tough way to spend the day, climbing hills on bikes." The Cookie Lady held out her hand. "Why don't you come sit on the porch and have a cookie or two until you get your breath back?"

Bicycle could think of no more wonderful words in the world at that moment. She let the woman help her to her feet and followed her a few steps to a small porch with big screened-in windows and colorful wallpaper. Set up on a table were packages of Oreos, Nilla Wafers, Chips Ahoy, Fig Newtons, Nutter Butters, sandwich cookies, soft cookies, chocolate-dipped cookies, and some weird little crispy twists covered in powdered sugar. Bicycle crammed three Oreos in her mouth and then turned red. She thought she'd been bad-mannered, but the woman laughed and handed her another Oreo.

"You help yourself there, child. You riding with a school group?"

Bicycle ate the cookie in two bites and shook her head. "I'm homeschooled." Sister Wanda had often used the same explanation to satisfy curious question-askers in D.C. as to why Bicycle was out and about on a school day.

"Ah. Where are your folks?" asked the Cookie Lady.

"Somewhere back there," Bicycle said, waving her hand to indicate the world outside the porch. She didn't like to lie, and as far as she knew, this was pretty much the truth.

The Cookie Lady nodded and eased herself into a nearby rocking chair with a couple of oatmeal-raisin bars. Bicycle helped herself to a handful of Nutter Butters and some Chips Ahoy. The two of them munched in silence.

When Bicycle could speak through the crumbs, she said, "Thank you. Really. I didn't know how much I wanted a cookie until I saw them all." She burped a small chocolatey burp, covered her mouth, and said, "Excuse me." She'd been yelling at Griffin when she crashed, so this woman must have seen her shouting at her own bicycle. She felt like she should try to explain. "I've been having a rough day. It's been harder riding than I thought it would be."

"I hear you, but you can take heart. It gets easier. And it's worth the effort." The Cookie Lady gestured toward the rear wall of the porch. "Hundreds of people have told me so. Some your age. Some decades older than you."

Bicycle looked more closely at the wall and saw that the inside of the porch was covered not with colorful wallpaper but rather with layer upon layer of picture postcards, some facing written-side out, some picture-side out. There were pictures of rock formations, of giant bridges, of snow-capped mountains and blue oceans. She read the nearest one: *Dear Cookie Lady, We made it to Oregon today. It is so beautiful! Thank you again for the oatmeal cookies. I think of them often. Love, Abigail.* The next postcard was written in Vietnamese. Another one said: *California at last! Cookies rule!*

"All of these people made it to the West Coast on their bicycles?" Bicycle asked.

"Well, not all of them had the same goal," said the Cookie Lady. "Some wanted to ride across Virginia, and lots come from the west headed east. Some rode here from South America and planned to head up toward Alaska! But most of them did what they set out to do." She poured another cup of lemonade for Bicycle. "Where are you headed?"

"To San Francisco," Bicycle said.

"Well, there's a bit of advice I've given before, and I'll give it to you: if you think you might give up before you get there, get off your bike, eat a dozen cookies, and think hard about it. Will you promise me that?"

Bicycle took the lemonade and washed down her last

bite. Now that she was full of chocolate and peanut butter and whatever Oreos are made of, she was feeling better. Energetic, even. She thought she could face climbing the hill again. "Yes, I promise. I won't give up hope without a dozen-cookie consideration first." She gave back the cup and stood up.

"Well, okay then," said the Cookie Lady. She looked satisfied, as if Bicycle was now guaranteed to make it to anywhere she set her mind to. "And send me a postcard from San Francisco. Address it to the Cookie Lady, Afton Mountain, Virginia, and it'll find its way here!" She got up from the rocking chair and opened the screen door.

"I will," Bicycle said. "I'll sign it 'A Girl You Rescued with Cookies and Lemonade.'" She waved as she went out. "Thanks again!" She knew it was her third thank-you, but she had to say it one more time.

Back on Clunk, Bicycle pedaled far enough beyond the Cookie Lady's house so that she didn't think the Cookie Lady could see her before whispering to Griffin, "Hey—you still there? Griffin?"

There was no answer.

"Griffin, listen. I'm sorry. I know I shouldn't have yelled. I'm not very good at being around people, you see. I've never had anyone to talk to before, at least not all day long."

Still no answer, but she felt like the handlebars were listening. "I haven't been out in the world much, you know.

I thought I had this trip figured out. But everything is just so . . . big. Crazy-hilly and big! There's a whole lot of difference between seeing a map of the Blue Ridge Mountains and riding a bicycle up and down the Blue Ridge Mountains." She tentatively patted the handlebars. "I'll try hard not to yell anymore—I mean it."

"You sure you mean it?" Griffin said. "You crashed me right into a signpost, you know. I was only trying to make you feel better."

"I know. I'm sorry."

Griffin held out for another few seconds of silence, then caved in. "Aw, it's okay. Wanna hear another song?" Griffin howled out a chorus of "Camptown Races" while Bicycle puffed up the mountain road.

That night, huddled in her rain-poncho tent with her flashlight illuminating the cool darkness, she jotted some notes in her tiny notebook. She thought it might help her muttering mind to calm down if she recorded which day it was and how far she'd come. She smiled when she added up her daily mileage and confirmed she had chipped away almost two hundred miles from her journey, but she hurriedly stopped writing after calculating the number of miles she still had to go. She shoved the notebook back in her backpack and pulled out *Wheel Wisdom* instead. The book contained a collection of quotes and advice from successful racing cyclists, a lot of them from Zbig. She flipped through the pages until a quote with his name caught her eye:

Most people who love to bike also love to eat. In fact, many bike racers I know took up the sport so they could eat whatever they wanted whenever they wanted but still stay thin. Sometimes these racers will be in the middle of a race, but they cannot resist stopping at a roadside restaurant for a meal and a bottle of wine. Each man eats like they have two or three stomachs. Roast beef! Pasta! Chocolate cake! It is a sight to behold. Sometimes, I myself cannot resist, and I will stop and eat with them. Yet we stay thin and trim and speedy, no matter how many roast beefs we eat. I think this is because calories have a hard time catching up with you when you are zooming down the road on a bike.

Bicycle patted her own stomach. Though the cookies had been digested miles ago, the memory of them still filled her with hopefulness. She wrote another postcard to the monastery and sketched a plate of Oreos topped by the words COOKIES RULE! in capital letters. She was sure Brother Otto would understand what she meant.

THE WAYWARD DOGS OF KENTUCKY

Bicycle came up with a new idea for her little spiral note-book. Instead of keeping track of how far she had to go, she started writing down the names of people she met and road signs that made her laugh, like WARNING: CATS SLEEPING and BED AND BREAKFAST AND EXOTIC ANIMALS. She wrote down some of the songs that Griffin taught her. She tried to wran-gle at least one jumbled word out of every town she camped in, like finding SAILOR in "Charlottesville" and NOOK in "Roanoke" and SUMAC in "Damascus."

On her seventh day, she began keeping track of how many other cyclists she saw and whether they waved to her, called out greetings, or seemed lost in their own little worlds. She saw kids in school clothes with neon backpacks, moms with babies in handlebar-mounted bike seats, folks in ratty clothes on old bikes like Clunk, and men and women wear-ing fancy jerseys that fit like gloves. Mostly they shared silent waves and smiles. She felt like a member of a secret society with whom she didn't have to share one word. Clunk's two wheels served as her membership card.

She also kept track of everything she ate and everything she wished she could eat. By her tenth day, she saw her food supplies weren't holding out like she'd hoped, and she was grateful for the generosity of strangers. When she stopped to fill her water bottles in the mornings at farm stands and country stores, farmers or folks who were shopping sometimes handed her snacks and fruit and waved away any offer of payment. Occasionally someone would give her over-stuffed backpack an odd look and ask if she was headed to school. Bicycle knew that with her regular clothes and old bicycle, she looked a lot like any average kid out for a neighborhood ride, so she always sidestepped any discussion of where she was headed by telling them what she'd told the Cookie Lady—that she was homeschooled and that her family was "back there," flapping a hand behind her. Then she'd thank them profusely for whatever munchies they'd given her.

Starting out on her eleventh day on the road, Bicycle climbed aboard Clunk without a single twinge of pain. Steady riding had toughened her up in places she didn't even know could be toughened. She still wished road builders would try harder to navigate around hills instead of constructing steep roads straight up and down them, but her muscles no longer complained quite so much about it.

Pedaling along and marveling at her pain-free body, Bicycle saw a large blue-and-white sign ahead in the distance. Feeling perky, she thought she'd sprint for it. She stood up on the pedals and raced down the road, Griffin yelling as her own private cheering section. "And, at the line, the winner is . . . Bicycle by a nose!" he bellowed.

She braked to a stop at the signpost and gave a happy whistle. "Griffin, we are really on our way."

"More than usual?"

"Read that sign."

She waited while Griffin slowly read out loud. "'Welcome to Kentucky. The Bluegrass State.'" He whistled, too. "Well, so long, Virginia, and helloooooo, Kentucky!"

"Eight more states to go," Bicycle said. Crossing the state line gave her a shiver of delight. She stopped at a gas station to buy a postcard of galloping horses. She had faithfully mailed a postcard to the monastery every other day through Virginia, and she really wanted to share the news of her completing one whole state by bicycle with Sister Wanda and the monks.

Kentucky State Line

Dear Sister Wanda and Mostly Silent Monks,

I've made it to the Bluegrass State! I wonder if they

68

have red and white grass here along with the blue? That would make for some patriotic lawns.

Nice people are everywhere. Folks honk their car horns and yell, "You go, girl!" out their windows. One lady flagged me down from her church bake sale to give me two whole fruitcakes. Don't worry—I said thank you, and I always brush my teeth before bed.

Bicycle

Riding in Kentucky offered Bicycle a new challenge: sharing the road with coal trucks. When she heard the rumble behind her that meant an extra-large vehicle was coming, she'd steer Clunk toward the very edge of the pavement and clench the handlebars tightly. Griffin would repeat, "Wow, that's big," over and over until the truck had passed them. He'd stopped hollering in surprise every time they saw a car, but after meeting a handful of coal trucks he announced that while cars were impressive, he preferred the peaceful whir of a bike wheel to the roar of an engine.

Bicycle kept a tally of coal trucks in her notebook, then scratched it out and kept track of wildflower colors instead. They had met up with the month of May in the Bluegrass State, and while her search for blue grass proved to be a disappointment, the pink honeysuckle, white magnolia, and purple violets made up for it.

In the middle of one afternoon, the first Saturday in May, she and Griffin found themselves on an odd stretch of road. The asphalt had dozens of sneakers strewn from one side to the other. Bicycle noticed as she biked through them that no two sneakers were alike. They'd made it more than halfway through Kentucky and hadn't seen anything like it before. She asked Griffin what he thought it meant, and he said, "Search me."

Bicycle came around a corner and saw a mailbox up ahead with a dog's face painted on it. An S-shaped dirt driveway led to a couple of barns and a ramshackle farmhouse with a wraparound porch. She decided she'd ask if she could fill up her water bottles there. So far, farmers hadn't said no when she stopped to ask for a drink of water and usually sent her on her way with a pint of raspberries or radishes. "Look at that cute puppy mailbox! I'll stop here for a drink and see if those people know about the sneaker thing," she said to Griffin.

Getting closer to the mailbox, she spotted a faded sign nailed to the trunk of a dead tree. She slowed down and squinted to read it. VISITORS NOT WELCOME. The next tree had another sign: WE SAID VISITORS NOT WELCOME. "Okay, I get the message," Bicycle said under her breath. "Not stopping here for any reason." She passed the mailbox and saw a hulking man and a shapeless woman sitting on the porch. They rocked listlessly side by side in two rocking chairs. Still pedaling, Bicycle lifted a hand and waved at them, but they didn't wave back. She was about to say something to Griffin when she heard a sound that turned her insides to cold jelly. It was a growl. No, it was three growls. Low, menacing, and coming from very close by.

She caught a glimpse of three furry shapes hurtling across the farmyard toward her. They were moving fast, and her instincts told her that she'd better move fast, too, if she wanted to keep moving at all. She stood up on her pedals and started pumping as hard as she could. "Griffin, we have to get out of here!" she yelled, tearing down the road away from the dogs.

"Wait a minute!" Griffin yelled back, but Bicycle was too busy pedaling to listen.

Bicycle raced down the road, dodging mismatched sneakers as she went, but the dogs were gaining on her. They were barking in excited, high-pitched yips. To Bicycle, they sounded overjoyed to have found a tasty little cyclist to eat for lunch. She dug deep into her body for more energy and pedaled faster. At the next fork in the road, she zigged off the main street and zagged onto a network of dirt roads. The dogs were close enough now that she could hear their toenails digging into the dirt. She could almost feel their hot doggy breath on her heels and felt a sudden certainty that these

71

beasts were the reason behind the single sneakers. Either the three dogs had pulled the shoes off cyclists who were trying to get away, or (gulp) the single sneakers were all that remained of unlucky cyclists who had wandered into their territory.

Griffin kept up his yelling. "Wait, Bicycle, stop for a minute! Trust me! Hold on!"

"No way, Griffin! I like my feet still attached to my legs!" Although her lungs were hot and hurting with every inhalation, she continued to pedal full-tilt. She kept zigging and zagging until she swooped around a corner and lost control of Clunk, tumbling off the bike into the road.

The dogs pounded around the corner behind her. When their furry faces came in sight, Griffin called out in a commanding voice that seemed to resonate through the whole frame: "Sit!"

The dogs, two big black-and-tan mutts and a grayish sheepdogish thing, looked shocked. They came to a stop and sat so fast, their back paws hit their front paws. Griffin bellowed, "Stay!"

The dogs stayed still.

"Good dogs! Shake!"

The dogs looked at one another as if to say, "Shake with a bicycle?" But they each lifted a paw in the air and offered it toward Clunk's frame.

"Roll over!" was Griffin's next command.

The dogs rolled back and forth on their backs in the dirt. "Dance!"

The dogs got up on their hind legs and started wobbling to and fro.

Bicycle would have laughed, but she was still trying to catch her breath from the chase.

"Good boys," Griffin praised them. Their long pink tongues lolled. "Go home!"

The dogs looked at one another again, shook the dirt from their coats, and turned tail to lope back the way they'd come.

Griffin waited a minute or two, and then said to Bicycle in his normal voice, "I think they're gone for good."

Bicycle came over to the bike, pulled it upright, and hugged the handlebars. "Griffin, you saved the day! That was incredible! How did you do that?"

The handlebars got a little warm, as though Griffin were blushing. "Shucks, I trained pups ever since I can remember. I know dogs, and I know that even the worst ones need a firm voice to tell 'em what to do. No dog was ever born mean. They only know how to act by the way their owners tell them to act."

"Oh," Bicycle said in a small voice. She thought about this while she put Clunk's kickstand down, then asked in an even smaller voice, "Why would anyone teach them to attack people on bicycles? What kind of dog owners would do that?"

"I can't imagine, Bicycle. People sure can be awful sometimes. It's not nice to think about, but it's true."

Bicycle sat down on the ground, suddenly shaken. "I . . . miss . . . my . . . monastery," she announced, tears welling up in her eyes. "What if . . ." She wiped her nose on her sleeve. "What if the next farm has something worse than dogs? What if they have attack wolverines, or pet grizzly bears, or robot sharks, and they send them out to chew up girls on bikes?"

"Bicycle," Griffin said, "if you think too much about how awful some people might be, you will never get anywhere. None of us would. Every person would stay home every day and hide under the bed. But there's this: that's the first time anything has tried to bite you in hundreds of miles. Think about the kind folks you've been meeting instead. Think about the ways you've been lucky, and you just forget about those rotten dog people. They ain't worth another thought, I'll tell you that, and they sure ain't worth you giving up your trip, no sir, no way!"

Bicycle wiped her face on her other sleeve. "We did cross the thousand-mile mark sometime today," she said in an unsteady voice. She'd done the math last night in her notebook.

"That's a thousand miles of good luck and hard work wrapped up together with cookies on top! Quick, what else can you think of that's lucky?" Griffin said.

"There was the all-you-can-eat church breakfast buffet where they wouldn't take any of my money," Bicycle said. "And the lady there who said I looked like an angel on wheels."

"Don't forget the deer and her fawn grazing grass right next to us when we woke up that time," Griffin added.

"And how it seems to rain only on warm days," Bicycle added.

"See? Measure that up against a few wayward dogs, and lucky comes out on top."

Bicycle sat and counted her blessings until she was feeling more herself again. She looked around. "Where are we?" she asked, pulling her map out of its plastic bag.

Griffin responded, "I wasn't paying a whole lot of attention when we were running for your life, but I think the road we were on is to the right somewhere. Take the next right, and let's see where we end up. How lost can we get?"

THE CANNIBAL TAKES OFF

Three hours and an unknown number of miles later, Bicycle repeated, "Yes, how lost *can* we get?" They'd gotten back on pavement and left the dirt roads behind, but so far, none of the towns they'd spotted were even on the map of Kentucky that Bicycle had brought. The cars she tried to flag down didn't stop. Around five o'clock, Bicycle heard a hullabaloo in the distance, so she pointed Clunk's front wheel toward that, hoping for some clues about their location.

Before long, they were at the edge of a huge assemblage of people. Everyone Bicycle tried to ask for directions was in too much of a hurry to respond. She gave up asking after a few minutes and decided to go along with the crowd.

She dismounted her bike and followed the streaming throng through a parking lot into a courtyard where one heck of a party was going on. A brass band played. Women wore the most astonishing hats: giant swooping affairs several times larger than their heads, some with ostrich feathers, some with ribbons or veils, glittering with color and flair. Men counted thick wads of money and made notes in glossy pamphlets. Bicycle murmured, "Where on earth are we?"

A boy no older than Bicycle overheard and answered, "You're at Churchill Downs racetrack. Today's the Kentucky Derby, duh! It's only the most famous horse race on the planet! Where did you think you were?"

The name rang a bell. Bicycle was pretty sure Sister Wanda had mentioned the Kentucky Derby when they'd done a math unit comparing the average racing speed of different animal species. She could remember that horses were a lot faster than humans and that cheetahs could outsprint them both, but she couldn't remember the name of the city where the Derby took place. She was going to ask the boy, but he was staring at her as if she were the stupidest person he had ever seen. So instead, she turned and wheeled Clunk away, cheeks red.

She leaned against a fence surrounding a grassy paddock and tried to get her bearings. "Griffin, tell me if you see a sign that says INFORMATION anywhere," she said.

"I can't see a thing but fancy dresses and fancy pants," Griffin said.

The crowd pressed closer around them, faces turned expectantly toward a line of horses clip-clopping into the paddock. Bicycle turned around to look at them, too.

The horses were grand, magnificent animals. Each one wore a different-colored saddle blanket with a big white number on it and was led by a handler wearing a matching numbered apron. Horses 1 and 2 had coats of a deep shiny brown. Horse number 3 was the color of a cloudy gray sky. Number 4 was truly enormous, midnight black, and walked with a proud, strutting gait. He was almost yanking his handler along until his gaze fell upon Bicycle and Clunk.

The black horse snorted and reared, muscles rippling. The crowd gasped. Ladies clutched their complicated hats, and men made more notes in their pamphlets. Number 4's handler pulled on his lead line and patted his neck to calm him down, but the horse rolled his eyes, showing the white around his dark pupils. He dragged his handler over to the fence and leaned his head over the top rail, breathing hot snuffling breaths down onto Bicycle's head. She looked up at him and he whinnied right at her. If he'd been a zebra, she would have been nervous, but as it was, she was more surprised. Finally, three extra people came to help his handler, and he was pulled away from the fence and back toward the other horses.

A dozen more horses joined the ambling parade. A bugler in a red coat trumpeted a brief melody, and the jockeys were boosted onto the horses' backs. Most of the jockeys sat easily, but Number 4's rider had to work to keep him under control for a final stroll around the paddock.

The parade proceeded toward a cordoned-off pathway. The big black horse kept turning to stare over his shoulder at Bicycle and Clunk, and his jockey pulled one rein to point the horse's nose in the right direction. Bicycle was startled away from watching him when the folks around her began to sing in unison about the sun shining bright on their old Kentucky home, and she felt Clunk's handlebars vibrate as if Griffin was humming along. When she looked back toward the pathway, all the horses were gone.

The mass of people standing around the paddock finished singing and thinned out. Bicycle glanced around for a friendly face—not a snooty boy—to ask for directions. Suddenly, a woman with the craziest hat of all, shaped like a life-size snow-white swan, came running up. The swan hat wore a tiny sequin-covered swan-shaped hat of its own.

"Oh my dear, my dear, you simply must come help us!" the woman exclaimed breathlessly, grabbing Bicycle's arm with both hands and pulling. When she said "dear," it came out in two syllables with no *r* on the end: "dee-ah." "It's The Cannibal! He's gone mad—you must help us!"

"Who's gone mad? A cannibal?" Bicycle shook the woman's hands off her arm and dug in her heels. "I'll listen to you if you need me to, but you aren't making any sense." The Mostly Silent Monks would have been shocked to hear her say that—they trained everyone to listen patiently to people whether they made lots of sense or none whatsoever, but Bicycle didn't like being yanked around.

The woman fanned herself with her hand, letting out little distressed gasps of air. Her swan-shaped hat was starting to slip to one side of her head. "Oh, oh, there's no time to explain. The Cannibal saw your bicycle and he's in a state. They can't get him near the gate. We're going to lose the race!"

She tried again to tug Bicycle along with her, but Bicycle hung on to Clunk's handlebars and stood her ground.

The lady let go of Bicycle and resettled her swan hat more firmly on her head, taking a deep breath. "I'm sorry, I am, but we've put every last cent of our money on The Cannibal to win the Derby, and he was sure to win until he saw y'all," she said. "When we bought him, the breeder warned us that bicycles might make The Cannibal act peculiar. He was raised in France, right next to the route where bicyclists ride that Tour de France race thingy. You know, where the cyclists race for weeks and weeks and miles and miles?"

Bicycle nodded. She sure did know the Tour de France thingy. It was the most important race covered in her cycling magazine every year. Zbig had won it on his first try.

The lady continued, "As a foal, he used to gallop along the fence whenever those Tour de France fellas came by, like he thought he was part of the race. I don't rightly know what's come over him now, but he seems to have gone out of his mind since he saw you. Can't you please come with me? I think if he sees you with your bicycle nearby, he'll settle down. It's the only thing I can think of!" She wrung her hands in frustration. "Please? I'm begging you."

The woman's distress was so clear, Bicycle couldn't just walk away. And her mention of the Tour de France had piqued Bicycle's interest. "Okay, okay," she said. "Where do we need to be?"

The woman cried out in relief and grabbed Bicycle's elbow, rushing her and Clunk past a side gate and through an underground tunnel. Coming out the other side, they were now standing on a huge circle of grass in the middle of a large racetrack. A white rail separated them from the area behind the starting gate, where the horses and their jockeys were milling around.

A bright and brassy trumpet fanfare cut through the air. Men in white uniforms guided several of the horses into the stalls of the starting gate. Bicycle saw The Cannibal rearing, kicking out with his front legs, and snorting, his jockey working hard to stay balanced in the saddle.

The woman put a lace-glove-covered hand to her mouth and let out a piercing whistle. The black horse twisted his head toward the sound and his hooves fell back to earth. He focused on Clunk and trotted over to the rail, flapping his lips at the bike. The woman said, "I think he wants to touch your bike, dear, if you wouldn't mind."

Bicycle wheeled Clunk right up to the rail, and The Cannibal touched his muzzle to the handlebars. He rubbed the handlebar grips with his nose, making a contented grumbling noise. The swan-hat woman stroked his forehead, murmuring encouraging things. The jockey on the horse's back raised his eyebrows at Bicycle. She shrugged as if to say "I have no idea what's going on."

An official came over and said to the woman, "Miss Annabelle, we need to get them in the gate. If The Cannibal won't go, we'll have to scratch him from the race."

Miss Annabelle nodded. The Cannibal, much calmer now, let his jockey lead him around toward the starting gate. Miss Annabelle leaned down to Bicycle and hissed in her ear, "As soon as he's out of the gate, we'll get your bike to the finish line. When he spots it from across the track, let's hope he decides to kick into high gear and sprint toward it."

They waited until every horse was in his slot at the starting gate. A bell rang, the gates opened, and the horses exploded forward in a tidal wave of pumping legs.

"And they're off!" called an announcer, and Miss Annabelle ran with Bicycle back into the tunnel until they emerged outside, near the white pole topped with a gold ball that marked the racetrack's finish line.

Miss Annabelle looked down the track to watch the race and clutched her swan hat, wailing, "Oh no, oh no, oh no!"

The Cannibal had made it through the first stretch but

was far behind the pack. He was jerking his head in all directions. The rest of the horses were racing single-mindedly along the inside curve of the racetrack, but he was running diagonally across the track. The crowd groaned to see this horse losing the race so terribly.

The announcer called out, "Mellow Johnny takes an early lead, followed closely by Jensie and Big Mig. On the inside, AlwaysComesInThird is moving up, neck and neck with Master Jacques and edging ahead of Cuddles, Bernard the Badger, Froomey, and long shot Red Lantern. Coming into the backstretch, trailing the rest of the pack by more than twenty lengths, is the favorite, The Cannibal."

"Don't you give up now, horse!" Miss Annabelle yelled. She put her fingers in her mouth and gave that piercing whistle again. Even though he was on the far side of the track, The Cannibal snapped to attention and looked their way. Bicycle thought his eyes lit up when he glimpsed Clunk. The enormous horse lowered his head and started charging down the track.

"Mellow Johnny is still in the lead with Jensie. Big Mig is falling back while Cuddles moves up and . . . Wait, hold on!" called out the announcer. "The Cannibal is gaining ground! He's caught the pack and is relentlessly moving up. As they turn for home, the Cannibal is passing Bernard the Badger and Master Jacques on the outside. AlwaysComesIn-Third is trying to edge over, but The Cannibal will not be stopped! Mellow Johnny and Jensie have dropped back two lengths and The Cannibal is on the rail now, on the heels of Cuddles. They're into the final stretch, and it's Cuddles and The Cannibal, it's Cuddles and The Cannibal, and at the wire—it's THE CANNIBAL BY A NOSE! THE CANNIBAL HAS WON THE KENTUCKY DERBY!" The crowd in the stands rose to its feet, yelling and screaming, throwing tickets and lavish hats until the air was a blizzard of color. Miss Annabelle jumped up and down, her swan hat shedding feathers.

When most horses cross the finish line at a race, they gradually slow down to a trot and then a walk. The Cannibal, instead, sped up and wheeled to the outside track, his eyes on Clunk. He jumped the rail that separated the track from the spectators, did a little wriggle and twist that caused his flabbergasted jockey to fall off in midair, and grabbed Clunk's frame in his teeth. Without even thinking about it, Bicycle seized the horse's thick black mane and pulled herself up into the saddle. Horse, bicycle, and girl galloped right through the crowd and away from Churchill Downs.

SLOWING DOWN FOR A
BITE IN ILLINOIS

Even after running the race, The Cannibal had enough energy to keep galloping. Bicycle had never ridden a horse before, so she had no idea how to control him. She tried clinging to his back like a starfish, but found she had better balance when she gripped the front of the racing saddle, put her feet in the stirrups, and bent her knees. *This is so much harder than riding a bike*, she thought. *How do people stand riding horses? There are no brakes, no gear shifters. And how do horses stand having people ride on them? Must be aggravating, something sitting on your back, telling you what to do. I wonder if Clunk ever feels that way.*

They careened along several roads until The Cannibal veered off on a dirt path into some woods, churning up the dirt with his fast-moving hooves. The path led them to a wide river, and the horse swung to the left, following the riverbank.

"Cannibal?" Bicycle tried asking. "Uh, Mister Cannibal,

sir? Can you slow down? Please?" The black horse was lathered with perspiration, and his breathing sounded ragged. He did slow his pace, trotting over to a flat sandy spot next to the river. He slowed further and walked along the river for almost an hour. Then he came to a stop, gently setting Clunk down on the ground before dipping his nose into the water and gulping.

Bicycle let go of her death grip on the saddle. The Cannibal kept drinking and didn't look like he was going to stop anytime soon. Deciding she'd better take her chance while she had one, Bicycle slipped off his back. Her cramped legs couldn't hold her up, so she fell to the ground and rolled like a stale bagel over to her bike. The Cannibal turned to look at her curiously. She continued to lie there, and the horse went back to drinking.

"Griffin? Are you still there? Is everything okay?" Bicycle asked the frame.

"Whooooooo," Griffin said. "I thought we were already having an adventure. Now, *that* was an adventure! Hooowee!" He sounded fine.

"Is Clunk's frame okay? Any dents or breaks?" she asked, pulling herself to her feet and feeling the top tube of the bike where The Cannibal had held it.

"No dents, no breaks. That horse held the bike like it was a little baby or something. I don't think he meant a bit of harm," Griffin answered. "Why, I think he wanted out of that crazy crowd with all those hats flying in the air so bad, he did the first thing that came to mind and took off with us."

Bicycle finished running her hands over Clunk's frame and was satisfied nothing was damaged. "Well, you heard Miss Annabelle say that he was raised in France and used to race cyclists along the road. Maybe he misses home." The Cannibal's ears had perked up when she said the word "France." She turned to him and said one of the few phrases she knew in French, *"Aimez-vous les bicyclettes?"* ("Do you like bicycles?") The horse waggled his ears and flicked his wet muzzle up in the air. He didn't look much like a cannibal. In fact, he seemed to be smiling.

Griffin commented, "I think that's a horse who prefers bicycles to other horses. His owners shouldn't have made him race like that if he didn't want to. But he showed them, I'd say. He's a free horse now. What should we do? Leave him here by the river?"

Bicycle had no idea what to do with a Thoroughbred racehorse. "We don't want him to starve, or get eaten by cougars or anything," she said.

The Cannibal looked from her to the bike and back again with great interest. He seemed to find a talking bicycle very entertaining.

Bicycle addressed him directly. "Okay, horse, here's the

thing—we were lost, and now we're probably even more lost. We need to get out of Kentucky and into Illinois." She unfolded her map and studied it in the fading light. "I think if we follow the river that way, we'll eventually end up back on track. It's getting late, so we're going to camp here hidden in the woods tonight. You can come with us in the morning if you like."

The horse flicked his ears back and forth again, and then put his muzzle down and blew Bicycle's wild hair off her cheeks. Taking this as a sign of agreement, she started setting up camp near the riverside in a grassy patch surrounded by skinny white birches.

The Cannibal whinnied and shook his head insistently, his bridle jingling.

Griffin piped up. "He probably wants that bit out of his mouth. Unbuckle those straps around his head and throat and take it off—he'll be a lot more comfortable."

The Cannibal stopped shaking his head and bent his neck low as Bicycle approached, standing stock-still as she gingerly reached up to undo the straps. Feeling them loosened, the horse shook his head one more time, and the reins and bridle dropped to the ground.

"Should I do the saddle, too?" Bicycle asked.

"Might as well," Griffin agreed.

Softly saying, "There's a good Cannibal . . . Who's a good Cannibal? You're a good Cannibal," she undid the buckles on the saddle girth while the horse patiently waited. She gave the saddle blanket a tug, and the whole thing slid off and thumped on the sand. The Cannibal turned and gave her a big horsey grin. She waited to see if he wanted anything else, but he just started cropping grass.

"Looks like he plans to stick around," Bicycle said. "I guess we have another traveling companion." She picked up the bridle and reins and put them neatly on top of the saddle and blanket. She liked the idea of someone coming upon the heap of racehorse accessories and trying to figure out how on earth they'd ended up here.

"The more the merrier," Griffin said. "Hey, you wanna hear me sing 'My Old Kentucky Home'?" He didn't wait for her answer and launched into it. "Oh, the sun shines bright in the old Kentucky home . . ."

Bicycle, Griffin, and The Cannibal continued to follow the river for several days. The weather was balmy and the river was bordered by a firm dirt path that made bike riding easy, so they were all in good moods. The horse seemed to particularly enjoy when Griffin would talk or sing, nodding and snorting in time to "She'll Be Coming 'Round the Mountain."

Toward the end of the fifth day, they crossed a metal bridge over the river. On the other side, there was another sign informing them in big letters that this was the Illinois state line and that THE PRAIRIE STATE WELCOMES YOU. A

smaller sign welcomed them in a smaller way to SHAWNEE-
TOWN, IL.

Bicycle parked Clunk against a tree and sat down, spreading out her maps to determine if they were where she thought
they should be. It was now getting toward mid-May and she
didn't want to fall behind in her schedule. "Hey, The Cannibal hijacking us could have been worse," she said to Griffin.
"We're back on the route I planned out. And check out all
the words jumbled up in the name 'Shawneetown,' there's
SWEET and SWEAT and . . ." She was about to tell The
Cannibal she'd found OATS when she heard wailing from
a small red house across the road. The Cannibal pricked up
his ears as the wailing got louder. A young woman dressed
in black-and-white checked pants, a double-breasted white
jacket, and an apron with a neat white cap over her short hair
burst out of the door and collapsed in a heap on the front
steps. "*C'est tout!* That's it! Ruined! I am ruined!"

Bicycle recognized her accent as French, and, apparently,
so did The Cannibal. He trotted over to the woman, who
had curled up in a miserable little ball and was rocking back
and forth. The horse leaned down to nudge her with his large
black nose. The woman looked up and called out to the heavens, "*Mon Dieu!* My God! It is *un démon noir*, a black demon,
come to devour me! Why not? There is nothing left to live
for! Go ahead, *mangez*, eat me, demon, it does not matter
anymore!"

The horse cocked his head to one side and looked over at Bicycle for some help.

"Excuse me, ma'am?" Bicycle pushed Clunk across the street and said, "It's not a demon, it's a racehorse."

The woman looked at her, sniffling and sniveling. "A racehorse? *Un cheval?*" She peered at The Cannibal. "*Ah oui,* it is as you say. Well, if your *cheval* would like to eat a French chef, he is welcome to. My life is over."

"I'm pretty sure he does not want to eat a French chef," Bicycle said. "I think he's a vegetarian."

The woman's eyes began welling with fresh tears. "A vegetarian. Ah! I could have made him such delicacies, but instead, I am *ruinée!* Ruined!" She took off her white cap and wiped her cheeks with it.

This was clearly a woman who needed to talk to someone. Bicycle slid her map back in its plastic bag, sat down, and gave the chef a look that said *"I'm listening."*

The chef poured out her story. "I am Chef Marie Petitchou, part of the Petitchou family, a proud family of chefs since forever. I am the first to branch out across the Atlantic Ocean and launch a series of restaurants in the United States. We had our grand opening last month. I foresaw such success. You see, these restaurants are not fast food. They do not serve the pig swill that people eat on the go, quick-quick, with no time to taste and enjoy." She made a face of disgust. "That is not food. So I open up my little restaurants. I named them the SlowDown Cafés because they are serving slow food instead of fast food.

"My chefs, I train them well—we make our food quickly, we serve it quickly, *but*"—she raised a calloused finger—"it must be eaten slowly and with delight." She stood up now, hat pressed against her chest. "I came to give my gift of slow food to the American people"—here she broke down again and crumpled back into a sitting position—"but no one comes. My business adviser says it is because I refused to put in an American drive-up window. Ha!" She scowled. "I will not allow people to drive their smelly cars up to my restaurants and drive away while eating." She paused. "But it seems he is correct. The restaurants are empty. I am a failure, ruined. What will I tell the rest of my family?" She took a big shuddering breath and sank into herself.

Bicycle patted Marie's arm and the horse nuzzled the top of the chef's head. Marie looked up and gazed at The Cannibal for a moment. The Cannibal gazed back and smacked his lips. "But I am being rude!" exclaimed the chef. "Here we are outside my very own café, and I do not invite you in to eat!" She got up, dusting off her white chef's uniform. "*S'il vous plaît*, please, come inside and let me feed you. My treat."

Bicycle liked this weepy chef, who reminded her of Brother Otto. She parked Clunk in the grass outside the little red building and let the chef lead her inside. The Cannibal ducked his head under the doorframe and came in, too.

It turned out that the red house wasn't a house at all, but a very homey café. Inside, there were small cloth-covered tables with sturdy wooden chairs, photos on the wall of the French countryside, and quiet accordion music playing in the background. "Please, make yourselves comfortable," Chef Marie said.

"Do you have a menu?" asked Bicycle.

"*Non, non*, that is part of the SlowDown Café philosophy, *n'est-ce pas*? There is no set menu. We cook whatever is in season," the chef explained. "Would you like a bowl of soup? Maybe some meat, vegetables, some fresh bread? Or *une salade*? I have many good lettuces today."

Bicycle's mouth began to water. "Anything is fine," she managed, swallowing hard.

"Very good," said the chef. "You leave it to *moi*, Marie Petitchou." She disappeared through a small door in the back.

Almost at once, the most astonishing smells started to waft into the room. Bicycle walked over to the door and pushed it open a crack to peek inside. The chef looked like a magician. She zoomed between cutting board, sauté pans, and tart tins. Bicycle had never seen anyone cook so fast. Before she knew it, Chef Marie was sweeping past her, back into the dining room, arms loaded with trays and plates. "*Asseyez-vous!* Sit! Eat!" She seemed much happier after her spin through the kitchen.

Bicycle fell on the food as though she'd ridden a thousand

miles. (She had, actually, ridden 1,175, to be exact.) The tender catfish in a tangy herb sauce melted in her mouth, and the panfried potatoes were crispy and golden brown. The Cannibal buried his head deep in a wooden bowl filled with chopped lettuce and sliced apples. There was silence for some time, broken only by the sounds of chewing, tasting, swallowing, and reaching for more. Bicycle had three helpings of the warm strawberry-cocoa tart and fell back into her seat, deliciously full. "How did you cook this so fast?"

The chef's face filled with pride as she put more lettuce in the wooden bowl for The Cannibal. "It is a technique passed down through my family, and I taught it to my SlowDown Café chefs."

Bicycle stifled a burp. "There must be a way to get people into your restaurants so they can taste this food. Once they try it, I'm sure they'd come back again and again."

The chef beamed. "You are very kind, *ma petite*. You appreciate a fine meal, I see this." Her eyes darkened. "But the fact remains that no one comes, because I don't have the drive-up window. And I will not bend on this. *Non!*" She shouted this last word and banged her fist on the table.

The Cannibal whinnied, smacking his lips around a piece of apple. He shuffled his hooves and knocked over a couple of chairs, which Bicycle jumped up to set right. As she was doing so, she looked thoughtfully at the large horse, who

took up most of the room. Then she glanced out the window at Clunk. "Chef Marie, you might be able to get a whole
bunch of people to come to your restaurants. Instead of a
drive-up window for cars, what do you think about a ride-up
window for bicycles and horses?"

Chef Marie stared at her. The she turned and stared
at The Cannibal, still crunching and munching. Bicycle's
mind was racing, fueled by the strawberry-cocoa tart. "You
could have outdoor picnic areas right next to the restaurant
where bicyclists and horse riders could eat their orders. You
could have big take-out bowls of salad for the horses! You
could advertise alongside bike paths and horse tracks and even
build little detours straight to your cafés. And people could
order at the window or come inside, whatever they want."

The chef's eyes got a faraway look. "*Les bicyclettes* and *les
chevaux* . . . This is not a bad idea. They do not belch smoke
on your food, and you cannot ride your bike or horse and eat
a meal at the same time. You must stop and enjoy it. And
people who ride bicycles, they are always hungry, *non*? And
horse riders and horses—who is more hungry than a horse?"
She began to get excited. "We must try it! I will call my manager *tout de suite*, right now, and see how fast we can do this.
We are ruined anyway if we do not try—what do we have to
lose? So we feed some bicyclists and some horses and their
riders before we go bankrupt. There are worse things to do

in life!" She grabbed Bicycle's hand and started pumping it up and down. "*Merci! Merci, merci, merci!*" she shouted, thanking her in French until The Cannibal drowned her out, whinnying insistently for more salad. Chef Marie filled his bowl one last time.

Bicycle said they needed to head out and started to explain about her trip to San Francisco.

Chef Marie interrupted. "How *merveilleux*, marvelous, that you have the chance to ride across the country. Everyone in my village in France rides bikes everywhere. You must have a good family like mine, eh? They let you stretch your wings and go where your heart leads you?"

Bicycle made a noncommittal noise that might have meant anything. Marie invited her to stay the night and Bicycle accepted.

The chef led The Cannibal into the fenced-in backyard while Bicycle wheeled Clunk into the café's backroom, where there was a sofa bed. Chef Marie came in with a stack of fresh white sheets, and she and Bicycle made up the bed. Then Marie gave Bicycle a couple of oversize postcards and wished her sweet dreams, excusing herself to make some phone calls to her business manager.

While listening to Chef Marie talking on the phone down the hall, Bicycle said to Griffin, "It's too bad ghosts don't have to eat. I wish you could have tried some of the things Chef Marie cooked."

"Me, too," Griffin said wistfully. "This whole place smells great."

Bicycle snuggled into the sofa bed and addressed one postcard to the monastery. The front of the postcard showed a U.S. map with a green star marking each SlowDown Café location, and the back listed forty addresses under the heading "SlowDown Towns." Bicycle noticed that there were at least two green stars in each of the six states she had left to cycle across. She wrote very small and squeezed in a note around the edge of the café list.

Please tell Brother Otto I think I'm beginning to appreciate eating as much as he does. I'll never take his pork chops for granted again.

Bicycle

In the morning, she devoured one of Chef Marie's fluffy cheese omelettes, along with several fruit-filled crepes and warm muffins. Bicycle was strapping her belongings to Clunk when Chef Marie walked over with a thick brown paper sack and a small card in her hand. "*Ma petite*, you have given me hope, and that is a precious gift. I offer you this in return." She handed Bicycle the sack, which was filled with foil-wrapped muffins and crepes, and the card, on which was printed in beautiful calligraphy:

❧

*The bearer of the this card is entitled to as many free
meals as she can eat at any SlowDown Café
across the United States.*

Chef Marie had signed the bottom in an elaborate curlicue script. "Wherever you find one of my cafés, you will be
welcome there. I hope enough of them will succeed with this
new plan that you may enjoy some more good food along
your way."

They hugged each other, and Bicycle whistled for The
Cannibal. She started pedaling down the road, but the horse
took no more than a couple of steps before turning back.
Bicycle stopped, too. The horse was gazing at Chef Marie
with a great deal of affection. He'd apparently found something that made him feel even more at home than a bicycle:
French cooking.

"Eh? You want to stay with Marie?" The chef reached
out and rubbed the horse's nose. "This is fine by me. You
can help me test the vegetarian recipes, *non?*" She looked at
Bicycle. "What is his name?"

Bicycle grimaced. "Well, his owners called him The
Cannibal, but he doesn't seem much like a cannibal to me."

Chef Marie was aghast. "They called a vegetarian The
Cannibal? This will not do! *Non, non, non.*" She put a hand

on the horse's mane and proclaimed, "I will call you Truffle. I think you will like this better." She turned back to Bicycle. "You don't mind if he stays? You will be all right on your own?"

Bicycle smiled to think of the powerful racehorse retiring and getting fat with Chef Marie. "I'm not on my own. I've got Clunk and . . ." She figured there was no easy way to explain Griffin. "And I've got my Free Eats card. I'm a lot better than all right. *Au revoir!* Good-bye!" Bicycle waved and pedaled away.

PIGS ON PARADE IN MISSOURI

If Bicycle had blinked while biking through Illinois, she might have missed it. She traveled through the very bottom of the state, where it came to a point, so two days of riding took her from one border to the other. Before she could get accustomed to Illinois's open fields and grand old houses, she was biking over the Mississippi River. She wasn't quite halfway across the country, but crossing the Mighty Mississippi was a milestone to celebrate. She stopped on the big metal bridge and gazed down at the wide swath of muddy water rushing far beneath her feet. Griffin hummed a patriotic song, and Bicycle solemnly saluted the rippling waves below. Clunk dropped a screw into the water.

On the other side, a green sign with curlicue writing announced WELCOME TO MISSOURI—THE SHOW-ME STATE.

Griffin shouted, "That's right! Show me my hometown! Show me the fried-pie shop!"

Around dinnertime, Bicycle pulled out the other oversize postcard Chef Marie had given her and saw that she was near a SlowDown Café. She told a passing man on a tractor the address, and he directed her toward the next street. The café had a blackboard out front with the words NEW RIDE-UP WINDOW chalked on it, with an arrow pointing around the side of the building. It looked like Chef Marie's café managers weren't wasting any time trying out the new idea for attracting customers.

Bicycle coasted up to order her food. The ride-up window was clearly nothing more than a regular window in the kitchen that the chef had slid open. She showed her Free Eats card over the sill and was surprised when the chef said he'd been hoping she'd stop by—Chef Marie had called and told him to be on the lookout for her. He handed Bicycle a heaping plate of the daily special, a crawfish meatloaf with asparagus and mashed potatoes. She balanced her plate on her handlebars with one hand and pushed Clunk around back to look for a picnic table. Three of the seven tables were already taken, two by groups of cyclists, and one by a couple who had come on horseback. Bicycle smiled to herself. Word about the ride-up café was spreading already.

She finished every bite of her dinner, licking the last of the potatoes right off the plate with a contented hiccup. Reluctant to leave such a hospitable spot, Bicycle set up camp next to a picnic table that night.

When she awoke the next morning, she waited until the chef opened shop for the day and ordered the breakfast special—lemon waffles and chicken-apple sausages.

"Let's get go-ing, let's get go-ing, let's get go-ing!" chanted Griffin while she ate outside. "We're in the Ozark Mountains now, we're getting real close!"

Bicycle finished swallowing a maple-syrupy mouthful and grumbled at Griffin, "Look, I have to eat if I'm going to pedal us anywhere, so just hold on."

Griffin tried to be patient while she ate, but he kept asking, "Are you done now? How about now? Now? Can you eat faster?"

Finally, she gave up trying to eat. "Okay, okay, let's get you home, Griffin G. Griffin," she said, folding up her leftovers in a napkin. Right before she left, the chef came out with a paper sack of extra breakfast goodies, calling it a "Feed Bag," and said Chef Marie had asked all the cafés to provide them to her. Bicycle added her leftovers to the sack and gratefully packed it up. She knew Chef Marie had said hope was a precious gift, but gifts of free food had to be just as precious. Probably more. Bicycle thought hope could take care of itself when her bike was stocked with homemade waffles.

The Ozark Mountains didn't seem exactly like a mountain range to Bicycle; they were more like a monster-sized roller coaster. There were lots of short, steep hills placed very close together. Bicycle could race down one hill and then coast almost to the top of the next one before she had to pedal again. It was a grand way to bike.

"It hasn't changed a bit, not a bit!" said Griffin as they roller-coastered along. Bicycle found this hard to believe, but she was full of waffles and in a good mood, so rather than argue with him, she said, "Yes?" and let him talk.

"The mountains go up and the mountains go down, same like I remember! It's better on a bike than walking 'em, though, and more fun to be heading back to Green Marsh than it was to be walking off to war. And there's trees, just like I remember! Trees!"

Bicycle was happy Griffin could find so much that made him feel at home. For every modern gas station or parking lot, the ghost also noticed old-fashioned fishing holes and kids playing ball. He cajoled her to stop and try something called a grasshopper shake, which he was sure would be full of grasshoppers. When she reported it was made from mint ice cream, he howled with laughter. When they camped at dusk, he begged her to catch spring fireflies. She put them in an empty water bottle to make a lantern, then let the entire twinkling bunch go at once to scatter in the darkness.

On the afternoon of their third Missouri day and twenty-fifth day overall, they coasted into Green Marsh. Griffin chattered the whole way into town. "Well, that farm over there, that was Old Man Roy's—he was mean as twelve snakes in a sack. And that notch over there, that's the top of a good trail for trapping raccoons. That mountain, that's where I spent my first night camping. And those clouds, the big puffy ones, those are the exact same clouds I used to see, I swear!"

When Bicycle pedaled up Main Street, Griffin was almost yelling about the things he recognized.

"That's right where the schoolhouse was, right there! Looks like it's a post office now. And that place that says Pet Shop, that used to be the general store—you could get everything there, clothes and candy and shovels and string. Boy, things sure have changed!"

"I thought you said everything was the same," Bicycle teased.

"Well, it's both! I know that tree over there, and that lilac bush . . ."

Bicycle was half listening when she noticed that not a single shop was open. Not a single person was on the street. Colorful ribbons and streamers were draped from the streetlamps, so the street had a festive feeling, but the complete silence was more than a little sinister. "Griffin," she interrupted, "where *is* everyone?"

"Huh?" He paused in his reminiscing. "You're right. Where is everyone?"

"I haven't seen anyone since we pedaled into town." Bicycle heard a sort of rumbling behind them. She turned to see a cloud of dust puffing up one of the side streets. "I wonder what that could be?" she said, shading her eyes with her hand and squinting toward it.

Griffin listened. "Last time I heard a rumbling like that must have been the pig stampede in '59 when Old Man Roy's pigs escaped from their pen and stormed the schoolyard . . ." He trailed off. "Oh no," he said in a small, horrified voice. Then he started shouting. "Bicycle, get out of the street! Get out now! I mean it, now! Pigs!"

"Griffin, get a hold of yourself," Bicycle said. "Pigs? Why should I worry about pigs? They're no taller than my knee, nothing to worry about—*Aieeeeeeeeeee!*"

Rounding the corner was a landslide of enormous pigs running at top speed toward Bicycle. They covered the entire road, pressed up snout to shoulder, a solid wave of pink-and-brown pig flesh. The rumbling sound of their trotters grew to a pounding thunder. Dust flew in all directions.

There was no time to ride to safety. Bicycle tried to jump off Clunk and get out of the way, but one sock caught on the edge of a pedal. She jerked her foot sideways in a panic. "Griffin, help!" she shouted. The dust started to swirl around her, blinding her. Then she was flying through the air and everything went dark.

When she opened her eyes, it was still dark, but the kind of dark that meant nighttime instead of unconscious. She was lying on a soft bed next to a window with a quilt tucked up under her chin. She sat up in the unfamiliar shadows. "Hello?" she called out. "Is anyone there? Griffin?" No answer. She pushed the quilt off and swung her legs over the edge of the bed. She felt a little dizzy, so she sat still until the feeling passed. She noticed a sliver of light poking under the bottom of a door. She got up and pushed on the brass doorknob.

The door creaked open to a large room with well-polished logs forming the walls and wooden beams crossing the ceiling. An old man sat in a rocking chair reading a cookbook. His skin was as wrinkled as a peach pit crossed with a prune.

He looked up at Bicycle's approach and his face wrinkled even farther with a smile. "You're awake! I'll be a monkey's great-granduncle. I didn't think we'd be seeing you until morning." He put down the cookbook and rose slowly to his feet.

Bicycle walked over to him, and he offered her his hand.

"Jeremiah's the name," he said, shaking her hand. "And you are . . . ?"

"Bicycle," she answered. "What happened? Where is my bike? Where am I?"

"Let's have some hot chocolate." Jeremiah started slowly toward the kitchen. "Not often I get an excuse to stay up late and have hot chocolate."

In the kitchen, he puttered over a pan with some milk and cocoa powder. Bicycle sat at a table covered in sloppy stacks of cookbooks. One was open and had some handwritten notes in the margin: *Meat fillings: Buffalo? Polish sausage? Frog legs?* She cleared a space for two mugs when Jeremiah brought them over to the table.

"Well, you're a lucky little thing. Folks checked the streets before that darn Parade of Pigs got started, but you must've slipped by. I was in my shop makin' sure everything was locked up tight when I saw you out the window, your eyes big as pie plates, watchin' the pigs hurtle right toward you!" Jeremiah blew on his hot chocolate. "I was gonna run out and see if I could grab you in time, but near as I can figure, looked like your bike sort of wriggled itself and pitched up in the air, throwing you into that big lilac bush near the sidewalk. Durndest thing, like the bike was alive, pitchin' around like that. Somehow your backpack came loose, too, and helped break your fall." He nodded toward a corner of the room where her backpack sat with her helmet neatly perched on top.

"What *is* the Parade of Pigs?" Bicycle asked.

"You never heard of it? Lord, I thought that stupid thing was famous everywhere." Jeremiah squinted his eyes and sipped a little hot chocolate. "Well, it's a long story. Handed down through my family for three generations, but we don't like to talk about it much."

Bicycle gave him a look of quiet encouragement that she had perfected in Intermediate Listening class.

"Fine, okay, I'll tell you the shortest version I can," he said. "One of the first mayors Green Marsh ever had was a feller named José Marquez. Came here from Spain. He was a farmer and brought a couple of piglets with him. His piglets grew up into big ol' pigs and had lots of little piglets. He started buyin' up land and raisin' more and more pigs until half of town was basically one big pig farm.

"He made a lot of money with his pigs, got elected mayor, and was sorta well-known and influential in Missouri, so he managed to get Green Marsh selected as the town to host the first Missouri Music Festival. All kinds of musicians were invited, banjo players and fiddlers and guitarists and singers, with judges from Saint Louis. It was a big to-do, I tell you. My great-grandpa, Joe Branch, was going to make fried pies for the event, and he figgered it was gonna make him world-famous. That was his dream, ever since he returned from the Civil War, to have a shop that sold world-famous fried pies. Even the governor of Missouri was comin' to hear the music and taste my great-grandpa's pies."

Bicycle's face lit up. She'd found Joe Branch's fried-pie shop! She scooted up to the edge of her chair, listening even closer. Despite his protest that he didn't like to tell the story, Jeremiah had gotten into storytelling mode—he had a far-off look like he could see the festival right before his eyes.

"My momma told me he didn't sleep, makin' fried pies day and night. He was going to sell them in a big tent he bought and put up right in front of the shop. Then the night before the festival, Mayor Marquez called a meeting and announced his big pig plan." Jeremiah stopped talking for a minute, looking at Bicycle to make sure she understood the importance of this.

Bicycle couldn't think of an appropriate response, so she echoed, "Big pig plan?"

"Ayup. He was from Spain, remember, and the town he grew up in was called Pamplona. He explained to everyone that in Pamplona, for hundreds of years, they'd been having this tradition called the Running of the Bulls. They get this big buncha bulls riled up and then they let 'em race through the streets of the town, chasin' people. It's how they start some festival there. Well, he wanted to do the same thing here, but with his pigs. Let 'em run down Main Street to kick off the festival. 'We'll call it the Parade of Pigs. It'll give the festival some class,' he said to the townspeople. I ask you, is there a battier idea than that in all of Missouri?" Jeremiah frowned and shook his head. "My momma said if Great-grandpa Joe had been at the town meeting, he woulda told the mayor not to do it. But he was too busy frying, so he missed the whole thing. The rest of this durn town, well, some voted for it and some voted against it. But I guess not enough voted against, and no one thought to tell my great-grandpa.

"The next day, people were streaming into town for the festival, the fried-pie tent was set up, and everything was lookin' good. Someone said they'd seen the governor arrivin' with his family. My great-grandpa went out to look, and what did he see? Well, same thing you saw, I reckon. A big ol' mess of crazy pigs running down the street straight toward his tent.

"Nothin' he could do." Jeremiah sighed. "Pigs ran right into the tent and knocked over the tables. Whatever fried pies they didn't trample, they swallowed down just like . . . well, pigs. Needless to say, the governor didn't eat any of Great-grandpa Joe's fried pies. No one did that day. The townspeople was real sorry about what them pigs did to the pies. But"—he sighed even more deeply—"the townspeople also seemed to think pigs runnin' through the town was as funny as all get-out. They decided to have the Marquez family do it again the next year, and the next, and they've done it ever since."

Jeremiah's voice got quiet. "My momma said Great-grandpa Joe was never the same after that. He still fried pies, and still sold 'em in the shop, but he gave up tryin' to become world-famous." Jeremiah's eyes were moist. He looked up at Bicycle. "More'n you wanted to know, I reckon, but that's the basic story of why we got pigs runnin' down our street."

Bicycle was lost in the images of pigs trampling pies. "Wow." Then she remembered why she'd wanted to hear the story in the first place. "But what about my bike?"

Jeremiah slurped a little more hot chocolate, then pursed his lips. "Well, missy, I'm sorry to be the one to tell you this. Your bike threw you off like I told you, but it stayed in the street. It got run over by eight hunnert and thirty-eight pigs. It looks about as good as a tent fulla pies looks after eight hunnert and thirty-eight pigs come through."

Bicycle gasped. *Clunk! Griffin!* "Where is it?" she demanded. "I need to see it now."

Jeremiah looked at her with sad eyes for a moment. He gestured with his mug toward a blanket-covered bundle. "Over there."

Bicycle pushed back from the table and flew to the blanket. She lifted it and dropped it to the side. Underneath, there was a heap of orange metal. If you knew what to look for, you could tell it was once a bicycle. Barely. Hoofprints had mashed the metal frame almost flat in places. The tires were no longer round, but semihexagonal. Bicycle felt a snap in her chest, like her heart had broken in two. She fell to her knees and put one hand on Clunk.

"Griffin?" she whispered to what she thought were the handlebars. "Can you hear me?"

No answer.

"Griffin?" she asked again, a little louder.

Silence.

"Griffin! You answer me!" she yelled, her voice cracking. "You can't leave now!" She started to cry, tears streaming off her face and onto the mashed frame. "I just got you home! You have to be okay!"

Jeremiah shuffled up behind her and put a hand on her shoulder. "Missy," he said, "I think you'd better go back to bed and rest. We can talk more in the morning. Then we'll have some pie. Everything looks better when you have a fried pie in front of you."

"Fried pie." She sniffled and snuffled, tears still flowing. "That's why I'm here . . . for fried pie . . . I was . . . supposed to . . . find Joe Branch's pie shop." Her voice was hitching in her throat.

"Well, you found it, all right. Great-grandpa Joe started our family's Paradise Pies fried-pie shop, and my grandfather and then my parents ran it after him, and I run it now. I made up my mind to try to make it world famous in his memory." He paused for a moment and then asked, "Now, how would a young thing like yourself know the name Joe Branch?"

Bicycle felt a new wave of tears welling up. "Never mind," she gulped. "It's not important . . . now." She stood up on wobbly legs as Jeremiah covered Clunk's frame again with the blanket. He guided her to the room where she'd been sleeping, making soothing clucking sounds with his tongue.

"Back to bed, missy. Things will look brighter over pie in the morning."

Bicycle took his advice and got into bed. *I let Griffin down. He took care of me when I needed help, but I couldn't do the same for him.* She felt like she might never sleep again, but her eyes closed on their own. Her dreams were nothing but black.

PARADISE PIES

It seemed mere moments had passed before sunshine was beaming into Bicycle's face through the bedroom's window. She heard familiar off-key singing coming from another part of the house. "Oh! Susanna, Oh don't you cry for me, for I come from Alabamy with a banjer on my knee—hee!"

"Griffin!" Bicycle shouted. She threw off the covers and ran to the kitchen. There stood Jeremiah in a flour-covered apron and polka-dotted oven mitts, peering into a pot of oil, singing in a gravelly voice. "The sun so hot, I froze to death, Susanna, don't you cry . . . Well!" He straightened up, grinning a grin filled with crooked but strong teeth. "Up already, eh? Just in time to try a hot batch of peach!" He used a metal net to scoop some little pastries from the pot and added them to a pile on a towel-lined cooling rack.

Bicycle's shoulders drooped and she half sat, half fell onto a chair. Jeremiah ambled over and put down a pocket of crispy dough on a plate in front of her. "Dig right in. Put some warm pie in that mouth, and it won't look so unhappy," he said.

Why do so many people I meet want to feed me? Bicycle wondered, thinking of the Cookie Lady and Chef Marie as well as the snack-giving strangers she'd met. Then her stomach gurgled as if to remind her how terrific it was that so many people wanted to feed her. Then it gurgled a little louder as if to remind her not to be impolite, so she picked up the pie pocket and bit into it. Warm peach and cinnamon flavors filled her mouth, and her stomach burbled in approval. She took another big bite and finished the pie in no time flat.

"Have another. As many as you like," recommended Jeremiah, plunking down another plate with four more fried pies on it.

Bicycle reached out and picked up two more, eating them with one in each hand.

Jeremiah's smile wrinkled his face so much his eyes nearly disappeared. "Yes, ma'am, my pies can cure what ails you. They're all I eat, breakfast, lunch, and dinner, and I got no complaints."

Bicycle realized that she was enjoying herself and felt ashamed. *Griffin's gone, and all you can do is eat pies? You're a rotten person.*

Jeremiah watched her face fall back into despair, and sat down at the table with her. "Now, it's plain as day that you're mighty upset. Maybe we better start from the start. I told you how those pigs got in that street yesterday—now can you can tell me how *you* got in that street in front of them?"

Bicycle said, "It's a long story, too, but I'll tell you as much as I can." She thought for a minute about where to begin, and decided she had better start from the start, as Jeremiah had suggested. "The day I was left at the monastery, the front door was missing . . ."

She talked through the whole morning, Jeremiah handing her fried pie after fried pie, listening to every word. She told him about the places she'd been before getting to Missouri: Washington, D.C.; Virginia; Kentucky; and Illinois. She told him about Griffin and her promise to return him to his hometown and his friend's fried-pie shop. Jeremiah's gray eyebrows raised way up when she related that part of the story, but he kept listening without comment.

And when she finished with the Parade of Pigs, she remembered that some of the last words she'd said to Griffin were to disagree with him. "And I said, 'Why should I worry about pigs?' Usually I'm a good listener, but I didn't listen to him until it was too late. Then he saved me, but I let him get run over eight hundred and thirty-eight times." She felt tears welling up again. "So I've lost my bike and Griffin, too."

"Losin' two friends in one go—that's tough on toppa tough," Jeremiah agreed.

Bicycle looked at him. *Griffin was my friend. I made a*

friend. She sat in silence, overwhelmed. After a few minutes, she shook her head like she was waking up. "Mister Jeremiah, I can't give up on Griffin. Is there a doctor in town? No, wait—some kind of a bike mechanic?" she asked. *Maybe Griffin isn't totally gone,* she thought. *He was a ghost, after all. Maybe he's just in some passed-out ghostly state.*

Jeremiah looked uncomfortable. He stood up and turned away. "Mebbe. I don't rightly know," he said gruffly. He busied himself cleaning up the dishes. After a few minutes of dish splashing and soapsuds, he turned back around. "I know who can help you, dagnabbit," he said, "but I don't know that she will. One lady fixes bikes here in Green Marsh, and that's Estrella Marquez Montgomery." He spat out the name. "But I ain't talking to her since it was *her* great-grandpa who ran those pigs all over *my* great-grandpa's dreams. We don't have nothin' to do with each other." He looked mad, and then lifted his shoulders in apology. "But it wouldn't be right to pretend like I don't know where you need to go. A word of warning: When we get there, don't tell Estrella that you're trying to revive a ghost who was a friend of Joe Branch's. She's mean as those pigs her family raises, so that probably wouldn't help you at all." He started toward the front door. "I'll pull the van around while you get your bike, and we'll head over there."

Bicycle ran to pick up the blanket with the remains of Clunk wrapped inside.

Bicycle and Jeremiah trundled down the street in a white bakery van labeled PARADISE PIES on the outside. The van moved as slowly as its driver, and Bicycle had to jiggle her legs up and down to defuse her impatience. After a while, Jeremiah turned left at a sign that said MARQUEZ PIGS and drove up a tree-lined driveway to a fine house with a large detached garage. He turned off the engine and said, "You run in alone and see if she's there. Tell her what you need. Be better if she don't see you with me."

But before Bicycle could hop out of the van, a tiny, wrinkled lady came around the corner of the house, hollering at the top of her lungs.

"You git that durn pie truck out of my driveway, Jeremiah Branch! You tryin' to poison an old lady with those awful fried pies? I ain't fallin' for it. You git, now!" She came up to the side of the truck and starting kicking one of the tires with her tiny foot. "Git, I say!"

Jeremiah climbed out of the front seat as fast as he could, which wasn't very. "You leave off kickin' my truck, Estrella, afore you break somethin'! I ain't here to give you no pies! You ain't never welcome to eat a single pie I fry—that's the honest truth!"

Estrella redoubled her tire-kicking efforts. "Jealous of my pigs, you are. I know you're up to something!"

Jeremiah yelled back, "I wouldn't even be here if it wasn't

for your pigs and the mess they make! Jealous? Ha! I'd like to see the day!"

Bicycle jumped out of the van and dashed around to open its rear double doors and pull out the blanket-wrapped bundle. She interrupted the squabble with one of the Sacred Eight Words: "Help!"

It did the trick. Jeremiah and Estrella stopped arguing as Bicycle lugged the bundle over to them. Jeremiah looked sheepish, but Estrella looked interested.

"Well, youngster, what have you got there? Appears to be a bike in trouble," she said. The blanket had fallen partially open, and Estrella was peering down at a piece of Clunk's frame.

Bicycle looked Estrella in the eyes. They were close to the same height, even though Estrella seemed to be a hundred years older. "It is. It's in a lot of trouble. Please," she said. "Please help me, help my bike."

Estrella smiled a puckered smile at Bicycle. She may have had fewer wrinkles than Jeremiah, but not by much. She touched Bicycle's cheek with a soft hand and said, "Bring it in the shop, honey, and I'll take a peek. Sometimes things look worse than they are." She glared at Jeremiah. "You," she warned, "stay out here and keep your poison pies with you."

Jeremiah glared back, but he saw Bicycle's pleading face and kept his mouth shut.

Bicycle followed Estrella into the garage and laid the blanket on a workbench to unwrap Clunk. Estrella put on a helmet with a spotlight on the top and magnifying goggles over her eyes. "Hmmmm," she hummed, examining the frame from a distance, and then up close. "Hmmmm." She plinked one spoke like she was playing a guitar string, then plinked another.

"Can you do something? Anything?" Bicycle said. "My friend might be trapped in there, and I need to know if he's still alive . . . well, not alive, because he's a ghost, but at least if he's awake. Oh, please, say you can help!"

Estrella glanced at her. "Think there's a ghost in your bike? You've been eatin' Jeremiah's pies, ain't you? They'll make you daft like that old man—you better watch out."

Bicycle shook her head, and then nodded. "No—well, yes, I had some fried pies, but I'm telling you the truth. I had a ghost haunting my bike frame because he needed to get to Green Marsh from a Civil War battlefield since this was his home. I need to know if he's still in there."

Estrella turned the spotlight on Bicycle's face and peered into her eyes with the magnifying glasses. "Hmmmm." A long moment passed. "All right, you're telling me the truth. But I mean it—don't have any more fried pies; they'll be the death of you." She turned back to the bike. "So I need to see if I can fix up this here bike and also wake up a ghost who may or may not still be in here, that right?"

"That's right. Can you do it?" Bicycle twisted her hands behind her back.

Estrella picked up a tiny wrench and leaned close to Clunk's frame. She tapped it lightly with the wrench and listened to the *clank*. She squeezed a tire. Then she sniffed at the bike, and sniffed again. "Run over by pigs, was it?" she asked. "Oh my, was this the bike that got caught in the Parade of Pigs? That's why we always clear the streets beforehand. Those pigs of mine sure can run, but they have a heck of a time knowing when to stop." She set her mouth in a hard line. "Child, if anyone in the world can help you, it's me—it's the least I can do, seeing as how it was my company, Marquez Pigs, that caused this damage to your bike. Whoops, almost overlooked my manners. I'm Estrella Marquez Montgomery, owner of Marquez Pigs and the best bike mechanic in town. And you are . . . ?"

"I'm Bicycle."

"There's a name I won't soon forget. You leave this to me, and we'll see what's what." She was all business now, and waved an impatient hand. "You go on and scat. I can't work with you staring moony-eyed at me. Come back around dinnertime, and like I said, we'll see what's what." She turned to the bike.

Bicycle started to back out of the garage, past a few other bikes awaiting repairs. "The ghost's name is Griffin, Griffin G. Griffin, if you find him," she said.

Estrella gestured distractedly over her shoulder, shooing her out, and Bicycle left her to work.

Jeremiah was sitting in his bakery van, grumbling to himself. "Call my fried pies poison? She's poison, and that's the honest truth there." He saw Bicycle and asked with concern, "Can she help at all? Hate to think we came down here to get yelled at by that old turkey and she can't help you."

Bicycle said, "There's a chance. She said if anyone could help fix Clunk and wake up Griffin, it'd be her." She climbed in the van. "But we won't know much more until dinnertime. I'll have to wait until then to find out what she can do."

Jeremiah grunted. "Best thing to do when you're stuck waitin' for news is to keep busy." He started up the van and they pulled away. "Pie shop's closed on Tuesdays, but there's always somethin' needs doin' there. Say, you can help me taste test some new pies I'm workin' on."

Without thinking, Bicycle said, "Estrella said not to eat any more of your fried pies or they'll make me daft."

Jeremiah spluttered, "Daft? I'll tell you what's daft: a woman who won't eat a single fried pie because of some family feud, that's what. Pies, fried or not, are the best thing for you in the world—they're the secret to a long life. I'm ninety-two years old, myself. I've eaten nothin' but fried pies for the last ten of them years, and I ain't got no complaints. It'll serve her right if she dies from a lack of pies." They drove back through town and parked in front of the pie shop. "You come on in and try my double-crispy apricot fried pie and then you tell me which one of us is daft."

"I'm sorry," Bicycle said as she followed Jeremiah into the kitchen at the rear of the shop. "I think your fried pies are delicious. I'd love to try a double-crispy anything." She thought she'd be too distracted to offer much assistance with taste testing, but she'd give it her best shot.

Jeremiah explained that he was designing some new fried-pie flavors and was having trouble coming up with combinations. "Apple, peach, blueberry, cherry, strawberry-rhubarb, raspberry, bumbleberry, turkey, chicken, pumpkin, peanut butter and sorghum, chocolate cream surprise, bacon and egg: we do those flavors better than anybody. But the only way we're gonna get world-famous is if we come up with some new fried pies no one's ever thought up before."

He walked over to a spread of fried pies he'd made the day before. "Now, over here I've got some turtle pie."

Bicycle wrinkled her nose.

"It's not what you think. It's full of caramel and pecans. Then over here we've got sweet potato, but that's not what you think either—it's got turtles in it." He spluttered a hearty laugh at her expression. "Naw, just kidding—it's sweet potatoes, I promise. Hey, how about a cutie pie?"

"What's a cutie pie?" Bicycle said.

"You are!" He laughed even harder.

Bicycle managed her first smile since she'd seen the Parade of Pigs coming her way.

"That's an old pie-seller's joke. My momma always used to use that one on me. Okay, down to business. Try this," he said, handing her a lumpy pie pocket.

She bit into it, and spat it back out into her hand. "What was that?" she asked.

"Celery and banana. Not so good?"

"Not so good."

Jeremiah sighed. "Let's hit the cookbooks."

The shop's kitchen table was loaded with as many cookbooks and recipe notecards as Jeremiah's home kitchen table. They pored over the recipes all afternoon, trying to mix the right combination of unusual and appetizing. They blended canned peaches with dried cherries, then toasted walnuts with ground beef, and agreed they were on to something interesting when they filled one pie with chopped blueberry muffin tops and tapioca pudding. They were so intent on their work that Bicycle was surprised when she glanced at a clock on the wall and saw it was past six.

A flutter of hope started flittering inside her, accompanied by a good dose of nervousness. "Jeremiah, can you please give me a ride back to Estrella's?"

Jeremiah grumbled, but agreeably. "Ayup, I'll drive you, but I'm not gettin' out of the van this time, even if she kicks a tire again."

A BICYCLE WITHOUT WHEELS

Back at Estrella's garage, Bicycle crossed her fingers and stepped inside. Estrella was bent over the workbench, her chin resting on one hand. Bicycle came up behind her and looked over her shoulder. "Holy spokes," she said, stunned.

Clunk looked as good as new. Better, in fact. The frame was shinier than it had ever been, gleaming like it was under a spotlight. The bike lay on the workbench like a polished work of art. "Estrella! This is incredible! How can I ever thank you?" Bicycle's flutter of hope had turned into a flying bird, soaring through her with happiness.

Estrella, however, wasn't celebrating. Her face was grim.

Bicycle felt the flying bird soaring through her turn into a frightened, fluttering thing once more. "Is it . . . did you . . . could there . . ." She couldn't ask the question, because she was afraid of the answer.

Estrella waved her closer and took her hand. "Honey,

this is something I never like to tell anyone. Your bike, it may look good, but . . ." She shook her head. "You're never going to ride it again. I was able to fluff out the frame so it would have the right shape, but it's weakened here"—she pointed—"here, here, and right through here. In fact, I strongly suspect it was getting toward the end of its riding life before it got to Green Marsh. This is an old, old bike, sweetheart. All it's ever going to be is a pretty shape to look at. I am so sorry."

Bicycle stared at the frame in disbelief. It looked perfect. "Are you sure? How can you be sure?"

Estrella rummaged through her tools and came up with a stethoscope. "Here, give a listen. Best way to tell if a bike is safe to ride or not is to listen to its frequency."

Bicycle put the stethoscope in her ears, and Estrella placed it against Clunk's frame, which she then tapped with a screwdriver.

"Hear that? That's weakness in the steel."

Bicycle heard a *twang* and then a *hum* in her ears.

"And listen here," Estrella said, moving the stethoscope to another part of the frame and tapping it again.

Another *twang* and *hum*.

"And even here." Estrella put the stethoscope up near the handlebars and tapped once more.

A *twang*, a *hum*, and Bicycle heard something else. Distant, like it was coming from several miles away.

"Sun so hot, I froze to death, Susanna don't you cry . . ."

"Griffin!" she shouted with joy, dropping the stethoscope and hugging the frame. "You're back!"

Estrella raised her eyebrows. "You hear the ghost?" She took the stethoscope and listened for herself. "Hmmm, I hear him, too. He's got a good singing voice."

Bicycle kept hugging the bike frame with one arm and turned and hugged Estrella with the other.

Estrella blushed but hugged back. "Shucks, woulda done it for any bike, haunted by a ghost or no." She finally disengaged from the hug. "Now, now, don't squeeze it too hard, it needs some time to rest before the frame's as strong as it's gonna get. I'm keepin' it here overnight, but you can take it in the morning, don't worry." She covered the frame with the blanket.

Estrella brushed aside Bicycle's thanks and offer of payment as they walked out of the shop together.

Jeremiah rolled down his van window and looked distrustfully at Estrella and questioningly at Bicycle. He saw Bicycle's happy face and asked, "All fixed up, then?"

Bicycle struggled with a funny feeling—a combination of disappointment over the terrible luck that she was never going to ride Clunk again, and elation over the terrific luck that Griffin was back. "Not exactly," she answered. "The bike looks normal, but Estrella says I can't ride it anymore. But Griffin—he's awake! He's still in there! He just needs to rest. I'm going to see him in the morning." Knowing Griffin had made it home—that seemed to mean more to her than anything. *So this is what it's like to help out a friend,* she thought.

Jeremiah took the information in stride. "Well, sometimes half-good news is good enough. Let's head home."

Estrella said, "She's had a hard enough time, I reckon, without havin' to sleep near the poison-fried-pie experiment laboratory you call a kitchen. She'll stay here with me tonight and have some proper food." She turned her back on Jeremiah.

"Hmph," Jeremiah said. He asked Bicycle, "That what you want to do? Stay here tonight?"

Bicycle didn't want to choose sides in any family feud, but she did want to stick around while Griffin recovered. "Yes, if that's okay with you."

"Anything you want to do is okay with me," he said. "Guess I should go get your backpack and bring it here so you have your stuff." He hesitated. He seemed torn between wanting to help Bicycle and not wanting to return to Estrella's house any more than absolutely necessary.

"No need," Estrella announced without turning around. "You think I can't take care of a guest? I got great-grandkids who visit. I'm stocked up with spare toothbrushes and pajamas, and I got the best dinner planned—ham steaks and pork ribs."

Bicycle smiled at Jeremiah to show she'd be fine for the night, and he nodded ruefully back, turning the key in his engine.

"I'll be back in the morning to check on you," he said to Bicycle. To Estrella, he added, "You do your best to show that girl some kindness, or you'll get an earful from me."

"I'm kind as the day is long," Estrella retorted, leading Bicycle toward the big, rambling house.

"Well, don't feed her too much pig meat—that stuff'll kill you!" Jeremiah shouted as he started down the driveway.

"I'm ninety-one and ain't got no complaints!" Estrella shouted back. She opened her front door. "Land sakes, that ol' man."

Bicycle and Estrella had dinner together, eating plates of ham, ribs, pickled pig's feet, and bacon. Estrella asked her about how she came to be in Green Marsh, and Bicycle told her the shortest version of the story that explained it all.

Estrella was impressed. "You know, when I was your age, I biked clear across Missouri—one of the best things I ever did. Good to know that youngsters still go on bicycle adventures in this day and age, what with video games and technopads and whatnot. When I wasn't learning the pig-raisin' trade as a teenager, the biggest favor my folks did for me was letting me mess around with tools and bikes out in that garage. I'm lucky to have a hobby that's so satisfyin' and useful."

Bicycle swallowed a bite of ham and asked a question that had been in the back of her mind. "Estrella, why are you mad at Jeremiah? He told me that his great-grandfather's pie business was nearly ruined by your great-grandfather's pigs, so I sort of understand why he holds a grudge. Why do you?"

"That man!" she said. "I'll tell you why I hold a grudge. I tried to make peace with him once. I brought over a nice pork-skin pie that I baked myself, thinkin' we could put our great-grandfathers' follies behind us and start again. At the least, we could be civil." She chewed angrily on another slice of bacon. "But that durned Jeremiah! I gave him my pork pie, and he threw it on the ground! Rudest thing I ever did see! I told him he was a dunderheaded lummox and stormed off. Haven't had a polite word between us since then. It's been"—she squinted and counted on her fingers—"seventy years now."

Bicycle asked, "He threw it on the ground?" Doing anything with a pie except frying it and eating it didn't sound much like Jeremiah. "Maybe he was upset because he thought you were trying to take over his pie business." She yawned. "Maybe you could try talking to him again someday, try to mend things one more time."

Estrella stood up from the table. "Mebbe someday," she said grudgingly. "After I turn a hunnert years old, mebbe I'll be more forgivin'." She took Bicycle upstairs and showed her to the spare bedroom. "You can sleep here. I reckon it's been a long day for you. You need me, come look in the garage. I'm going to sleep out there on my cot in case the bike or the ghost needs somethin'."

Estrella headed downstairs, and Bicycle climbed into bed.

Bicycle was up at dawn, too impatient to stay asleep. She splashed some water on her face and went straight into the garage. Estrella was snoring on a cot in the corner and didn't wake up when Bicycle came in and removed the blanket from the bicycle frame on the workbench.

"Griffin?" she whispered.

The response was immediate. "Hey, Bicycle, where've you been? I've been stuck here on my side, thinking you'd forgotten to take me with you or something. That lady over there's been snoring all night, way worse than you do."

"I do not snore!" Bicycle said, and then immediately giggled as relief washed over her. "No, I'd never forget you, Griffin. You can count on that. The town was having their annual Parade of Pigs—it started after you left—so more than eight hundred pigs ran over you and Clunk, and I think you passed out. Then Estrella over there found a way to wake you up. She also fixed Clunk's frame, but the bike isn't safe to ride anymore."

"Whoa. Then how are you going to get to San Francisco?" he asked.

"I'm not sure," Bicycle said. She'd been so focused on getting Griffin back, she hadn't thought about herself.

"Well, how about the pie shop? Did you find out if Joe ever started frying pies?" Griffin said.

"Yes, he did. Joe's great-grandson Jeremiah runs the shop now, and I've eaten about forty fried pies already," Bicycle said, ready to list the flavors.

Before she could start, Jeremiah's van pulled up in the driveway outside.

"I'll tell you later," Bicycle said as Jeremiah shuffled in and whistled when he saw the bike frame.

"My oh my, I almost hate to admit it, but Estrella did a fine job on that bike," Jeremiah said. "You say it won't ride? It looks pert' near perfect, shiny as a new penny."

Griffin piped up from the handlebars, "Thanks!"

Jeremiah started. "That the ghost?" he asked Bicycle in a low voice.

She nodded.

Jeremiah cleared his throat and stood up a little straighter. "Er . . . greetings to you, Griffin the Ghost. I'm Jeremiah Branch. Bicycle tells me you were a friend of my great-grandpa's, and any friend of his is certainly a friend of mine."

Bicycle lifted the bike frame down and set it on the ground, facing upright. Griffin announced, "Jeremiah, I sure am glad to meet you and happy to be home again. I hope

I can come help you out at the pie shop. I've been thinking about it ever since I met Bicycle."

Jeremiah took one handlebar in his hand and wiggled it in greeting. "It would be my pleasure to have you in my shop. Now, are you in that bicycle for good, or you plannin' on hauntin' my pie plates, or what?"

Griffin made a grunting sound like he was trying to lift something heavy. "You know, I don't have a clue how to get out of here. When Bicycle found me, I decided kinda on a whim to haunt her bike, and it was easy. Now that that lady over there fixed up the frame, I'm feeling more locked in somehow than I was before."

Jeremiah waggled his head. "Well, Estrella does do a decent job fixing bikes. I wouldn't be surprised if she fixed you in there real tight. She don't do nothin' halfway. I've always admired that about her. When we were much younger, I admired her a great deal, in fact."

The little trio was so intent on their conversation that they hadn't noticed the snoring had stopped.

A sour voice piped up behind them. "You admired me so much that when I came to your shop to make amends with you, you threw my pork-skin pie right on the ground? That don't strike me as any kind of admiration."

They turned to see Estrella standing behind them.

Jeremiah's blush rippled through every one of his wrinkles. "Shucks, Estrella, I was so nervous that a beautiful woman was giving me a pie, I dropped it. I was all thumbs when I was a youngster. Then you called me a big dunder-headed lummox and ran off, so I thought maybe you gave me the pie to show me you didn't need me and my pie shop. Thought you was bein' mean."

Her face softened. "Well, don't that beat all! For seventy years, I ain't talked to you for throwing my pie in anger, which you didn't do, and you ain't talked to me since I gave you a mean-spirited gift, which I didn't do. Jeremiah, we been such fools as that all that time?"

Jeremiah, still a bright shade of pink, shuffled his feet. "Seems so."

Bicycle looked from one wrinkled face to another and decided to leave them alone in the garage for a while. She wheeled the bike out into the sunshine.

"Griffin," she said, "what am I going to do without Clunk? Is this the universe telling me I should stop now and give up? That I should call Sister Wanda and tell her I made friends with a ghost, and hope that's enough to get me out of being sent to any friendship-making camp?" She scuffed a toe at the ground. The idea of going back made her feel disappointed and low. And the idea of pressing onward without Clunk and Griffin was overwhelming.

Griffin whistled a few wistful notes. "Bicycle, I was so excited to be coming home, I never thought about us parting ways. Maybe you could stay a while, fry pies with me and

Jeremiah? I know! We'll park Clunk next to the deep fryer, and I'll tell you how to mix up the pie fillings. Then we could mail special pies to Zbig, the bicycle racer fella, spelling out different messages in pie dough to convince him to come visit us, or we could . . . Wait—if you stay here with us, that's giving up on your own adventure," he said. "You'd be the one with unfinished business then. Nope, nope, that won't do. If you stayed here, you'd always wonder whether Zbig mighta been the best friend you ever could have. You've got to keep going. And then you'll come back and tell us about what you saw and how amazing it is! You never know what's around the next corner, or across the next state line, right?"

"That's for sure." Bicycle thought about it. "I remember what the Top Monk once told me: 'Always finish what you start.' At least, I think that's what he told me. He said 'Sandwich,' but I'm pretty sure that's what he meant. And Zbig really does seem like the perfect person for me to have as a friend. Nobody's happier on a bike than he is." She envisioned Zbig waving to a cheering crowd.

"'Cept maybe you," Griffin added. "You just haven't had a chance to ride as many places as him yet. If you get out to California, and you win that contest to ride with him, well, you're bound to end up as happy as a ghost in a fried-pie shop."

Bicycle thought, *Probably the first time anyone in the world has used that expression.* "I do know if I go home now,

I wouldn't be even close to finishing what I started. The reason I ran away from the Friendship Factory bus was to prove to Sister Wanda that I could make my own kind of friend my own kind of way. And now I've got you. But I think I've got to prove I can make a friend on purpose, or Sister Wanda will just send me off again." Bicycle shivered, thinking about it. "Whatever lies between me and California has to be better than that. So I guess that's my answer. I'll figure out a way to keep heading west." She patted the handlebars. "I'll miss you, Griffin. You were the best traveling partner, dog trainer, and singing accompaniment to hill climbing a girl could ever ask for. And I pinky-promise to come back and visit as soon as I can." She wrapped her pinky around the bike's brake cable and squeezed.

Jeremiah and Estrella came out of the garage. It sounded like they might be arguing about something again, and Estrella was poking Jeremiah in the arm with one tiny finger. But then they proposed that Bicycle stay the summer in Green Marsh.

Estrella said, "We'll call that Sister Wanda of yours and clear it with her. You could help fix bikes—"

"And fry pies," Jeremiah interjected.

"And raise pigs. What more does a girl want out of life?" Estrella finished.

"Oh no! I mean, thanks anyway, but Sister Wanda doesn't change her mind very easily," Bicycle said. "If we called her now, she'd have me locked in the Friendship Factory in no time at all. She'd probably chain my ankle to three other kids. Maybe even chain herself to my ankle, too. This is the only chance I'll ever have to try to make friends with Zbig and prove I can do this my own way. There's no going back now."

"Sounds like you don't change your mind very easily yourself," said Estrella. "Sounds like you're determined to see this thing through."

"You don't know anything about stubbornness like that now, do you, Estrella?" asked Jeremiah.

"You're one to talk!" Estrella said.

They looked at each other, and Bicycle held her breath. Then they brayed laughter, and Bicycle exhaled in a big whoosh.

"All right. Well, as one stubborn mule to another, here's what I can do to help you on your way," Estrella said. "My grandnephew's driving a pig delivery truck to Midway Station, Kansas, in a few hours. You're welcome to ride with him, and that'll get you down the road a piece. I've got a secondhand bike—it's been hanging around my workshop ever since I repaired it, but the owner never paid her bill. Should be a good fit for you, plus it's got one of those adjustable seat posts. I'll have my nephew stick that bike in the back of the truck for you, so once you get to Midway Station you can start pedaling on your way again. Better a neglected bike goes with you than ends up collecting more dust in my garage." Estrella brushed her hands together twice and walked toward her front door, saying over her shoulder, "That's settled, then. I'll go call my nephew and tell him to come meet us at Paradise Pies after he loads up the truck. I'm so glad to help you out, child."

"Thanks," Bicycle said, a little nervous about getting a lift on four wheels instead of two. Somehow driving seemed like cheating, but after two days in Green Marsh, she was seriously behind schedule. Accepting Estrella's generous offer seemed like the best thing to do, especially since no better plan was presenting itself.

"If she gets you a ride, then I can get you pied," Jeremiah said. "Hee! Get it? Pied? I'm gonna fill up that backpack of yours with some of them tapioca-muffin ones, plus whatever else you want. You need some money, too?"

"Pies will be great," Bicycle said. She still had some money left, plus her Free Eats card, so she thought she was in good shape. "Sister Wanda always says, 'Neither a borrower nor a lender be,' and I think she means I shouldn't use anyone else's money if I can help it. But I will take a postcard if you have one to send to her and the monks."

Jeremiah said, "Let's head to the shop and I'll see what I can find. I've got your backpack and helmet ready for you there, and I invited Estrella to join us for lunch." He helped Bicycle load Clunk in the van, and when Estrella came back out of her house, the three of them squeezed into the front seat.

Back at Paradise Pies, Griffin tried un-haunting the bike one more time, but he seemed good and stuck.

Estrella said, "I don't know much about ghosts, but I made sure every little piece of that bike was screwed in, tightened down, and firmly in place. I do think you are permanently in there, Mr. Griffin."

Griffin didn't mind much. He'd gotten to appreciate how the metal of the frame echoed with his singing voice.

Before starting lunch (a chicken pot pie, baked this time, not fried), Jeremiah hunted up a postcard from the Marsh County Rolling Pin Museum. Bicycle wrote it out and asked him to put it with tomorrow's outgoing mail.

Green Marsh, Missouri

Dear Sister Wanda and Mostly Silent Monks,

It turns out I made a friend but it wasn't like I thought it would be. It sort of snuck up on me while I wasn't paying attention. But it shows that I'm on the right track.

We should come visit here during fried-pie season, which I learned is any day of the year that doesn't have a Parade of Pigs.

Bicycle

After they ate, Bicycle wheeled Clunk out front. Jeremiah set up a stepladder next to the Paradise Pies shop door and asked a strong neighbor to give them a hand. The neighbor climbed up the ladder to the portico over the door, and Jeremiah and Bicycle lifted Clunk up to him so he could mount the bike atop the portico. Jeremiah called up to Griffin, "How's that?"

Griffin hollered down. "The view is great!" A family was walking past on the sidewalk and Griffin sang out to them, "Hey there, folks, you should come on in and try some fried pies! They'll make you happy today and live longer tomorrow!" They stopped in their tracks, gawking at the talking bicycle. "What's on the menu today, Jeremiah?" asked Griffin.

"Oh, we've got peach, and apple. We got some real good blackberries in, too—I could whip up a few of those. Or you could try some of our new experimental flavors—chicken noodle or mashed potato."

Griffin started singing a silly song about a magical fried pie that saves the world, and the family headed into the shop, chuckling with delight at the singing bicycle. Another couple went in shortly afterward. A whole troop of Boy Scouts was coming over to see what the fuss was all about when the Marquez Pigs delivery truck pulled up next to the sidewalk.

Estrella came out of the shop with Bicycle's backpack and helmet, and she helped Bicycle climb up into the passenger's seat. She gave her grandnephew strict instructions to take good care of the girl all the way to Kansas, talking loudly to be heard over the sound of pigs snuffling and groinking from the cargo container.

Jeremiah and Estrella both waved good-bye as the truck started to pull away, saying, "Don't forget us!" and "Come back soon!"

Bicycle yelled back, "Invent some really good fried pies. I'll be back to eat some of them when I can!"

Griffin called out, "Take care, Bicycle! Don't let any more pigs run over you!"

The truck started down the street, and Bicycle craned her neck out the window. The Paradise Pies shop crowned by a singing, talking bicycle was starting to draw a crowd. *That place might actually be on its way to becoming world-famous,* she thought. She waved a final good-bye, sorry to leave the town of Green Marsh behind her.

MIDWAY TO NOWHERE

Estrella's grandnephew's name was Dan. That was the first thing that Bicycle learned about him on the five-hour drive to Midway Station, Kansas. The second and final thing she learned was that he didn't talk much. Dan answered each of her questions with an unrevealing grunt, tugging on the brim of his baseball hat. Bicycle gave up after a few tries and lapsed into silence, watching the countryside pass by outside her window. She didn't know how accustomed she'd become to Griffin's nonstop chatter until she realized that sitting in Mostly Silence now made her uncomfortable.

Before long, they came upon a big white sign that announced WELCOME TO KANSAS: THE SUNFLOWER STATE in green-and-red letters decorated with streamers and painted confetti. *Seems nice enough,* Bicycle thought, but for the first time on this trip, her heart wasn't much in the traveling. She felt she'd left it back in Missouri with Griffin and Clunk.

Dan didn't drive very fast. Even so, driving on a road in a truck is a lot faster than pedaling on a road with a bicycle. The scenery shot by. Bicycle saw fields of something golden like wheat, and something green like corn, and several big windmills and tall storage silos. The flat horizon stretched out forever. It looked like an excellent place to bike.

Bicycle slumped in her seat and let herself feel a little bit sad. She missed Clunk. Clunk had been a part of her life so long that losing him was like losing a part of her body. *It's like I was a centaur,* she thought, *one of those half-human, half-horse creatures you see in mythology books. But I used to be half-human, half-bicycle. Now I'm just a plain old regular human.* She sighed. It was hard to imagine riding the rest of the way to California on some other bike.

Mile after mile sped by. She unwrapped a couple of the turkey-and-tater-tot fried pies that Jeremiah had stuffed in her backpack and shared one with Dan. Fields of giant, yellow-headed sunflowers nodded as they passed, and the day wore on. The sun finally began to light the clouds with orange and pink. Bicycle gazed at the multicolor sunset and hardly noticed that the truck had slowed down until they were pulling into a parking lot in front of a general store. "Are we here?" she said.

Dan, unsurprisingly, grunted. He got out of the truck. Bicycle slung her backpack over her shoulder and followed him into the store.

She hung back near the racks of bubble gum and candy bars, waiting until Dan had handed his paperwork to the distribution manager. The two of them went into the parking lot to unload the pigs, and Bicycle followed to retrieve her secondhand bike. Dan extended the truck's ramp and opened up the rear gate. A passel of pigs tired of being cooped up in a cargo container galloped down the ramp into a holding pen.

The manager locked up the pen and went back inside the general store. Bicycle came to stand next to Dan as he closed up the back of the truck. The cargo area was empty.

"Where's the bike Estrella gave me?" Bicycle asked.

Dan scratched his cheek and then pointed at the wide gap between the top of the rear gate and the ceiling of the cargo container. The rear gate was high enough that no pig could jump over it. But it was low enough that a bicycle could have fallen over it. Only, however, if some resourceful pigs had gotten underneath it and shoved.

"You think the pigs might've pushed the bike out of the truck?" Bicycle asked. "Really?"

Dan nodded. He took off his baseball hat and held it respectfully against his chest. Then with a brief "I guess that's that" kind of grunt, he replaced his hat, got in the driver's seat, and drove out of the parking lot.

I suppose that's all I'll ever know about Dan the grunting truck driver, Bicycle thought. *He would make a great Mostly Silent Monk.*

Bicycle went inside to talk to the distribution manager. He sat at a small desk, adding up numbers on a calculator. She cleared her throat.

The manager, whose name tag said ON DUTY: MR. PITTS-BURG, looked up and smiled. "What can I do for you this evening, miss?"

Bicycle smiled back, trying to look as nice as possible. "Hello, sir, I came in the truck with Dan. Estrella from Marquez Pigs in Green Marsh sent me. It looks like my bike fell—well, maybe got pushed out of the back of the truck somewhere back in Missouri, so I'm hoping you can help me find a way to head west."

Mr. Pittsburg shook his head. "West, you say? Sorry, Midway Station is used exclusively for eastern deliveries and distributions. Nothing from here goes west toward the Rocky Mountains. In fact, I've never been west of this spot in my life. Let's see . . ." He thumbed through a calendar on his desk. "I could get you a ride to Ohio tomorrow if you like, or"—he thumbed some more—"to South Carolina on Friday."

Bicycle ignored the tiny claws of anxiety seeking to climb up her throat. "Is there someone else in town who might be able to help?"

Mr. Pittsburg bunched his lips together in a regretful way. "There isn't much of a town to speak of. We just have the general store here, a gas station, and the delivery pens. That's the extent of it."

Bicycle said, "Let me make sure I understand. No town. No trucks. No way west." The anxiety clawed its way farther up her throat, and she swallowed hard.

Mr. Pittsburg nodded. "I'm sorry I can't be of more help. There is a train station about fifty miles away. I'd take you myself, but I don't have a car. I live right around back of the gas station, and I never did learn to drive." He bunched up his lips again, thinking. "Are you hungry? I know I feel better on a full stomach. Got a hammock out back; it's a good place for a snack. Help yourself to anything you like." He gestured to the racks of canned and packaged foods. "On the house. Then let me know if you'd like that ride to Ohio."

The door jingled as another customer walked in. Mr. Pittsburg started talking delivery business with him, leaving Bicycle to contemplate her situation.

Stuck in Midway Station, Kansas. According to her cycling maps, she'd covered almost half the distance to California. She started pacing up and down the aisles, wondering if the universe was once again trying to tell her to give up and go home. She noticed a bag of assorted cookies. She thought of her promise to the Cookie Lady, and decided it couldn't hurt to eat a dozen cookies and think about what to do. She took the cookies and her backpack and went out the back door, where she saw the hammock tied up between two cottonwood trees surrounded by a picket fence. The moon was beginning to rise as she climbed into the hammock.

Bicycle tore open the bag and ate one lemon cookie. *Universe, if you're trying to tell me to give up, I don't agree.* She ate an oatmeal ring and a jam-filled sandwich cookie. *Besides, it might not even be the universe that's trying to tell me to give up, only Estrella's pigs. I'm not letting a bunch of pigs tell me what I can and can't do.* She chewed a peanut butter swirl. *Things could be worse. I'm not in danger, not lost. The one thing stopping me right now is a lack of wheels. I know where I need to go, right down this road. There's a train station fifty miles away. Maybe I could get that far somehow.* She popped two chocolate chip cookies in her mouth. *Hey, I've still got legs. If I can bike fifty miles down a road, I guess I can walk fifty miles down a road to the train station. Maybe I have enough money left for a train ticket, or maybe I can talk a train conductor into giving me a ride to California.* She ate another six cookies, feeling more resolved and more relaxed with every bite. *That Cookie Lady knows her stuff,* she thought. *Cookies do help put a sweeter perspective on things.* She yawned, and before the moon was up she was fast asleep in the hammock, crumbs festooning her shirt.

Morning came with the snorting of pigs from the delivery pens. Bicycle washed up in the store's restroom and shouldered her backpack. She went in to tell Mr. Pittsburg that she was going to head out on foot, half expecting him to try to talk her out of it. She'd met a few people in her travels who thought it was ridiculous to try bicycling across the country, and walking fifty miles through Kansas would probably seem one step past ridiculous and well into preposterous.

Instead, he shook her hand and wished her well. "Boy, I wonder what's west of here?" he mused out loud. "Canyons, rivers, gorilla farms? Could be darn near anything, for all I know. Listen, could you do me a favor? When you make it to the train station, maybe you can send me a note and let me know what you've seen? I'd love to get a postcard from the west." He gave her a book of stamps, a handful of blank white postcards, several bottles of water, and a corn muffin in a cellophane wrapper.

Bicycle started walking on the side of the road facing the oncoming traffic. She remembered how her first day biking had felt so great and wondered if she would have a similar experience today.

After two hours of walking, she had her answer: *no*. Her feet hurt, and her back and shoulders were tired from carrying her backpack. She trudged with one hand over her eyes, shielding her face from the sun, looking down the road. She'd been walking next to sunflower fields, and as far as she could tell, she hadn't made much progress. In front of her: a strip of road rolling flat as far as she could see. To the left of her: nothing but sunflowers. To the right of her: nothing but sunflowers. And behind her: sunflowers, sunflowers, and more sunflowers. She couldn't see the general store at Midway Station any longer. No cars had passed her yet. Except for the road, she felt alone on a planet populated by nothing but sunflowers. "I'll never take wheels for granted again," she grumbled.

To cheer herself up, she started eating things out of her backpack as she plodded along. She ate the corn muffin. Then a tapioca-muffin fried pie. Then two chicken-noodle fried pies and a chocolate cream surprise. She saved the rest of Jeremiah's pies and took long pulls from her water bottles to wash down the last crumbly bits of the beef jerky she'd brought all the way from Washington, D.C. She wiped her mouth and felt less cheerful than she'd hoped and more ready for a nap.

The sun climbed higher in the sky. Even with the extra bottles of water from Mr. Pittsburg, she was starting to run low on moisture. If she didn't come upon a town or a farm soon, she was going to get thirsty in a hurry. *Maybe it'll rain?* she hoped, scanning the sky. Vast blue without even a whisper of a cloud. She poured a little water on her head to cool off and kept putting one foot in front of the other.

The sun hit its peak and started to sink toward the horizon. The road was pointed due west, so Bicycle now had the sun shining directly into her face. She felt like it was bleaching out the back of her eyeballs. The sunflowers rustled and shifted in a slight breeze, and Bicycle could almost see their big seed-filled heads turn to follow the sun in the sky. Clearly, sunflowers loved living in Kansas—the plants were healthy and green, and most were taller than Bicycle herself. Taking a break, she found a bit of shadow between the thick rows of flowers and sat on the warm earth to finish her water.

As she was sitting there, a blue sports car with a rumbling motor flew by. It was going so fast that the sunflowers bowed and rustled in the wake of its passing. The driver slammed on the brakes with a screech and, to Bicycle's surprise, took a sharp turn right into the sunflower field ahead of her. She sprang up and limped (her feet were really hurting now) to where the sports car had turned. There, cut through the flowers, was a skinny dirt road. A carved wooden sign marked the turn with the words ALVARADO ESTATE. A smaller hand-printed paper had been taped to the signpost to announce ESTATE SALE TODAY. Bicycle downed the very last dregs of her water. Whatever the Alvarado Estate was, she hoped they wouldn't object to her refilling her bottles. She started up the dirt road.

Bicycle followed the road deep into the sunflower field and was beginning to wonder if it went anywhere when it opened up to a lawn in front of a large house. *More of a castle than a house, I suppose*, thought Bicycle, since the building had elaborate turrets and walkways. It even had a moat and a wooden drawbridge. The blue sports car was parked outside the drawbridge, as were other fancy vehicles like Rolls-Royces and limousines. Bicycle crossed the drawbridge into an open courtyard.

"We have a five-hundred-thousand-dollar bid for this twelfth-century jade-and-emerald wastebasket. Do I hear six hundred thousand? I've got six! Do I hear seven? The bid is up to seven hundred and fifty thousand with the gentleman in the back. Going once, going twice . . . Sold for seven hundred and fifty thousand dollars!" A tall, stiff-necked man in a tuxedo knocked a hammer on a gavel in an authoritative manner. "We'll move on to the next item, a carved Greek marble statue . . ."

Bicycle checked out the scene. A dozen folding chairs had been set up in the castle's courtyard and were filled with elegant people holding numbered paddles. Women wearing silk dresses primly crossed and uncrossed their legs, and men in gray suits adjusted the knots on their dark ties. They seemed bored and lifeless until the man in the tuxedo started the bidding for the statue. Then they raised numbered paddles, flapping them in the air to bid, frowning fiercely at each other as the price got higher and higher.

On a table over in the corner, Bicycle spied a bowl filled with orange punch and several pitchers of ice water. She made her way over to the table, poured water into a plastic cup, and drank enough to feel sloshy inside. She refilled her water bottles, glancing around to make sure she wasn't getting any disapproving looks for taking excessive advantage of the free drinks. No one seemed to care. She saw an empty folding chair at the very back of the gathering. Running her hands through her hair and brushing the dust from her clothes, she tried to look like she belonged as she sat down. A young woman came over and brought her a bidding paddle with the number 15 on it in red.

"Um, thanks," Bicycle said, taking the paddle.

"This next item," the tuxedo man said, "is quite a . . . find, indeed. This bicycle . . ."

Bicycle sat up and took notice.

"Has many . . . interesting features, like . . . er . . . wheels, and . . . this bell." The auctioneer tapped the handlebar bell and it rang with a silvery jingle.

The bike's frame was gracefully shaped, glittering in blue and yellow paint. It even had flames painted on the top tube. Bicycle scrabbled in her backpack and counted up the money she had left.

"Shall we start the bidding at one thousand dollars?"

Bicycle groaned.

No one raised a paddle. One man yawned. Another flicked a fly off his trousers. Bicycle couldn't believe it.

"Do I hear one thousand? One thousand, I say? No? Do I hear five hundred, five hundred dollars for this very . . . ah . . . unique . . . piece." The auctioneer put a finger under his collar and harrumphed. "Made from an unusual metal alloy, the parts for this bike are worth three hundred dollars alone. Do I have a bid for three hundred?" More of the audience was yawning now, and people were getting up for punch. "All right, I'm sure there's someone interested in this item for two hundred . . . one fifty . . . one hundred dollars?"

Nothing. Bicycle clenched her hands around her bidding paddle.

The auctioneer shrugged in defeat. "Do I have any bids at all?"

Bicycle leapt up with her paddle, aching feet forgotten, and yelled, "Seventy-three dollars and twenty-two cents!"

The crowd turned to stare.

The auctioneer said, "I have, er, seventy-three dollars and twenty-two cents. Are there any other bids? No?"

Bicycle looked around, clutching her paddle with white knuckles, terrified that someone was going to jump in and steal the bike out from under her.

A bony woman in a black dress twitched her bidding paddle thoughtfully, turning toward Bicycle. Her lips were shocking red against her pale face. Her huge sunglasses hid her eyes, but Bicycle could sense the woman's gaze crawling over her skin like a hungry little snake. Then the woman turned to examine the bike, tapping her red lips with one long fingernail.

The auctioneer was hurrying along, eager to get to his next wastebasket or marble statue. "Going once, going twice . . ."

The woman twitched her paddle again and the auctioneer paused.

"Miss Monet-Grubbink?"

Miss Monet-Grubbink slipped off her sunglasses. Her green eyes were as cold and creepy as a swamp in winter. She took a last calculating look between Bicycle and the bike on the auction block, then sneered dismissively and dropped her paddle into her lap.

The auctioneer said, "Sold to the dusty girl in the last row." He tapped the gavel lightly and waved someone over to move the bike off the auction block and take it to the payment table.

Bicycle hurried toward the table, worried the woman in the black dress might realize she'd missed bidding on the best thing at the whole auction and try to sneak it away from her. She plunked her paddle and money down in front of the cash box and said, "I bought the bike."

The deeply tanned lady manning the cash box looked down her nose at Bicycle. "Yes. You did." The lady would have been beautiful if not for the sour look that dominated her face. She picked up the crumpled dollars and handful of coins, placing the money in the cash box, which was nearly full to bursting with hundred-dollar bills from earlier sales. She scrawled out a receipt, pushing it across the table at Bicycle.

Next to her, an equally tan, slouch-shouldered man with carefully arranged black hair added, "I'm surprised anyone wanted that thing." He would have been handsome except for the unnaturally tight, smooth skin around his mouth and eyes—it looked like he never smiled and probably couldn't if he tried. He was filing his nails with a tiny golden file, and he flicked his eyes up momentarily toward Bicycle, focusing on her purple T-shirt with the word BICYCLE in bold letters. "But if anyone would buy it, I suppose it would be someone like you," he sniffed. A gust of wind blew by, pushing his carefully arranged hair from one side of his head to the other. He smoothed it down and sculpted it back into place.

Bicycle hardly heard what they were saying as she gazed in delight at the bike. She said, "I had to leave my bike in Missouri and didn't know what I was going to do. I need to get to California as soon as I can, and this new bike is going to make it possible. It's terrific luck that it's here and that I found it when no one else wanted it. Really, incredibly good luck!"

The slouching man sat up a little straighter. "Luck, you say?" He and the woman exchanged a glance. "Funny you should say that. Our father, the man who built that bike, his name was Luck. Dr. Luck Alvarado."

"That name was an obsession with him," the woman said. "He spent far too much of our—er, his—money study-ing luck, or fate, or destiny, whatever you want to call it. Trying to understand how you can measure a person's luck, whether you can alter it, and whether luck somehow controls the path of our lives. What a waste of time! He would have been better off focusing on his inventions."

Her brother interjected, "Father did invent things used by every household in the country: the automatic gift-wrapper, the self-propelled pancake-flipper, hedgehog repellent, to name a few. The money from those inventions bought all of this." He gestured around at the estate.

Bicycle was intrigued. "Did he ever figure it out? About whether luck controls the path of our lives, I mean."

The man slouched back in his seat and started filing his nails again. "Who knows? Father disappeared almost three years ago, just after he finished building that bike. He thought he could program it to collect data about luck. Ridiculous. We haven't seen him since." He pretended to pout with sadness, but he cheered up as he eyed the full cash box. "We figured we'd have a little sale here, get rid of some old things. Spring cleaning, really, and what's the harm in making some money in the process? Father would have wanted it that way."

The auction was wrapping up. The final item, a solid bronze statue of a very ugly cat, had been sold, and the remaining auction attendees were getting ready to pay for their items and gathering their belongings to leave.

The woman grimaced at the blue-and-yellow bicycle. "I'm glad this thing is sold. I know Father was fond of it, but it seems so useless to me. Why else were cars invented?" Bicycle couldn't comprehend how the woman could look at the bike as though it had no value at all. Emblazoned on the side of the frame was a name in gold: WHEELS OF FORTUNE 713-J. "Should we wrap it up for you?"

"No, ma'am," Bicycle answered. "I'll ride it like it is." She couldn't wait to get in the saddle and pedal the beautiful thing. She slipped her water bottles into the bike's bottle cages, secured her pack to its built-in rear rack, and stroked its smooth leather seat.

"Fine," the woman said, dismissing her as she started to collect payments. "Good luck with it—if you believe in luck." She and the slump-shouldered man shared a nasty laugh.

Bicycle was going to thank them but then thought better of it. She was so eager to leave, she didn't notice until she wheeled the bike past it that the bony woman in black had been hiding behind a tall potted plant, listening to the whole conversation.

THE WHEELS OF FORTUNE
SPIN IN KANSAS

The dirt road from the estate was bumpy and rutted, so Bicycle had some trouble maneuvering the Wheels of Fortune 713-J until she coasted out of the sunflower field and back onto pavement. She pointed the front tire west and started pedaling. The bike leapt forward, tires spinning like they were powered by some unseen engine. "Wheee!" shouted Bicycle. The frame of this bike was thirty or forty pounds lighter than Clunk's frame. With Clunk, she'd sometimes felt as if she were dragging an invisible suitcase full of rocks along behind her. With this bike, someone had cut the suitcase free.

Bicycle sprinted like a two-wheeled cheetah for several hours before the sun dipped below the horizon and she had to stop for the night. There was still no end in sight to the sunflower fields, so she steered the Wheels of Fortune 713-J into one of the rows between the waving stalks and made camp beside its feathery-light frame. *No room for a ghost in this bike. It's got to be filled with helium gas or something to make it seem so weightless.* She patted it with intense gratitude, and then blushed with guilt. *I don't think I should feel this way so soon after losing Clunk,* she thought.

As she slipped into a dream, she promised, *Clunk, don't worry—I'll never love another bike more than you.*

She thought she heard Clunk answer in Griffin's voice: *Of course you won't. Besides, this bike's so new, it has no personality yet. You show it some adventure; break it in, turn it into a good bike, like you did to me.*

The next day dawned warm. But Bicycle was far from the overheated, exhausted thing she'd been when walking the day before. Today, she stayed cool and comfy by making her own breeze as she skimmed along the ground.

The Wheels of Fortune 713-J had a small computer screen mounted on the handlebars, and after pushing several buttons, Bicycle found that it could calculate her speed and distance traveled. She was amazed to find she was pedaling over twenty miles an hour. Every now and then a car would come driving up behind her, and she'd stand up on the pedals and start to sprint, racing alongside the car until it pulled away, going as fast as possible before her leg muscles burned too much to continue.

The next five days were just as swift and sweet. The straight, flat road made it easy to move right along. She found a SlowDown Café and saw that it had new logo: a horse and a bicycle standing over a big bowl of food, the bicycle with a napkin tucked into its front wheel. The horse looked very familiar. Bicycle was glad to know The Cannibal, retired racehorse, had found new work as Truffle, café mascot. Once again, she left the café with a full stomach and a Feed Bag for the road.

Only one unpleasant note arose: the lady in black from the auction reappeared. Munching lunch outside her second SlowDown Café in Kansas, Bicycle felt a crawling sensation on the back of her neck, like an overly familiar beetle trying to nuzzle into her hair. She turned and saw the bony lady at a picnic table, this time dressed in a tight black tank top and wide-legged pants. The woman's big sunglasses didn't disguise the fact that she was staring at Bicycle, a sunflower-seed burger and fries sitting untouched in front of her. When the woman started to get to her feet, Bicycle grabbed her gear and left.

Bicycle told her imagination to get a hold of itself, that the lady was not following her, that anyone would stop at a SlowDown Café for its awesome food. She also reminded herself of Sister Wanda's admonishment never to judge a book by its cover. But she had to admit, this lady's cover was stamped in big letters with the word CREEPY.

Her thirty-fifth day on the road, finding she missed Griffin's singing, Bicycle thought she'd start working on a song of her own about her trip. She sang, "Oh, I am the fastest bicyclist that you will ever see, I ride as fast as water flowing down into the sea, Tomorrow morn in Colorado I will surely be, I'm not afraid of mountains there—they'll be no match for me!"

On the handlebar-mounted computer screen, the miles-per-hour display disappeared. In its place, one word started blinking:

False.

Bicycle tapped the display a couple of times. She pressed a button, and the words on the screen changed:

Probability of tailwinds increasing your speed: 94.5%.

Bicycle slowed down and pulled off the road between two dense rows of sunflowers. She liked watching the display show her how fast she was going and wanted to find a way to fix it. She pressed a small red button on the side of the computer, and the display changed once more:

Do not press that button again.

Bicycle's eyebrows raised. She pressed the red button again.

Do not press that button again. Red button will activate missile launch sequence if you press it a third time.

Bicycle thought, *Okay. So I've gone from a bike haunted by a ghost that could talk to a bike that can write and launch missiles.* "Er, sorry," she said. "Is this the Wheels of Fortune 713-J I'm talking to?"

Yes, the display said.

"Hi! I'm your new owner, Bicycle. I'm traveling from my home in Washington, D.C., to San Francisco for the Blessing of the Bicycles. You are a really fast bike. I'm so happy that I can ride you," she began.

"Bicycle" is not a human name, but a noun describing a machine like myself. You are a human, not a machine. Therefore "bicycle" is not your name.

"Hold on a minute!" Bicycle said, annoyed. She thought she had a great name, memorable and pretty. "Bicycle *is* my name, because humans can have any names they want. They can call themselves Bob or Muffy or Englebert or Kansas or anything!" she lectured the computer screen.

Please wait. The screen blinked. Processing. A few moments passed. Potential human names include Bob, Muffy, Englebert, Kansas, and Bicycle. Data saved. Greetings, Bicycle.

Mollified, Bicycle said, "Okay, greetings to you. So you are a bike that can think?"

I can do better than think. I was designed to be the perfect long-distance traveling machine, and my circuitry is state-of-the-art in every way.

Bicycle read the screen and thought it sounded pretty smug for a computer. "So how come you haven't said anything to me before now? We've been riding along for almost a week, and I never knew you could communicate."

We have been riding along for precisely five days, five hours, and forty minutes. You did not say anything worth discussing up until now.

Clunk was wrong, Bicycle thought, remembering her dream. *This bike does have a personality. Unfortunately, it's an annoying one.* "So . . . what did I say now that made you start blinking 'false' and something about tailwinds?" she prompted.

Tailwinds are winds that blow from behind you. There has been a very strong wind blowing right up the middle of the road. Therefore, your loud musical statement that you're the fastest bicyclist one will ever see is false. Our current high-speed cycling is due not to you but to the good luck of strong tailwinds pushing you forward.

"What?" Bicycle exclaimed. "There hasn't been any wind for days! I've been riding along super fast on my own! Look, the sunflowers aren't even moving." They weren't.

False, it blinked again. This tailwind does not disturb the sunflowers because they are planted so closely together. You can feel it only when on the road. Since you were moving in the same direction as the wind, you would not be able to notice it unless you were remarkably perceptive. You are clearly not remarkably perceptive.

"Hey!" said Bicycle.

Step into the road and turn around. You will feel the winds that are pushing you.

"Hmmph!" Bicycle huffed. "I don't believe you!"

The screen simply blinked back at her, showing the same message as if waiting for her to do as it requested.

Finally, she threw her hands up. "Okay, look, I'm going in the road, and there's no wind—" As she stepped out from between the sunflowers onto the pavement, her last word was snatched away by a brisk wind gusting straight out of the east. It whooshed through the vents in her helmet like it was trying to blow-dry her hair.

She ducked back into the shelter of the tall flowers and walked over to the Fortune, whose screen had gone blank. Nonetheless, she felt the bike had written I TOLD YOU SO in some internal database. Bicycle decided to call it a day.

The next morning, Bicycle rode past a roadside traffic sign warning CAUTION: STRONG WIND CURRENTS. The sign had been blown flat. Today, she'd tested the wind before she'd started out. There wasn't even a light breeze, and she noticed she was riding more slowly than she had during the past few days. She was still miffed at being called unperceptive by the Fortune, but she figured that it had been right about the tailwinds pushing her along the road after all. She tried starting up a conversation.

"Fortune, can you tell me how far it is from where I started in Washington, D.C., to here?"

The display replied: 2,102 miles from the center of Washington, D.C., to this spot.

"Do you know how far we have to go until we reach San Francisco?"

Exactly 1,841.67 miles. With good luck, probability of reaching San Francisco, California: 99.63%.

Bicycle was encouraged by this. "You think it's that probable that we'll make it there?"

Unless there are unpredictable hazards of bad luck in our path, the display read.

This troubled Bicycle. She contemplated the unpredictable hazards of bad luck that might be lying in wait down the road. Escaped circus zebras with a taste for young bicycle riders? She was relieved when her contemplation was distracted by a yellow-and-purple sign announcing WELCOME TO COLORADO, MOUNTAINS AND MUCH MORE! She occupied her mind searching for anagrams inside "Colorado" and was enormously pleased to find the whole state name could be rearranged into the two words COOL ROAD.

When she crossed the state line, she scanned the land ahead with excitement. She'd read about Colorado and its snowcapped Rocky Mountains. She expected the minute she entered the state, she'd see them rising dramatically in front of her. Instead, the landscape looked more like Kansas than Kansas did. A long, flat prairie studded with grain silos stretched out on either side of the road. A few sunflowers bowed their heavy heads as Bicycle passed by. She squinted into the distance but couldn't see anything even vaguely resembling a mountain. "How hard can climbing the Rocky Mountains be if I can't even see them yet?" she said. "I won't need a tailwind to bike over them."

Probability of Rocky Mountains being very difficult for you to cycle over: 86%, announced the Fortune.

"Great, thanks for the vote of confidence," Bicycle answered.

The next four days were much the same. Each day Bicycle expected the flatlands to give way to some purple mountain majesty, but each day she saw more flat flatness surrounded by pancake-like flats. Every time she'd question whether the Rocky Mountains were ever going to appear, the Fortune was quick to point out You will be climbing mountains before you are ready for it.

She still sent postcards back to the monastery so that Sister Wanda and the monks would know she was okay, but she found it was hard to word them so she didn't sound cranky. Her new traveling companion was getting under her skin. She thought she might have given in to serious grouchiness if not for the yummy food at the two SlowDown Cafés she found. SlowDown business looked like it was booming in Colorado, with full bike racks in front of each café and plenty of horseshoe tracks outside the ride-up windows.

One afternoon, when the Fortune blinked: Probability of

heavy rain 92%. Seek shelter soon, Bicycle chose to ignore it because the sun was shining overhead. But a few minutes later, it clouded up and a light drizzle began to fall. Bicycle put on a rain poncho and kept riding. She'd experienced drizzling days before, and the wetness didn't slow her down. The Fortune blinked again: Rain will become dangerously heavy. Seek shelter immediately.

Bicycle snapped at it, "Look, a little rain is no problem for me. I'll go ahead and ride through it, so how about you just keep telling me my speed and distance traveled?"

The Fortune kept its message on the screen for a few moments longer, then went blank. Bicycle started tapping the computer screen with annoyance. She didn't notice the vicious black thundercloud that had blown in from the north, until a colossal sizzle of lightning lit up the horizon. She clenched the brakes when a clap of thunder followed a few seconds later. The heavens opened in a downpour as she put her feet to the ground.

Bicycle was soaked to the skin in less than a minute. "Fine!" she shouted at no one in particular, looking around for some kind of shelter. The rain doubled its efforts, forming a layered curtain of water and obscuring her vision. She thought she might have glimpsed some buildings up ahead, so she sat back on the saddle with a squish and started pedaling again.

After one wet mile, she reached . . . someplace. She could

see about as clearly as if she were biking underwater, but there were definitely a few buildings near the side of the road. She turned off the pavement toward them, and the Fortune's tires slid and splashed in deep puddles. She dismounted, sneakers sinking into a soft splat of mud. She yanked her feet up with loud sucking squelches and pushed the Fortune over to the closest building she could see. It looked like a store. The door was locked tight, and a hand-lettered sign in the window read CLOSED.

She put her hands up against the glass to look inside. With the next flash of lightning, she could see that this store's sign hadn't read OPEN for a long, long time. There was nothing inside but a couple of broken chairs and one table littered with the tiny bleached-white bones of some long-gone animal. Old advertisements were peeling off the walls, and everything was covered by a thick layer of dust.

She squelched through more mud to the next building. This one had a sign declaring HOTEL—MEALS AVAILABLE, and she tried the door. This one was locked, too. She shook the door in frustration, and it rattled in the frame. With a *pop*, a couple of rusted hinges gave way and the door leaned sideways at a drunken angle, offering a view into the gloomy interior. Bicycle hesitated until another flash of lightning lit the sky. She pushed the leaning door aside and wheeled the Fortune into the old hotel.

The rain drumming on the roof echoed through the large

front room. Water dripped on one key of a rotted upright piano with an insistent *plink-plink-plink*. Bicycle heard rustling from the ceiling and saw a row of black-and-white birds nestled on an old chandelier, fluffed up against the chilly air. They chirped and chirruped, and she felt a little better. At least something was alive in this spooky place. She put down the Fortune's kickstand and looked for the driest spot to set up camp until the downpour moved on.

A section of the back wall was covered with small wooden cubbyholes where hotel guests once kept room keys and received messages. A faded poster still advertised ROOMS—$1. THREE MEALS—75¢. LEAVE ALL SHOTGUNS AT THE FRONT DESK. She found a decaying old couch with a faint pattern of flowers still visible on its fabric. She touched it with one finger, and the fabric rustled and squeaked. Before Bicycle could react, a furry gray mouse and seven mouse babies squirmed out of a hole in the fabric and skittered away into the shadows. Bicycle hurried back over to the Fortune 713-J.

"Let's get out of here. There's got to be somewhere else to stay," she said.

The Fortune seemed to take some sort of electronic pleasure in disagreeing with her. Probability of finding better lodging in this ghost town is extremely low. I recommend staying put and drying off.

"Ghost town, huh?" Bicycle had read about these old, abandoned frontier towns, homes to nothing but birds, rodents, plenty of dust, and maybe a couple of pioneer phantoms. "Fine, I've done the ghost thing already, so that doesn't bother me." Bicycle took off her dripping helmet and poncho and started unfastening her backpack from the back of the bike.

If you require shelter, you may press the green button under the seat.

Bicycle wrinkled her forehead. After the missile-launch moment with the red button, she'd stopped pressing any unfamiliar buttons or switches on the Fortune's frame. But with water still trickling down her neck, her clothes clinging to her skin, and her shoes covered in mud, she said, "What have I got to lose?" and pressed the green button.

The Fortune hummed for a moment, and Bicycle took a step backward. A panel slid open within the bike's seat post. Out popped a small square of plastic, and, with a whooshing sound, the square inflated and expanded extravagantly into a blue-and-yellow tent shaped like an igloo that encircled the Fortune. An unzipped half-circle entryway pointed toward Bicycle. She looked inside and saw that a tarp was unfurling onto the floor.

"Now we're talking," she said.

Bicycle peeled off her sneakers and socks and climbed inside, zipping the entryway closed behind herself. The tent was tall enough for her to stand up, and it had pockets stitched to the walls for storing items.

"Is it okay if I sit down? I'm pretty wet. I don't want to get the tent gross and soggy."

The Fortune replied with another low hum. Jets blew warm air onto Bicycle's skin. It felt like a dozen gentle hair dryers were pointed right at her until she was dry. The tent was lit by oval lights embedded in the ceiling, and the Fortune's computer screen lowered and tilted sideways until it was facing Bicycle.

She sat down on the padded tarp with a smile. "Wow, what else can you do?"

The 713-J model is equipped with many features. To list them all would take seven hours and eighteen minutes. Shall I begin?

Bicycle shook her head. "Nah, I guess I'll find out more about you as we go." She felt her stomach rumble and looked at her damp backpack, still attached to Fortune's rear rack. What if the downpour had soaked through the second rain poncho into her stuff? She wasn't too excited about eating waterlogged leftovers. "Well, there is one thing. Can you make any food? Maybe some soup, or hot chocolate?"

Press the purple button.

Bicycle did, and the bike ejected something from the end of one of the handlebars. She picked it up with interest. Wrapped inside a napkin was a little brown pellet that looked like a Tootsie Roll. It was vaguely warm, and she put it in her mouth and chewed. The pellet tasted precisely like it had come out of a bike: greasy, rubbery, and metallic. She discreetly spit it back into the napkin. "What is this, um, food thing?"

Efficiently packaged complete nutrition. Twenty-six essential minerals and vitamins, high-quality protein, lipids, and simple and complex carbohydrates in an easy-to-swallow pellet. It will sustain human life for twenty-four hours at a time. Plus it has a chocolate coating.

Bicycle thought of Brother Otto and Chef Marie and Jeremiah. She knew what they'd think of this life-sustaining pellet: any kind of life that got sustained by eating pellets wouldn't be much of a life at all. "Uh, great." She hid the napkin-wrapped pellet in her pocket. "So, did your inventor, Dr. Alvarado, program you to carry tents and make food?"

My inventor built me to be perfectly suited to long-distance travel, providing shelter and sustenance to my rider. I can even ensure that your shelter has a pleasant, relaxing scent.

The Fortune released a puff of lemony-scented mist into the air, and Bicycle sniffed appreciatively. "Wasn't your inventor famous for trying to understand luck, too? Is there really a way to compute whether good or bad luck might happen to us? Dr. Alvarado's children didn't seem to think so."

Dr. Alvarado added an experimental program to my central processing unit to monitor my rider's luck while traveling. The cursor blinked for longer than normal before Fortune continued. He ceased work on this model two years, ten months, and twelve days ago. I have not been able to travel until now, so I do not know if I will be successful in monitoring good or bad luck, or computing whether either will happen to us.

Bicycle wasn't sure, but she thought the bike might have been embarrassed by its lack of experience. "That's okay," she reassured it. "We've got quite a ways to go, so you'll collect a whole lot of data on the way to California."

She unzipped her backpack to find a snack. The rain ponchos seemed to have protected everything inside well enough, but even so Bicycle figured she'd unpack everything after she ate to make sure nothing had been damaged by the cloudburst. She found a Feed Bag with some brownies, bit off a hunk, and asked the Fortune, "How about music? Can you play any music?"

I am equipped with recordings of music from every world culture, including eighth-century religious chants. Here is a list of options. Listing all music items will take four hours, thirteen minutes, and fifteen seconds.

Bicycle waved away the options that started to scroll down the screen. "Just pick something upbeat," she said.

The Fortune started to make a blatting noise that sounded to Bicycle like a tuba swallowing a goat.

"Whoa, whoa, that is not what I meant by upbeat!" she yelled.

Bronze Age Lusations would describe that music as very invigorating and upbeat. Perhaps you would prefer I play it more loudly?

The blatting got louder, sounding now like an army of goats fighting their way out of a sea of hungry tubas.

"No, no, stop! How about some non-Bronze Age music instead?" She tried to think of a suggestion, and Griffin popped into her mind. "Do you know anything like 'Oh! Susanna'?"

Stephen Foster. Of course. I contain his whole catalog.

The bike started playing a quiet version of "Swanee River" sung by a beautiful soprano voice with a piano accompaniment.

Do you prefer this?

Bicycle lay back, arms folded under her head. The music made the tent very homey. "Much."

ON TOP OF THE WORLD IN COLORADO

The rain let up sometime in the night, and the next day dawned fresh and cool. Bicycle crawled out of the zippered opening and stretched. "How do I put the tent back in the seat post?" she asked.

You say "Please put the tent back in the seat post."

"Okay, please put the tent back in the seat post."

The Fortune sort of inhaled the whole tent back inside itself. Bicycle gathered up her belongings from the floor of the hotel lobby where she'd spread them out. The only thing that had been damaged was the waterproof pocket Polish-English dictionary, which turned out to be more water absorbent than waterproof. Its pages were glopped together. Bicycle had stuck it inside her packet of Spim's Splendid Sponges to see if the sponges might suck out the moisture overnight, but it was still pretty soggy. *Oh well, it'll dry out eventually*, Bicycle thought, and packed it back up with the rest of her stuff.

She hoisted the Fortune on one shoulder and the backpack on the other, then carried them outside and over the muddy track and back to the paved road. She was ready to leave the ghost town in her dust.

"On the road again," she started to hum as she attached the backpack to the rear rack, and was pleasantly surprised when the Fortune chimed in with guitar, harmonica, and a rhythm section. They continued pedaling west.

After a few hours of dodging tumbleweeds, Bicycle saw something big in the distance. It looked like a thick layer of low-lying clouds, grayish-purple topped with white, resting against the horizon. She studied them until she grasped that these weren't clouds at all. The Rocky Mountains lay dead ahead.

Bicycle stopped that night outside a town surrounded by rough hills. The Fortune inflated the tent in no time flat. Before the sun set completely, she climbed up one of the smaller hills to watch the last rays of light sink in the west behind the Rocky Mountains. The line of peaks was sharply clear now. They looked like the fangs of a massive sleepy wolf yawning at the sky. Tomorrow, she was going straight into the mouth of those fangs. Bicycle felt a little thrill of anticipation shiver up her spine. She wondered if the road builders in Colorado worked like the road builders in Virginia and

constructed roads that went straight up and down whatever slope was in their way. That night, she flipped through
Wheel Wisdom for advice on climbing mountains and found
this passage by Zbig:

> *I think that mountains are like surprise parties: they*
> *are more fun if you don't know they are coming. For*
> *example, when I am in a race and I know a mountain*
> *is coming up, I worry, I sweat, I can't sleep the night*
> *before. But when I am busy riding, enjoying the sun*
> *and fresh air, and then, unexpectedly, there is a moun-*
> *tain to climb, this is no problem. Climbing up is just*
> *one more fun way to make the wheels go forward.*

As soon as the sun lightened the sky Bicycle was up and
on the road. As she pedaled, the incline gradually got steeper
and steeper, but she focused her energy on turning her pedals
steadily, as a real professional bicyclist would do. Breathing
hard, she started to imagine what it would be like to ride in a
crowd of other cyclists, everyone jostling for position, trying
to win an important cycling race to the top of the mountain.
She could almost hear competitors in her head, calling out
to their teammates in Italian and French and Spanish and
Belgian and Polish and Dutch, trying to intimidate her so
she would lose her nerve and slow down. "Never!" she said
to herself, standing up in the pedals as if she were sprinting

to get away from the other riders. She was pulling ahead. The other riders were astonished at her burst of speed. Could anyone challenge this American girl's incredible speed and stamina in this race?

"She's all alone! She's broken away from the pack and no one has the strength to follow! Who is this . . . amazing . . . American girl . . . on her way . . . to becoming Queen of the Mountains?" Bicycle panted out loud to herself, still standing up in the pedals. She pretended the red and yellow wildflowers lining the road were adoring fans, come there to watch her win.

"Yes, who is this amazing American girl?" said a voice at her shoulder.

Bicycle thought, *Boy, my imagination is extra intense— must be the thin air.*

But the wiry cyclist on her left was as real as the road itself. He gave her a salute, accelerating to pass her. Behind him came six more riders, three young men and three young women, dressed in identical neon yellow jerseys labeled KING TUTTER'S BUTTER POPCORN CYCLING TEAM. Each one smiled or saluted as he or she passed.

The last woman, with a long braid, turned as she passed Bicycle and waved her onto her back wheel. "Stick with us! If you stay right on my wheel, it'll be easier to make it to the top," she said.

Bicycle focused her eyes on the woman's rear wheel. She

178

positioned the rubber of the Fortune's front tire within an inch of the other rider's tire and pumped her legs like crazy to keep a steady speed. The cyclists ahead of her rode in a smooth line, each rider keeping close to the person ahead. *So this is what it's like to ride with a team!* she thought. *Cool!*

The rider at the front of the pack maneuvered to the left and eased up, letting the rest of the riders pass him by on the right. He pulled in behind Bicycle and started riding close on her back wheel. "So, Amazing American Girl, how do you like riding in a paceline?"

"I love it!" shouted Bicycle. She'd seen professional cycling teams ride like this in the films back at the monastery, in a perfect compact line, trying to achieve the most efficient speed possible. It took a lot of concentration and focus to stay right behind someone's back wheel without bumping into it. The Fortune showed her speed and distance as the road got steeper and steeper. Bicycle wasn't sure, but she thought the screen might have blinked the word impressive for one split second.

One by one, the other riders took their turn pulling at the front of the pack. After a few minutes, each of them peeled to the side and let the pack pass by, latching on to the very end of the paceline. The woman with the long braid was now at the front, riding hard. She called over her shoulder, "Ready to take the lead?"

"Ready," Bicycle replied.

The woman gave Bicycle a thumbs-up sign, peeled to the left, and dropped back. Bicycle was alone at the front of the team, leading the way. Bicycle felt her legs burning and her lungs calling out for her to slow down, but she kept pushing up the steep incline. The road curved around in a snakey switchback, and when she came around the next bend, she had a clear view of the road ahead and saw the top of the pass.

Bicycle let out a whoop of excitement with one searing breath. "Yahoo!"

The rest of the team joined in, hooting their own happy words: "Yippee!" "Whoo-hoo!" "Yeah doggies!"

Bicycle stood up on her pedals and used the last of her energy to roll under the big sign marking the top of the climb. WOLF CREEK PASS, ELEVATION 10,857 FT. YOU ARE STANDING ON THE GREAT DIVIDE, it said. She was panting so hard she thought she might throw up. The team encircled her and started patting her on the back and shoulders, talking over each other.

"You did great!"

"Just keep breathing—thinner air up here, you know?"

"Did you know what makes the Great Divide great? If you spit off one side of the Divide, your spit will flow down to the Atlantic Ocean, and if you spit off the other, it'll go to the Pacific."

"Dude, I think your spit would just sit there and eventually evaporate."

"What I mean is, if you could spit in a river running down one side, it goes west. But if you spit in a river running down the other, it goes east."

"Everyone stop talking about spitting! Hey, Amazing American Girl, want a snack?"

The wanting-to-throw-up feeling wavered and passed. Bicycle couldn't do much more than pant and nod in thanks.

The team rested long enough to share some buttered popcorn and chug some energy drinks. "Gotta get down the hill, our coach will be waiting. Want to come along?" asked the woman with the braid.

"I think I need some more time to recover," Bicycle said.

The woman gave Bicycle half a dozen popcorn packets and energy drinks, saying it would save them carrying the weight since their sponsor, King Tutter's, supplied them with all the popcorn and corn-based drinks they could stand and then some. Then, like a well-oiled machine, they formed a new paceline and pedaled out of sight down the other side of the pass.

Bicycle was alone on top of the evergreen-covered mountain with a view of the whole state of Colorado below. It smelled great up there. Sipping an energy drink, she pulled out a couple of postcards. She wrote a celebratory note to the monastery, letting them know she had made it as far as the Continental Divide, as well as one to Mr. Pittsburg in Midway Station, Kansas. She sketched a mountain with a big smiley-faced bicycle wheel on its crest.

On Top of the World

Dear Mr. Pittsburg,

I'm writing to you from two miles up in the sky. Sunflowers and flat roads are certainly wonderful, but mountains are full of wonder, too. Someday you should come west if you can. And whatever you do, bring a bike.

Sincerely,

Bicycle

After a few more breaths of thin, pine-scented air, Bicycle coasted down the other side of the mountain, admiring the crisp scenery of green valleys and burbling streams that she'd missed while working her way up to the top. At the bottom of the mountain, she rolled into a town called Pagosa Springs and found a SlowDown Café near a natural hot springs pool. She parked the Fortune in a bike rack and began to poke through her pack to find her well-worn Free Eats card from Chef Marie so she could dig into a colossal post-mountain-climbing meal. However, she couldn't seem to find the card. She was getting hungrier by the minute and her stomach let out a loud liquid growl as she kept looking.

The Fortune blinked, Why do you produce such a noise?

"Oh, I'm so hungry I can't think straight!" Bicycle answered, still searching. Her stomach rumbled again, a long gurgle with a bubbling squeak at the end. The nearby hot springs pool blorped out a similar bubbling gurgle. Her stomach responded more loudly, as if it were dueling with the pool for most unpleasant noise.

If money is required to obtain food, I can be of assistance. The Fortune popped open a small slit on the side of its computer screen and hummed. Out of the slit scrolled three pieces of paper that floated to the ground.

Bicycle picked one up. It was a one-hundred-dollar bill. Her eyes opened as wide as bike wheels. "Okay, Fortune, that's enough," she said, grabbing the money and ripping it up. She threw it away and glanced around. Luckily, no one was outside the restaurant to notice a bike spitting out hundreds of dollars. "I don't need any counterfeit money, thanks anyway."

It is identical in every detail to genuine United States currency. I can also print yen, pounds, euros, złoty, rubles—

Bicycle cut it off. "Never mind! Let's talk about this later." She decided to bring her backpack into the restaurant and search for her Free Eats card inside.

After pawing through her pack a bit more, she was relieved to peel the card from the back of the still-damp Polish-English dictionary. She sat down at a table near the window, asking the chef to cook her something befitting a cycling champion.

She was sticking her fork into a plate piled high with rainbow-trout spaghetti when the chef, a woman wearing a red bandana covering her hair, came over to sit at her table. "You're Bicycle, aren't you?" she asked.

"Correct, yes, that is me!" Bicycle said, slurping her spaghetti and getting trout on her chin.

The chef grinned. "Nice to finally meet you, girlfriend. Your inspiration got Chef Marie to make some smart changes to our cafés. Business is great! I swear, hungry bicyclists are the best thing to happen to any restaurateur. We had a bunch come in to eat earlier with their coach, and they requested three kinds of dessert." The chef leaned closer, lowering her voice. "But I'm not talking to you just to thank you. I'm wondering if anyone's told you about the lady in black."

Bicycle stopped slurping pasta.

The chef continued. "We SlowDown Café chefs talk every week, discussing recipes, that sort of thing. The other chefs have been reporting on your progress to California. But lately, there's been someone asking questions at the cafés, questions about *you*." The woman peeked around and lowered her voice again, almost whispering now. "She's always dressed in black clothes. She comes in and asks, 'Has anyone seen a young girl, wild hair, riding a bike?' The other chefs say that the lady is pretty scary, that her eyes freeze your heart to ice. So far, no one's told her anything. We think maybe this lady in black is bad news." She sat back. "Do you know her?"

Bicycle froze. *The lady from the auction. What did the auctioneer call her again? Miss Monet-Grubbink. I was right to be creeped out when I saw her at that café in Kansas. She was following me.* Her eyes fell on the Fortune outside the window.

She remembered how Miss Monet-Grubbink had looked her up and down with those cold, calculating eyes when Bicycle had bid on the Fortune 713-J. The more Bicycle had learned about the Fortune, the more valuable she'd realized the bike was. Especially now that she knew the Fortune could print up enough fake money to buy Dr. Alvarado's entire estate. It'd be worth a literal fortune to anyone dishonest enough to take advantage of it. Bicycle put her cheek down on the table and groaned out loud.

"I knew it." The chef nodded. "She is bad news, isn't she? Don't worry—none of us will give her any information about you. You can count on us." She stood up. "Now I'll let you eat."

Bicycle lifted her head and sighed. Her appetite was a lot less than it had been. She took a halfhearted bite of her trout. The incredible flavor perked her up a little. The chef brought a basket of warm, fresh bread with soft pats of melting butter, followed by a slice of caramel cake as big as her head. Bicycle cheered up a little more. *Well,* she thought, surveying the calories laid before her, *if she wants the Fortune, she's got to catch us first.* She popped a big hunk of buttered bread in her mouth. *I sure won't make it easy for her.*

TO CATCH A THIEF IN UTAH

Bicycle spent the first week of June camped in the most out-of-the-way spots she could find, trying to keep a low profile. She rode through Colorado's western frontier towns with her bike helmet pulled down to her eyebrows, not talking to anyone, determined not to give her would-be bike thief a single hint about where to find her and the Fortune. Whenever she heard a car approaching behind her, she gripped her handlebars and steered into roadside drainage ditches, crouching protectively beside the Fortune until the car passed. She was extra grateful for the Fortune at night, after the bike informed her it could camouflage the tent to match the scenery and ensure they were well hidden once the cover of darkness had fallen.

The riding was tough. Craggy mountains rose up like ancient soldiers standing at attention along her route, eventually giving way to open plains once more. After that week of tense travel, a painted billboard welcomed her to

UTAH—STILL THE RIGHT PLACE. The billboard showed a broad swath of blue sky, pale orange desert sand, and a big rock formation with a big hole in it. A smaller sign below let Bicycle know this was THE BEEHIVE STATE.

Several miles ahead, she spotted a huge, uneven red shape by the side of the road. Bicycle was not a fan of bees, having been stung on the very top of her head one summer, so she rode very cautiously toward the shape, ready to speed past if it turned out to be some giant hive for mutant red bees. As she drew closer, she discovered it was a tall arch eroded out of red rock. A handful of people stood beneath the arch, snapping pictures, oohing and aahing at its titanic size. Bicycle heaved a sigh of relief, and then let out some oohs and aahs of her own. Past the arch, she saw rocks in shades of scarlet brown and dusty pink carved by the wind and weather into smooth towers, arches, spires, and rounded knobs. Bicycle pedaled the Fortune right through man-made tunnels hollowed through some red rock cliffs. As the day wore on, the sun lit the sandstone formations from different angles and they glowed with the colors of old bricks and new bricks, of underripe raspberries and just-right chili peppers. Everything darkened to deep browns and silent blacks as the sun disappeared, and a million stars filled the sky.

Early the next morning, her eyes peeled for any black-clad figures, she slunk cautiously into a visitors' center to snag a free postcard with a rock arch on it. She tried to describe this new scenery for Sister Wanda and the monks:

I don't think the songwriter for "America the Beautiful" knew what to say about this part of Utah. It hasn't got amber waves of grain, purple mountains, or fruited plains. It's more like a playground molded from red Play-Doh. How lucky am I to be able to bike through an alien's playground?

Bicycle

A few sandy, cactus-filled miles later, she regretted saying she felt lucky. The red rocks were lovely, but they left very little room for trees to grow. Shade was in drastically shorter supply than it had been at the start of her trip seven weeks ago. The Fortune's thermometer hit 100°F before lunch and stayed there past dinnertime. The following day, it hit 101°F.

Bicycle tried to count her blessings and appreciate now that the sun rose earlier and set later, she had more hours in the day to ride. However, the trade-off for more hours of sunlight was keeping company with the sunlight itself: for three days in a row, it glared down on Bicycle's head from above while the parched ground reflected the heat right back up at her from below. Bicycle thought she now knew how a pie felt when it was baked in an oven or fried in a deep fryer.

The wind blew frequent clumps of tumbleweeds like fluffy wagon wheels across the road. Bicycle filled up her water bottles whenever she could, from gas-station faucets and hoses in front of people's houses, but the water never seemed to be cold. At best, it would feel slightly cooler than her dried-out mouth, and after a few minutes of sloshing around in her bottles, it would turn as warm as bathwater. The warm water was awful on a hot day, but she worried that if she didn't drink it, she might dry up and fly away like a tumbleweed herself.

She slept fitfully. She was plagued by restless dreams of being chased by skinny women in black police uniforms riding atop big, drooling farm hounds. One sleepless night, Bicycle pulled out a flashlight and opened up *Wheel Wisdom*, searching for advice on handling the heat. Unfortunately, she didn't find any passages about cycling in hot weather and had to settle for a quote from Zbig about cold instead:

Sometimes, you ride in freezing rain or snow. This is a whole new challenge. You lose feeling in your feet first. They become like lumps of ice that glue your legs to the pedals, nothing more. Your face will go numb—you cannot feel your nose, your lips, your cheeks. Then your fingers become icicles. When you lift them up to wipe your face, you can't tell if you are wiping your face because your face cannot feel anything and your fingers cannot feel anything. This is why it is good to have teammates. "George," you will ask, "am I touching my face?" And George will watch you and say, "Yes, you are—but be careful! You keep sticking your hand in your mouth—you might bite off a finger by mistake." So teammates are very important to have around you.

Bicycle read and reread that passage until she had it memorized, trying to picture herself riding through freezing rain and snow with her bitterly cold teammates. It helped her stop sweating and fall asleep.

Suspecting the lady in black might try to ambush her at a SlowDown Café, she didn't feel comfortable going in for free meals and Feed Bags, and ended up eating the nasty Complete Nutrition pellets that the Fortune provided. Every time the bike gave her one, it advertised the pellets as filled with all necessary nutritional elements, packed with vitamins. Choking down a single greasy pellet was almost worse than starving, and Bicycle began fantasizing endlessly about ice cream—ice cream sundaes in glass dishes with towers of whipped cream, ice cream cones decked with rainbow sprinkles, ice cream milk shakes too thick for straws.

Ice cream wasn't the only thing she started to crave. In her entire life, Bicycle had never dreamed that avoiding people could make her feel lonely. To her, being silent and alone had always been a good thing. But the sun beating down seemed to have burned a lonesome hole in her midsection. She missed Griffin and his chatter. She missed meeting interesting people in snug little towns. Her notebook pages, usually full of funny observations and anagrams of town names and comments on what she'd eaten, recorded nothing more than the Fortune's report of her daily mileage and the high temperature.

After a few more days of heat and hiding, Bicycle's cravings for real companionship and real food became too powerful to ignore. She rode straight into a tiny town at dusk and stopped at the Cool Cone Shake Shack, almost drooling with anticipation. She'd order a double-dip—no, a triple-dip! Heck, she'd tell the ice cream scooper to load as much ice cream as the cone could hold without disintegrating. She'd argued with herself all day about whether it was wrong to ask the Fortune to print her a counterfeit five-dollar bill. She'd finally ended her mental argument by telling herself, *It's absolutely wrong, so I will have to make it right after my trip is over and mail real money and an apology to the ice cream shop.* She didn't feel great about pocketing the bill the Fortune agreeably printed for her, but she wrote down the address of the Cool Cone Shake Shack in her tiny spiral notebook, underlining it three times before she went inside.

The place was empty except for the teenager behind

the counter, who popped his gum and stared off into space as Bicycle ordered nine flavors (mint chip, chocolate bean, mocha choker, extra-rocky road, peanut butter ripple, praline scramble, maple almond, fudge brownie surprise, and black vanilla). He gave Bicycle her towering cone, and she handed him her money. Hoping to distract him from the fact the bill was so crisp and new, she said nervously, "So, why are there beehives on the Utah state road signs?"

The boy put the money in the cash register and turned toward her with vacant eyes. "Wha'?" he asked.

"Your state road signs? Have a beehive on them? I haven't seen any bees, though. Is Utah famous for honey, or something like that?" Bicycle tried to engage his brain.

It didn't work. "Beehives, yeah." The boy scratched his stomach. "I dunno. The signs just have 'em." He lapsed into silence and stared at a point on the wall. He popped his gum again.

"Okay, then," Bicycle responded, giving up on the conversation. At least her monster cone would satisfy one of her cravings. She sat at a small table and settled into some serious licking.

Three gangly teenagers came into the Cool Cone Shake Shack together, swatting at one another with mountain-bike helmets. They slid onto stools at the counter and ordered banana splits, talking loudly about their day biking out on the rock formations in the national park.

"Did you see me jump that wash? I was flyyyyyyying," the one with blue hair was saying.

"Uh, flying like a ladybug must be what you mean, since you were about an inch off the ground," another said sarcastically, a gold ring pierced through his nose.

"At least I tried jumping it, you doofus," Blue Hair retorted, punching his friend's arm. "What were you doing, besides complaining about leaving your sunblock at home? And then talking to that creepy lady—were you inviting her over to your house for tea?"

Bicycle's ears pricked up.

The third one, a small tattoo of a flying bird on his arm, laughed. "Inviting her over for tea, good one. What was up with her, though? I couldn't believe she asked us if we'd seen a girl riding a bike around there. Lady, what do you think? There's lots of people riding bikes. School's out for summer, and it's the perfect place to ride!"

Bicycle blurted out, "Was she wearing black? And did she have eyes that made your heart go cold?"

The three of them swiveled their stools around to stare at her.

"Dude, her eyes were wicked—" Blue Hair started to respond, but Bird Tattoo nudged him into silence with his elbow. Bird Tattoo seemed to be in charge of the group.

"You know her? Man, she was creepy and a half. She your mom or something?" he asked in a tough voice.

Bicycle gave them her fiercest look. "No, I think she's after my bike. She's been following me for a while, and if she finds me she's going to try to steal it."

The boys' eyes widened, and Bird Tattoo said, "She wants to steal your *bike*? That is *not* okay. That is so far beyond not okay." He came over to Bicycle's table, and the other two followed. They pulled out chairs and sat down. "Do you need some help?"

Bicycle licked a drop of mint chip dribbling down her cone. She looked across the table at the mountain bikers and felt how awfully tired she was becoming. Tired of riding in the heat, tired of being alone, but mostly tired of hiding. The tiredness reached deep down inside, where even nine scoops of ice cream couldn't fix it. It had been two long weeks since the SlowDown Café chef in Pagosa Springs, Colorado, had warned her about Miss Monet-Grubbink. She didn't want to keep skulking in the shadows. It didn't suit her one bit. "I might. I don't know how you could help, though. I think she figured out that my bike is pretty amazing, and I'm scared she won't give up until she's got her hands on it."

The boys made exasperated noises over that.

"We've all had bikes stolen from us. It's the worst feeling in the world," said Bird Tattoo. "This lady—maybe we can figure out where she is and set a trap for her. We could catch her and make it clear to her what we think about slug-sucking bike thieves, and guarantee she'll never bug you again."

"I don't know, Carlos, we've never done anything like that before," Nose Ring said uncertainly.

Blue Hair looked like he wasn't sure which of his friends to agree with.

Bird Tattoo, apparently known to his buddies as Carlos, wouldn't let his friends back down. "Guys, we can do this. Just think. It would be like getting revenge for our stolen bikes, for all stolen bikes everywhere!"

Blue Hair mused, "I always wished I could find whoever stole my first bike and make them feel as bad as they made me feel. Okay, I'm in."

Nose Ring looked at the other two, then nodded at Bicycle. "Me too," he said.

Bicycle noticed Carlos's bird tattoo was the temporary kind that washes off after a few days. The boys weren't as tough as they pretended to be, but they were passionate about bicycles. She thought she could trust anyone who was passionate about bicycles. "Okay," she said. "Tell me what you think we could do. How can we make the creepy lady leave me alone? I don't want to hurt anybody or anything."

"Nah, we're not going to hurt anybody. We'll come up with some way to convince her that she's better off giving up bike thieving," said Carlos. "We saw her out in the park. When she left on her bike, she headed this way, so she's probably still in town. It's getting too dark to ride anywhere else tonight."

"Wait, what? She was riding a bike?" It was hard for Bicycle to imagine Miss Monet-Grubbink perched on a bicycle. Hold on—maybe she could. It would be black and angular and stolen from some other poor person. "That means I'm not the only one she's been after. She's probably been stealing lots of bikes! What can we do?" Bicycle's tiredness from hiding and her nervousness about the Fortune being stolen blurred into a new feeling of righteous outrage.

Carlos said, "First, let's bring our bikes inside so we can keep a close eye on them." He called to the boy working the counter, "Bobby, you don't care if we bring the bikes in, do you?"

Bobby popped his gum and shrugged.

After the mountain bikes and the Fortune were wheeled inside and parked against the back wall, Carlos rubbed his hands together. "So, how about this for a plan . . ."

The four of them stayed at the ice cream shop for more than an hour, eating more ice cream and working out their idea. They were so intent on discussing bike justice that Bicycle never thought to ask Blue Hair's and Nose Ring's real names. When it was time for the ice cream shop to close, the three boys formed a protective triangle around Bicycle and rode with her and the Fortune back to Carlos's parents' house, where they cleared a space for her in a cluttered gardening shed.

Carlos said, "You'll be safe here. My parents haven't

gardened in years. I'll come out and knock three times in the morning so you'll know it's me, and we'll go meet up with the guys. Got everything you need?"

Bicycle patted the Fortune's seat. "I sure do."

Carlos smiled and closed the shed door behind him. Bicycle pressed the green button, climbed inside the tent, and told the Fortune about what they were preparing to do.

Your plan is interesting. It may require some good luck to succeed. May I offer my abilities when confronting this person? I have a high-density fishing net that may be of use, as well as the missile launcher.

"No missiles," Bicycle said hurriedly. "Nothing like that. We just plan to scare her so she leaves me in peace to get to California. Maybe we can use the net if we need to keep her from getting away before we're sure she's going to give up her bike-stealing ways."

Understood. The Fortune blinked placidly. I will be ready.

Bicycle and Carlos met up with the other two mountain bikers in the Cool Cone Shake Shack parking lot the next day.

"Okay," said Carlos. "Let's head to that shortcut to the main road out of town."

They rode through the rock formations, sunburn red in the morning light. Bicycle saw the thin ribbon of road several miles ahead, cutting through an empty area of sand, rocks, and desolation.

"There are a couple of billboards up there that will give us perfect cover," Carlos said, sitting up straight and pedaling with no hands on his handlebars. "We'll be able to see her coming from miles off, and then when she rides up to us, whammo!" He knocked one gloved fist into his palm and patted the strap of the worn backpack he had slung over his shoulders. "She won't be bugging you anymore!"

They rode hard, reaching the spot Carlos had in mind. The two billboards stood alone in the bleak terrain, one on either side of the road. The faded advertisement on the left side told everyone to BRUSH WITH SUPA-KLEEN TOOTHPASTE—WHITER SMILES FOR MILES AND MILES! The ad on the right appealed to those who preferred tooth decay: CHEW SUGARTIME TOOTHSOME TAFFY—STICKS WITH YOU THROUGH THICK AND THIN!

They pulled their bikes behind the toothpaste billboard, making sure everything was out of sight. The sun already blazed down like a blast furnace, and it was a relief to find a little shade behind the tall sign. A small hole (camouflaged by the letter I in the second MILES) allowed Carlos to peer out from behind the billboard and see the road.

He watched for a minute and then let out a whistle. "She's fast—I'll give her that."

"She's here already?" Bicycle felt a surge of alarm. Facing her stalker had sounded like a good idea until this moment. Now she wanted to change her mind and keep running away instead. Blue Hair saw the terrified look on her face and patted her helmet.

"Yep," answered Carlos. "Maybe four miles back. It's definitely her. Our bike-thief lady in black." He unzipped his backpack and handed a bag of squishy red things to Blue Hair. "Head over to the other sign and wait for my signal."

Blue Hair and Nose Ring scuttled across the road and hid behind the taffy billboard. They looked over to Carlos and Bicycle, and gave a thumbs-up. Bicycle squinched her eyes closed and whispered a Mostly Silent prayer. They waited for what seemed like an eternity.

Carlos whispered, "She's getting closer . . . closer . . . Wait for me . . ." Then he shouted and waved his hand in a circle in the air. "Now! Go, go, go!"

Blue Hair and Nose Ring came rushing out from behind the taffy billboard, hollering nonsense. They began pelting the lady in black with rotten tomatoes. She yelped in surprise and came to a stop, shielding her face. Then Carlos started pelting her with more tomatoes from behind, getting her with a big squishy splat on the back of the helmet.

"Leave this girl alone! Her bike is *her* bike, and you are *not* going to steal it!" bellowed Carlos.

Blue Hair hurled another tomato. The woman ducked this tomato and mounted up to ride away from the attack.

"Where do you think you're going?" Nose Ring yelled.

Bicycle's eyes popped open. What if the bike thief got away and kept chasing her? She'd have to keep hiding. She wouldn't be able to stop in ice cream shops or SlowDown Cafés. She'd have nothing to eat but the Fortune's Complete Nutrition pellets.

She swallowed her fear and wheeled the Fortune into the road toward the retreating figure. "Fortune, *now!*" she shouted, and the bicycle popped open a panel in the top of the seat and shot out a weighted net toward the woman. It covered her from head to toe and tangled around her bike. She started struggling and kicking.

Bicycle hid behind the boys while Carlos put on his toughest tough-guy expression and said, "Listen, lady, you need to promise to stop following this girl and leave her and her bike alone for good."

Blue Hair chimed in, "We don't take kindly to bike thieves around here." He hooked his thumbs in his belt loops and looked for a moment like a punk sheriff.

The woman spoke for the first time, exclaiming, "What? Bike thieves? How dare you suggest I'm a bike thief!"

Her voice gave Bicycle a weird feeling. She peeked around Carlos's shoulder.

The woman had managed to turn partway around, still tangled in the net, one hand braced on her handlebars. "I'm not here to steal anything from anyone. I'm here to rescue a girl!" She wiped some of the tomato goop and plastered hair off her face to glare at the boys, and Bicycle gasped in utter horror.

It was Sister Wanda.

The nun's frosty blue eyes zeroed in on her. "That girl right there, in fact."

Bicycle swallowed hard.

Carlos sneered. "Yeah, right." He pushed Bicycle forward, saying, "You go ahead and tell her to leave you alone. We won't let her do anything to you."

Sister Wanda had bits of rotten tomato stuck like nasty-smelling glue all over her black Nearly Silent Nun's robe. This wasn't her everyday robe, though, but one that was cut shorter and snugger for use when exercising. It looked like she was wearing black spandex cycling knickers underneath. Bicycle tried to make her mouth say something.

"I'm . . . sorry . . . ," Bicycle managed to whisper.

"Sorry? Sorry?" demanded Nose Ring. "What are you talking about? Isn't this your bike thief we got here?"

"No," said Bicycle miserably. "This is Sister Wanda. She's a nun from the monastery where I grew up." She stuttered, "A-a-actually, she's the one who taught *me* that stealing things is wrong."

"*Sister* Wanda? This is a nun?"

The three boys' eyes went wide.

"Holy cow—we're breaking like seven different commandments!" shouted Carlos. "Let's get outta here!"

The boys scrambled for their bikes and rode off in a cloud of dust. Bicycle was left alone under the silent gaze of Sister Wanda.

NO OVERRIDE FOR THE MISSILE LAUNCH

For one fleeting moment, Bicycle thought about hopping on the Fortune and riding off after the boys. Instead, she found her backpack and fished out the penknife she had packed. She brought it over to Sister Wanda, who used it to make short work of the net. Before long, she was standing before Bicycle, her pink cruiser bike leaning against the billboard. Despite the tomato guts trickling down her skin and clothes, the retired nun was as imposing as ever.

"You thought I was some other person, someone trying to steal your bicycle?" she asked, arms folded.

"Yes, ma'am," Bicycle said miserably.

"So you got your comrades back there"—she waved in the direction the boys had disappeared in—"to set up a trap for a bicycle thief. Is that correct?" She walked over to the Fortune. "And this machine here somehow shoots out nets to capture people?" She tapped the Fortune's frame with one finger and then focused her skin-melting gaze back on Bicycle.

"I hardly know those boys—I met them yesterday in an ice cream shop—but that's about right." Bicycle looked down and shuffled her feet in the sand and sparse grass. "I'm so sorry, Sister Wanda, I had no idea it was you." Her apology sounded woefully inadequate in the presence of the smell oozing off Sister Wanda. "Really."

"Mmmm-hmmmm," said Sister Wanda. "Well." A small smile crept over her slime-splattered features. "It looks as though you hardly needed rescuing at all." She suddenly reached out her arms and grabbed Bicycle, pulling her into a warm, gooey hug. "You foolish girl!" she said.

Bicycle exhaled in a huge, relieved *whoosh* and hugged Sister Wanda back. "You forgive me?"

"Of course, my dear. I'm not a monster. Now, if you had known it was me and you did this, that would be another story," she said. "You would be in trouble so thick you could spread it on toast. But as it is, I'm rather impressed. You know what I have learned here? For a twelve-year-old who has never traveled before, you have some very good survival instincts. Plus a knack for finding help in unexpected places." Sister Wanda let Bicycle go. "Well, we both need to clean up before this old-spaghetti smell becomes permanent. I remember seeing a sign advertising a gas station that's supposed to be around this next bend."

Sister Wanda arranged her exercise robe primly over the top tube of her pink cruiser bike. The bike had three speeds and looked like a real antique, old enough to have been ridden on a road from ancient Egypt through the Middle Ages to finally reach today.

Bicycle mounted up to follow her, full of questions. "How did you get here, Sister Wanda? I didn't think you could leave the monastery with no one to run things. And why are you on a bicycle? Did you ride here from D.C. like I did?" Sister Wanda had often worn her exercise robe to jog, but Bicycle had never seen her ride a bike before.

"Trying to track you down has been an adventure in and of itself," replied Sister Wanda, starting to pedal on the dry stretch of road. Bicycle fell into place next to her. "After I read your note about leaving for California, I thought for sure you'd give up and come home that first night. Then I was sure you'd be back the following day. Then I did call the police to go look for you, but you were nowhere to be found in D.C. And several days later, what turns up in the mail but a postcard itemizing the number of cows in Virginia!

"So I called the police in the town in Virginia where the postmark was from, and they informed me that finding a girl on a bicycle would be like finding a needle in a haystack because there are kids on bikes everywhere you look. I convinced them to try, but to no avail. I kept using your postcard postmarks to call police from one end of Virginia to the other, but I suppose we were always a step behind. You moved faster than we anticipated."

Bicycle grinned with pride but quickly closed her mouth and tried to look more penitent.

"After nearly two weeks of your absence I thought there had to be a better way. Then your postcard arrived from Kentucky. You know the Mostly Silent Monasteries don't believe in owning cars."

Bicycle did know that.

"So I took money from the emergency fund to pay for a train ticket to Louisville, Kentucky; borrowed this bike from a nun at a Nearly Silent Nunnery there; and took matters into my own hands. I figured you'd want to watch the Kentucky Derby, but what a crowd! I scarcely paid attention to the race, searching for you, but I didn't see you there."

Bicycle figured after she got her own questions answered, she'd explain what had happened at the Derby with The Cannibal. She asked, "You said you borrowed that bike to find me?"

"That and some camping gear. It wasn't as though you were going to ride next to the train tracks so I could see you out of the window. I asked myself: *If the police can't find her, what can I learn from that?* I answered myself: *The proper way to track down a bicyclist is to become a bicyclist.* I thought with the same wind in my face and the same cows in my view, I'd get the best sense of where you might be."

Bicycle nodded, seeing the logic.

"I left Brother Otto in charge, and the Top Monk absolved him of his Mostly Silent vows until I could get back. Honestly, he seemed much happier as soon as he was allowed to talk whenever he wanted to without getting the Mostly Silent Shush from the other monks. Anyway, I kept calling from pay phones to check in with him. (Along with cars, the Mostly Silent Monastery didn't believe in cell phones.) He reported on your postcards, and I added every new postmark from you to my own map to judge when I was getting close."

"So you've been riding behind me since Kentucky? But how could you be sure you'd pick the right roads?" Bicycle asked.

"Who taught you to read a map, hmmm?" Sister Wanda asked. "Who explained to you that the thickest, straightest lines are the interstate highways, where no bicyclists are allowed, and that the skinnier, wiggly lines are the more scenic ways to travel? Plus, by using your postcard postmarks, I was able to estimate your average velocity and likely route. And once you sent that big SlowDown Café postcard from Missouri with a map of the restaurant locations, I had Brother Otto forward that to me under General Delivery to a post office in western Missouri.

"Somehow, though, you got way ahead of me in Kansas, because Brother Otto started getting postcards about a hundred miles farther along than where I estimated I'd find you.

I tried, but I couldn't seem to ride fast enough to close the gap. I ended up getting a lift at the Colorado border from a nice woman who was visiting her Nearly Silent twin sister at the nunnery there. She loaded my bike into her trunk and drove me across the Rocky Mountains. And now here I am."

They arrived at the gas station and convinced the clerk to let them use the restroom to clean off the tomato splatters. A few minutes later, both cyclists emerged from the restroom in fresh clothes. Sister Wanda had rinsed her face and hair in the sink, and put on a clean exercise robe and new knickers, plus a neat pair of sky-blue socks with the Sacred Eight Words embroidered around the cuffs. She'd cleaned the tomato off her white sneakers as well as she could, although a few pink splotches remained.

"Much better," she sighed. "Now, what's this about a bicycle thief?"

"A SlowDown Café chef in Colorado told me that a lady dressed in black was asking about me. I thought it was this woman I saw at an auction in Kansas who wanted my bike. I've been trying to avoid getting caught since then," Bicycle said.

"Have you? Well, that explains the difficulty I had pinning you down. I kept thinking you'd be right around the next bend in the road." She was about to swing a leg over her pink cruiser when the front tire let out a loud *pop!* and a violent hissing noise.

"Let me," Bicycle offered. "It's the least I can do to make up for catching you in a net like a tomato-covered fish."

"Indeed, the very least," agreed Sister Wanda.

While Bicycle located her flat-fixing tools and set to work, Sister Wanda walked over to the Fortune leaning on its kickstand.

"This isn't Clunk. What is the story on this bicycle? It looks fancy."

Bicycle yanked the flat tube from the inside of the tire and pondered how to explain the Fortune. "Clunk got run over by a pig parade, and I had to leave him behind. I got this one at that auction in Kansas. It's got some neat features, like a tent and emergency food supplies." She checked the inside of the empty tire and found two small thorns embedded in it, pulling them out and tossing them far into the brush.

"Clunk was in a parade, you say?" Sister Wanda commented absently as she examined the Fortune's computer screen. "Look at all these buttons. So high tech. I wonder what this one does?" She tapped the red button on the side. When nothing happened, she tapped it again and again.

Missile launch sequence initialized. Countdown begins: Ten . . . Nine . . . Eight . . . Seven . . .

"Missile launch? Missile launch! Bicycle, how do you shut this thing off?" Sister Wanda yelled as the bike began counting down.

Bicycle rushed over and frantically jiggled the red button, then pressed every other button on the bike she could see. Nothing made any difference. The bike kept counting.

"I don't know how to stop it! Fortune, what are you doing?"

There is no override for the missile launch. Four . . . Three . . .

Sister Wanda grabbed the bike's handlebar stem and shook it back and forth like she was choking it. "You stop counting down this instant!" she commanded.

Two . . . One . . . Launching now.

Sister Wanda released the Fortune and took a big step backward, pushing Bicycle behind her. The Fortune fell to the ground and buzzed, opening a panel in its frame. Out of the panel emerged a long shaft of silver metal, pointed skyward. The buzzing became a *whoosh*, and a long, spotted tube shot out of the shaft. It flew straight up in the air for several hundred feet, slowed down, and then started to fall right back toward where they were standing.

Sister Wanda yelled, "Look out!" and she and Bicycle dived into the dirt.

The spotted tube landed in a clump of weeds, and they squeezed their eyes shut and clapped their hands over their ears, waiting for the blast. None came. Minutes passed.

Bicycle half opened one eye. She watched Sister

Wanda climb to her hands and knees and creep over to the clump of weeds. The nun bravely pushed the weeds aside. Then she snorted. She reached down and plucked out a spotted rubber snake, the springy kind that pops out of trick cans of peanuts.

Rubber snake dangling from one hand, Sister Wanda walked over to the Fortune and pulled it back upright. Then she gave it a look. Bicycle thought the Fortune, inanimate object or not, could sense the danger in that look.

"What is the meaning of this?" Sister Wanda asked.

My inventor failed to include missiles in my frame. Rubber snakes are all that was loaded before he discontinued work on me.

Sister Wanda slapped the snake against one palm. "If you ever pull a stunt like that again, Mr. Fancy Bike, you're going to be missing more than missiles. Do we understand each other?"

Yes.

The Fortune didn't add anything else. Bicycle didn't blame it. Getting on Sister Wanda's bad side would make anyone or anything go quiet.

Bicycle finished fixing the flat, and Sister Wanda climbed on the pink bike.

"So." She gazed around her, orienting herself. "We will continue west."

Bicycle let out an "Oh!" of relief. She had been so focused

on apologizing to Sister Wanda for the tomatoes, and then the Fortune's rubber snake launch, that she hadn't let herself think about what was going to happen next. "You mean you're coming with me to California? Thank goodness! We're not too far from the state line, and the Blessing of the Bicycles should be pretty amazing, and I can't wait to see the Pacific Ocean—"

Sister Wanda cut her off. "You misunderstand me, child. We're not continuing west to California. Only to Calamity, Nevada." She began pedaling and Bicycle had no choice but to jump on the Fortune and keep up. "The Friendship Factory was very understanding. They agreed to transfer your credit toward attending camp to whichever of their facilities was closest when I caught up with you. I have a catalog of all of their locations, and the closest is in Calamity. I'm delivering you there. It is no more than four days' ride from the Nevada border. You'll stay there for the six-week summer intensive and the three guaranteed friendships. Once you are done, you'll take a train home to the monastery."

Bicycle's mouth dropped open. "What . . . what? . . . Friendship Factory? . . . *Me?*" The last word ended in a squeak. She couldn't put together a sentence. She didn't want to understand what Sister Wanda had just said.

Sister Wanda wagged her finger as if they were back in the monastery classroom. "You know how much I worried about you, a child in that silent place, spending all your time with quiet old monks and a rusty old bike. It wasn't healthy. Running away from your problems never solves anything, Bicycle. You must face them. You will learn to make friends, period. I would be remiss in my duty as your guardian if I didn't see to that, and I am *never* remiss in my duties, as I'm sure you realize by now."

"But . . . but . . . I'm not running away from my problems, I'm biking toward the solution! I'm going to make friends with Zbigniew Sienkiewicz, Sister Wanda. You don't have to do this."

"I beg to differ, my dear," the nun said.

Bicycle tried to think of a way to convince Sister Wanda otherwise. "I already made friends with a ghost, and he'd be here with me now to tell you so, except for the eight hundred and thirty-eight pigs that ran over him!" As the words left her mouth, she knew they were not helping.

"Making up stories about imaginary friends is not going to change my mind. There is nothing more to be said," Sister Wanda answered.

"But I—"

Sister Wanda silenced her with a look that was part pity and part steel. "I know you do not want to do this. However, you are too young to make such decisions for yourself. You need to be guided by the wisdom of your elders, dear, and that is *that*." Sister Wanda ended her lecture with the tone of voice that meant discussion of the matter was closed.

Bicycle's eyes filled with tears, blurring the vision of Sister Wanda's black-clad form, pedaling before her, blocking her way. This was much worse than being followed by a bicycle thief. Bicycle pushed her pedals mechanically. For the first time, she dreaded her progress. She was going to be sent to the Friendship Factory after all. Her escape had been futile. Her adventure was at an end. With Sister Wanda watching over her, this time there was truly no escape.

THE LONELIEST ROAD

After a long, fully silent afternoon, Sister Wanda announced, "I don't see anywhere better to camp. This will have to do." The nun and the girl slowed and pulled their bikes off into an RV park. Sister Wanda checked in with the front desk and was assigned a plain dirt campsite near a cinder-block bathroom. They saw no other tents or bicycles, only motor homes ranging in size from cozy to battleship.

"Come help me set up my tent, and we can share it," said Sister Wanda, unclipping a pannier from the side of her bike's rear rack.

The Fortune beeped to get Bicycle's attention. Tell her to press the green button. Tell her that my tent is of the highest quality. Tell her there is room for you both, and tell her I can ensure that your shelter has a pleasant, relaxing scent.

"The Fortune wants you to come over and try pressing the green button," Bicycle said.

Sister Wanda walked over to the bike and asked, "Oh? Can you promise there will be no snake missiles this time, Mr. Fancy Bike?"

Please press the green button, the Fortune replied—somewhat meekly, Bicycle thought.

Sister Wanda, a sleeping bag in one hand, looked at Bicycle, who nodded, and the nun pushed the green button. They stepped back while the Fortune did its tent-exhaling trick and Bicycle followed Sister Wanda inside the blue-and-yellow gumdrop.

"My, my," Sister Wanda said once inside. "This is quite the luxurious setup."

The Fortune puffed out its lemon-scented mist and started playing a cello concerto. It blinked, I also have Beethoven and Brahms if you prefer that to Bach. The Fortune seemed to know better than to offer Sister Wanda any Bronze Age music.

"Your bicycle can play classical concertos? We have a lot to catch up on, my dear. You were going to tell me something about Clunk and a parade?"

Sister Wanda unrolled her sleeping bag and pulled out her own tiny spiral notebook. She started flipping through it, and Bicycle could see it was filled with precise pencil marks and sketched maps showing Sister Wanda's route.

"Let's start comparing notes and see what we can learn from this," Sister Wanda said. "Then we'll figure out some dinner."

Bicycle dug through her pack and brought out her yellow notebook. She looked at its scruffy, chocolate-stained cover and thought about all the miles contained within its pages and felt like she might cry. She handed it to Sister Wanda. "Here, you can look at this if you want, but I'm too tired," she said sullenly, pulling her blanket out of her pack and lying down on the far side of the tent. She closed her eyes and pretended to be asleep until she really was.

The next day offered some long downhill stretches that ought to have been a blast to barrel down, but Bicycle couldn't enjoy them. She stuck to the Sacred Eight Words when Sister Wanda tried to engage her in conversation. The nun finally gave up and lapsed into an I-know-what's-best-for-you silence as they cruised along.

They passed a big black-and-red WELCOME TO NEVADA billboard with the image of a pickax-holding prospector. Bicycle didn't care. Sister Wanda stopped at a gas station and bought a postcard of a jackrabbit with miniature antelope horns glued to its head and GREETINGS FROM NEVADA! scrawled across the top in big yellow letters. She wrote a brief note letting Brother Otto and the Top Monk know that she'd found Bicycle and would be depositing her safely at the Friendship Factory soon. Bicycle got a postcard to send to Green Marsh and couldn't think of anything else to write except:

Dear Griffin, Jeremiah, and Estrella,

Sister Wanda found me. I'm doomed.

Bicycle

The sun rose higher and began baking the world around them. Bicycle was wiping small rivers of sweat from her face, and it wasn't even ten o'clock yet. "Holy spokes! I thought Utah was hot," she said.

"If my memory serves me, and it usually does," Sister Wanda said, "you've not seen anything yet when it comes to heat. I've read about southwest topography and terrain, and the desert and mountains ahead won't be any roll in the park, let me tell you. This part of Nevada is like a big rumpled carpet. We'll climb up a mountain, coast down the other side, then ride a long, flat stretch. A few miles later, another mountainous rumple in the carpet of the desert to climb, then another stretch of desert flatness.

"I'm sure you're wondering why I don't just buy us bus tickets to Calamity and be done with biking," Sister Wanda continued.

Bicycle wasn't. She didn't want to get to the Friendship Factory any faster than she had to.

"But this area of Nevada isn't like Washington, D.C. There isn't a subway or bus that can take us where we need to go. So we'll make do with the four wheels we've got. We've both proved we have the muscle power to make it another three days, haven't we?"

Bicycle didn't answer.

"Just make sure to drink enough water. And don't provoke the wild cows," Sister Wanda admonished.

The Fortune beeped as if to support Sister Wanda's suggestion. This desert region of Nevada routinely averages over 100 degrees Fahrenheit. My sensors indicate extremely low humidity. Drinking plenty of water and not provoking the wild cows would be wise.

"I'm not going to provoke anything!" Bicycle said. She muttered to the Fortune, "You don't have to agree with everything she says. Can't you be on my side?"

The Fortune blinked quietly for a few moments and then replied, I cannot be on your side. I would be unrideable from that position. But I will always be underneath you.

Bicycle considered that. "Thanks," she said. "I think."

Bicycle didn't want one more thing to worry about, but she couldn't help keeping her eyes peeled for wild cows, whatever they might be. She saw plenty of yellow road signs warning of roaming cattle, elk, and antelope, but the land seemed devoid of any animal life. Only the furry wink of a single rabbit tail hinted at creatures active in the bone-dry stillness.

If Nevada animals were few and far between, Nevada people were equally as scarce. They didn't pass any towns for a very long time. The sole signs of human habitation along the highway were tiny convenience stores attached to tiny casinos with names like Fat Chance and Lucky 7. They camped their first night in Nevada down the street from an establishment called the Jailhouse Motel.

The next day, Bicycle continued to ride in silence, her emotions cycling through despair, to anger, to regret, to brief stints of frenzied escape-plan-making, leading back to despair when she looked at the upright and unyielding figure riding beside her. Even when the pair went to a SlowDown Café for a late lunch, Bicycle found she didn't have much of an appetite. She mechanically chewed and swallowed her tumbleweed lasagna and elk chops until she couldn't stand to put another forkful in her mouth. What was the point in eating? It would only give her energy to bike. What was the point in biking? It would only bring her to Calamity. There was nothing fun about riding across the country when your destination was nowhere you wanted to end up.

The chef who came to check on how they'd enjoyed their meal gave her a long look as she pushed lasagna noodles around with her fork. "Are you Bicycle? The girl everyone's been keeping track of, headed to California?" he asked.

"Yes, sir," she said. She hoped he'd understand that her lack of appetite had nothing to do with the quality of his cooking and everything to do with the heavy feeling in her stomach.

"I am Bicycle's guardian, Sister Wanda," Sister Wanda

introduced herself. "How kind that you have been looking out for her. Your food is tremendous."

"Thank you. We are pretty proud of it," the chef answered. He dropped a dish towel on the floor and as he bent down, he whispered to Bicycle, "Are you okay? Is this the lady in black that has been asking after you? She doesn't look as bony as some of the other chefs said, but they were right when they said her eyes bore right through you."

Bicycle tried to think of some way to tell the chef the mess she was in, to ask for help. She opened her mouth and nothing came out, like a monk-in-training who couldn't pick which of the Sacred Eight Words to use. Without much conviction, she eventually said, "I'm okay."

The chef tilted his head. "If you say so. I'll wrap up those leftovers and make a Feed Bag for you." He took her food back to the kitchen.

Sister Wanda stood up as the chef brought back Bicycle's leftovers and Feed Bag and headed for the door. "Come on," she said. "We've miles to go before we sleep."

Sister Wanda spent that evening comparing her maps with the Fortune's navigation system and confirming their route to the Friendship Factory. The next day a road sign informed the pair that they were traveling on HIGHWAY 50—THE LONE-LIEST ROAD IN AMERICA. They pedaled past the Loneliest

Hardware Store in America, the Loneliest Golf Course in America, and they got some bagels at the Loneliest Jewish Deli in America. Finally—it was bound to come along at some point—they rolled into the Loneliest Town on the Loneliest Road in America. It had a casino, three restaurants, and an opera house.

"An opera house is lovely, to be sure, but let's see if they have the real measure of civilization: an ice cream parlor," Sister Wanda said. "We're nearly to Calamity. We'll stop here to have a treat before finding a campsite, and I'll use their pay phone to call the Friendship Factory and tell them to expect us tomorrow."

It didn't take long to hunt down Lonesome Licks, where they each sat at the counter with a peanut butter hot fudge sundae piled high with handmade whipped cream. Bicycle knew Sister Wanda was trying to be nice by treating her to ice cream, but as soon as the sundae was sitting in front of her, a sick-to-her-stomach feeling rose up. She unenthusiastically poked at the whipped cream with her spoon, tummy gurgling and lurching, and knew she couldn't eat it. She decided she should choke down a vitamin pellet from the Fortune so she wouldn't waste away to nothing.

"I'm going to get something from the Fortune," she said to Sister Wanda, who was already deep into her own sundae.

Bicycle shuffled out the door and over to the bicycle rack, eyes watering from the intense heat. She didn't even see the man standing next to their bikes until she bumped into him.

"Excuse me, sir," she apologized.

He didn't answer. He was staring at the Fortune as if he were in a trance.

"Uh, excuse me?" she tried again. "I need to get to my bike, please."

The man swam out of his trance and focused his eyes on Bicycle. "Hmmm? Oh, certainly, go ahead." He stepped back, looking dazed.

Bicycle got close to the Fortune, checking that her pack was still secure. Nothing seemed to have been touched, but she felt nervous about the attention the man had been paying the bike. She kneeled down and pretended she was adjusting her brake cables, but instead she shifted to the side and peered discreetly at the man behind her.

The dapper gentleman was still standing there, looking off into space. His well-trimmed hair was glossy black shot through with a few strands of gray. He was dressed in a dark blue suit, a pale blue shirt, and a silver tie. The tie was decorated with little shapes that Bicycle made out to be question marks. She gave him one more look and decided he seemed harmless enough. She stood up, pressed the purple button for a vitamin pellet, and returned to the air-conditioned comfort of her stool in Lonesome Licks. Sister Wanda had already made short work of her sundae and was over in the corner, using the pay phone to call the Friendship Factory.

The door jingled as the gentleman came into the parlor. Bicycle chased the vitamin pellet down her throat with a gulp of ice water as he sat on the stool next to her. He ordered a double-thick cactus milk shake. She tried to look at him out of the corner of her eye, and noticed he was looking at her out of the corner of his eye.

He then whispered to her out of the corner of his mouth. "Did they send you to find me?"

She turned to face him. "Excuse me?"

He agitatedly flapped his hands at her and whispered more loudly, "No, don't look at me! Pretend we're not talking. Just tell me: Did my children send you? Or the government—do they want me to try inventing something else for them?"

Unnerved, she quickly turned her head to face forward and whispered back to him out of the corner of her own mouth. "Uh . . . no idea who you are, sir. I need to be going now." She started to inch off the stool, ready to dash for the safety of Sister Wanda's side.

The man dropped the pretense of secrecy and faced her, speaking in a regular tone of voice. "You mean you showed up on *that* bike in *this* town without looking for me?" He clapped his hands together like a toddler on Christmas day. "The Wheels of Fortune got a chance to spin after all! Please allow me to introduce myself. I am Dr. Luck Alvarado. My dear, are you all right?"

Bicycle's jaw had dropped down onto her chest. "D-D-D-Dr. Luck Alvarado? Inventor of the Wheels of Fortune 713-J?" she stuttered.

He nodded happily.

She attempted to recover some politeness. "Hello. I'm Bicycle." She didn't know what else to say, so she just kept staring at him.

"I'm sorry, this is probably very startling for you," he said. "I forget sometimes that not everyone ponders the worldwide currents of luck. And this is quite a surprise, even for me."

Sister Wanda had noticed their conversation, and now she came over to introduce herself as Bicycle's guardian, a retired Nearly Silent Nun.

"I am the inventor of Bicycle's bicycle," Dr. Alvarado said, standing up. He suavely kissed Sister Wanda's proffered hand. "Always a pleasure to meet a Nearly Silent Nun, retired or not. Your work is so valuable. Come, come, we must get to know one another better. You will tell me your story? And I will tell you mine? And we will find how our stories came to intertwine here at Lonesome Licks."

"I don't know . . . ," Sister Wanda began.

"Oh, please, you must humor me. It isn't often that I get to delight in the company of two lovely ladies." He took her hand again and gave it another peck, and Sister Wanda turned the faintest shade of pink.

"I suppose we have time for a chat before we have to set up camp for the night," she said. "You're an inventor, you say?"

He ushered them to a table, and the waiter brought over his milk shake. Between long pulls on his straw, Dr. Alvarado explained how he'd ended up on the loneliest stretch of Nevada. From what Bicycle understood, he'd been given a big pile of money by the government to work on the Wheels of Fortune project. However, after official inspectors checked out Dr. Alvarado's finished prototype, the government withdrew their money.

"Apparently, when they requested that I invent the perfect long-distance traveling machine, they were envisioning armor-plated tanks with various guns and explosives. Not harmless blue-and-yellow bicycles." He shrugged. "What can I say? I'm not a tank sort of person. However, that was not why I left Kansas." He looked pained, pausing in his tale to slurp some cactus milk shake.

"It didn't matter much to me that the government withdrew their money. However, when my children found out about it, they went through the roof. They have been living off my invention money their entire lives. Never had jobs or families of their own. Their mother passed away when they were very young, and I am sorry to say I do not seem to have been a good father. Do you know the expression 'He is a good egg'? It is a compliment—it means someone is a good person. My children are the opposite. They are rotten eggs." He sighed.

"Anyway, it turns out my son and daughter had big plans to spend that government money on some extremely expensive cars with hot tubs and movie screens built into them. We had a fight. They demanded that I get the money back. I told them they could live without their movie-star cars. Then my son, pretending to be me, called the government representative and agreed to build a huge tank with machine guns and grenade launchers if they would send another check. My daughter was coaching him through what to say on the phone when I came upon them. I grabbed the phone, canceled the plans, and told my children that was the last straw.

"I left everything behind—including the Fortune 713-J, even though it could have helped me in my travels—and took off with nothing but the clothes on my back and the brains in my head. I did not tell my children where I was going. I did not even know myself where I was going. I felt certain that as long as I was around and they could sponge off me indefinitely, my rotten eggs would stay spoiled. It seemed like the right thing to do. I needed a fresh start."

As he'd been talking, he'd taken several straws from the straw dispenser and was absentmindedly weaving them together into a delicate bracelet.

Bicycle said, "They still seem to care an awful lot about money."

Dr. Alvarado raised his eyebrows. "You've met my children?"

"I have. I bought the Fortune from them," she said, thinking back to the brother and sister gloating over the cash box at the Alvarado Estate auction. "I think you did the right thing."

Dr. Alvarado handed her the plastic straw bracelet. "I continue to hope so. At any rate, I walked away from my home and hitchhiked the highways of America, looking for a place where I would be free to pursue my studies, someplace my children could not track me down. All I needed was peace and quiet to begin again. I wanted to find a location far away from everywhere." He spread his hands to indicate the town around them. "I settled here. I still invent things and sell them, but now I focus more on my real passion, trying to scientifically understand luck." He drank the last of his milk shake and said, "Now it's your turn. What twists and turns of fate brought our fortunes together?"

Bicycle caught him up on the auction in Kansas and her adventures in the Wild West. Sister Wanda explained that their journey would be ending tomorrow at the Friendship

Factory in Calamity. Bicycle added, "The perfect name for a disaster," and Sister Wanda gave her a warning look.

Dr. Alvarado made charming and sympathetic noises that somehow convinced both Sister Wanda and Bicycle that he understood and agreed with each of them, and invited them to stay in his guest room for the night. He wanted to take a look at the Fortune in his workshop, explaining, "I am very excited to see how my invention has been working."

Sister Wanda said, "I never turn down an opportunity to learn something or teach Bicycle something new. Lead on, sir."

THE BEST OF LUCK IN NEVADA

They walked from the ice cream parlor toward Dr. Alvarado's place, a modest one-story house at the end of a nearby cul-de-sac. He ushered them through the front door and told them to make themselves at home. Sister Wanda was immediately captivated by his library, opening a manuscript entitled *The Physics and Chemistry of Luck*. Dr. Alvarado hoisted the Fortune over one shoulder, and he and Bicycle descended a staircase to his workshop. The cool and cavernous basement workshop was full of projects in various states of completion. Electronic tidbits, drills, and soldering irons littered two long workbenches.

Dr. Alvarado clamped the Fortune up on a stand where he could see it better, dragging over a tall lamp for more light. He pulled out a cable and hooked up the Fortune to a computer with an oversized monitor. He started tapping keys, glancing back and forth between the bike and the monitor. "Well, well," he said, beginning to type more feverishly. "Well, well, *well!*"

Bicycle tiptoed up close to a chest-high gray metal box that resembled a filing cabinet crossed with a squid. Black cables sprouted tentacle-like from its base, some plugged into nearby electrical sockets, others lying in coils. One big red button sat in the middle of the box's rounded lid. She was tempted to push the red button, but she'd learned her lesson with the Fortune. "What does this do?" she called to Dr. Alvarado.

Dr. Alvarado looked over, distracted. "What? Oh, that, yes. Go ahead and push the button and let's see if it is working."

Happy to have the go-ahead, Bicycle pushed the red button. The machine clicked. It sat for a minute, then started to produce a sizzling noise and an enticing smell. After about a minute, it emitted a soft *bing* and the lid opened. Inside the machine was a perfect grilled cheese sandwich. Dr. Alvarado came over and looked at it. "Mmmmm. That invention came out quite nicely."

"What is it, exactly?"

"It makes grilled cheese."

"Oh," Bicycle said. She'd been expecting something more sciencey.

Dr. Alvarado turned back to the bike stand. "But I must ask you about the Wheels of Fortune 713-J! You have been riding it for how long?"

Bicycle counted back the days. "Three and a half weeks."

"Curious," Dr. Alvarado said. "Very curious indeed."

"What?" Bicycle asked.

"Well, I originally loaded the Fortune's computer system with everything a long-distance traveler would need—maps, music, weather information, that sort of thing. Then, as soon as the government rejected the whole project, I decided to tinker around and add an experimental program to the Fortune. I wanted to see if it could keep track of its rider's good and bad luck. I left home before doing anything more." He tapped a few more keys. "Now I find a whole new data table, and it looks as though the bike has been storing not only your experiences of good and bad luck but also your opinions and observations. The Fortune seems to have geared itself to learn everything it can about you. I'd say it regards you as . . . really interesting."

Bicycle cocked her head. She actually thought the bike had been having a good time making her look silly.

"I love when something I've invented surprises me," Dr. Alvarado said. "I expect I will be up into the wee hours tonight trying to understand this."

"Speaking of trying to understand things, can I ask you about your research?" Bicycle asked.

"Scientists always want someone to ask about their research," he said, twiddling some mechanism under the bike's seat with a screwdriver.

"Well, what kind of control does luck have over us?" she asked, perching on a stool. "Is it, like, all-powerful? I've hit a wall of bad luck, and I don't know what to do about it. Is there any way I can push back when bad luck starts shoving me toward places I really, really, really don't want to go?"

Dr. Alvarado put down his screwdriver. "The question of the power of luck is a big question. You know my first name is Luck? My name was the reason I became so interested in the topic. I was born in the back of a taxi on the way to the hospital. My father got this idea that I should be named after the taxi driver, but he failed to get his name, only his license plate: LUK477. So my parents put it right on my birth certificate: 'LUK477 Alvarado.' At least they called me 'Luk' for short when I was a small child, and I was able to go by 'Luck' at school. My name seemed like bad luck until I considered what my name *could* have been if the license plate had been ZXW983. Or—what if my father *had* gotten the driver's name and it turned out to be Hambone Squiggs the Third? Then my name seemed like pretty good luck, all things considered. Have you ever noticed that? Something seems like bad luck at one point, but it turns out to be good luck later on? Or vice versa?

"Luck is a very tricky thing. So as a scientist, my formal answer about the power of luck is: I don't know." He leaned conspiratorially toward Bicycle. "But here is my hypothesis:

luck is something like a river. Good and bad luck flow through the world, and we're floating in its currents—you, me, the 713-J, Sister Wanda, that spider in the corner, the grilled cheese sandwich, everything. If you do not pay much attention to your life, luck swirls you along like a leaf or twig. However, if you choose to put a paddle in the river and steer, or even paddle against the current—ah!" He raised his hands. "Then you may be able to change where you're headed." He picked up the screwdriver and pointed at Bicycle. "Please do not quote me on that to any respected scientific journals."

Dr. Alvarado's explanation sparked the first glimmer of hope inside Bicycle's heart since Sister Wanda had informed her that she'd be going to the Friendship Factory in Calamity. "Luck flows around us like a river, but we have our own paddles. Thanks, Doctor. Now, do you mind if I eat that grilled cheese?" In the cool of the basement, her appetite had returned.

That night, tucked in Dr. Alvarado's guest bedroom with Sister Wanda sleeping next to her, Bicycle tried to imagine a way she could dip her paddle in the river taking her to the Friendship Factory tomorrow. She couldn't seem to come up with anything beyond running away into the desert night and finding a family of wild cows to live with. She decided to keep her eyes peeled for a way to turn her luck around on the way to Calamity.

The next morning, Bicycle awoke alone. She rubbed her eyes and followed a breakfasty smell to the kitchen, where Dr. Alvarado stood in front of the stove. He was wearing the same sort of stylish suit jacket, pressed shirt, and silk tie that he had been wearing the day before, but his dress shirt was neatly tucked not into pants but into a pair of black spandex bike shorts. Bicycle watched him pour pancake batter onto a hot griddle. When a pancake started to steam, an upright freestanding spatula on wheels scooted around the edge of the griddle, scooped it up, and flipped it over.

"Good morning," Sister Wanda said from the kitchen table, where she was already halfway through a stack of the pancakes. "I thought the smell of these ginger pancakes might draw you out of bed."

Dr. Alvarado turned around and said, "It is a good morning indeed! I studied the Fortune's records last night, and I would be honored to ride along with you today to observe how the bike is collecting data, if you would not mind my company."

The pancake-flipper flipped three steaming ginger pancakes out of the pan and onto a plate. Dr. Alvarado handed them over to Bicycle, who found that her appetite had again disappeared. She wanted nothing besides a glass of cold water.

Sister Wanda said, "That would be fine. Perhaps you can teach us more about your work as we ride."

"I'm just glad you're letting me keep the Fortune," Bicycle added, pushing the pancakes around on her plate with a fork so she wouldn't seem rude. Then she stopped. "You are letting me keep it, right? You don't need to take it back?"

"Take it back?" Dr. Alvarado repeated. "Most certainly not. You bought it fair and square. That bike is yours, maybe more than you realize. Besides, I'm going to make my own copy of it. I created a copying program years ago based on the process by which cells replicate and divide to make new cells." He left the self-propelled pancake flipper to its self-propelled flipping and walked across the kitchen to the adjoining foyer, where the Fortune was now parked. "Want to see?"

He pressed a sequence of levers and buttons, and the Fortune started to quiver and bulge outward, like a bike-shaped balloon being filled with more and more air. When it was twice as thick as normal, the frame and wheels divided neatly in two with an audible *pop*. There were now two nearly identical blue-and-yellow Fortunes standing in the foyer. Bicycle noticed that the second Fortune was labeled WHEELS OF FORTUNE 713-K. Dr. Alvarado returned to his pancake griddle. "It's much easier than building a whole manufacturing plant. I don't know why all bike builders have not invented something like this yet."

"Where are the Wheels of Fortune 713-A through I?"

asked Bicycle. A whole fleet of Fortunes was an impressive thought.

"None of them worked exactly as I wanted them to, so I removed their circuit boards and gave them away to local children who couldn't afford bikes of their own. A bike without all the bells and whistles of the Wheels of Fortune may not be the perfect traveling machine, but it is still fun to ride. Syrup?" He sat down to breakfast, digging into his own towering, buttery stack.

The trio hit the road before nine, and the sun already showed no mercy. Dr. Alvarado turned out to be a very unstable rider. In fact, the first thing he did was to crash into a cactus. He seemed unconcerned by this, picking himself up, brushing spines off his jacket, and remounting his bike.

"Are you sure you want to do this?" Sister Wanda asked uncertainly. "Cycling may not be your strong suit."

"Nonsense!" exclaimed Dr. Alvarado, his tie flapping over one shoulder as he missed a clump of sagebrush by mere inches. "I've got this. I merely need to refresh my brain's neural pathways." He stuck the tip of his tongue out of the corner of his mouth as he tried without success to steer in a straight line.

They spent the morning riding the rumpled carpet of Nevada together. Tiny tornadoes—dirt devils, Dr. Alvarado called them—spun themselves around and around in the wasteland. The riders thought they'd find somewhere to stop for lunch until they saw a sign that informed them NEXT SER-VICES 75 MILES.

"Not a problem," said Dr. Alvarado. "We can enjoy a Complete Nutrition tablet from the Fortunes. Enough vitamins, minerals, and calories for all." He wobbled over to the side of the road and tried to find a comfortable place to sit among the spiky, crunchy desert bushes. There wasn't one, so he contented himself with sitting in the middle of the road. No cars had passed by for hours, and they could see for at least ten miles in any direction anyway if a car happened to show up. Sister Wanda folded her knees beneath her. Bicycle plopped down. She looked up at the sky, watching tiny puffs of cloud scuttle by as though they had urgent appointments elsewhere. She didn't blame them. She didn't want to stay much longer in this desert herself.

Dr. Alvarado pressed the purple button on his bike three times and doled out one napkin-wrapped pellet apiece. *"Bon appetit!"* he said, popping his into his mouth. He chewed vigorously with a broad smile for a few moments. The smile faded away and was replaced by a look of horror. He stood up and ran to the bushes and spit out a whole mess of vitamins, minerals, and calories in an impressive spray of goo. "My heavens, how exceedingly vile! Do they always taste like that?" he asked Bicycle, wiping his chin with his napkin.

She nibbled at the edge of hers. "Yes, sir, they do. The chocolate coating doesn't help much at all."

He pulled a notebook out of his suit-coat pocket and started scribbling. "Rework . . . vitamin tablet formula . . . *without delay,*" he muttered to himself. "My most sincere apologies. I never got around to testing the final product," he explained to Bicycle and Sister Wanda, who politely tried to protest that the pellets were really not *that* vile. In place of lunch, they had to satisfy themselves with long drinks from their water bottles instead.

When she was reluctantly climbing the fourth small, rumpled mountain of the day, Bicycle felt decidedly not herself. The climb was hot and windy, and when she reached the top, she stopped and dismounted to wipe the sweat from her forehead. Her hand came back from her face as dry as sandpaper. Somewhere along the climb, she'd stopped sweating. *Huh,* she thought. *I wonder if that's a problem?* She turned to tell Dr. Alvarado about it. However, once she started turning, she found she couldn't stop.

She spun around in a slow circle and collapsed in a dead faint.

CALAMITY

"Bicycle!" yelled Sister Wanda, who had stopped for a drink at the top of the climb herself. "Can you hear me? What's wrong?" She dropped her pink bike at the edge of the road and ran to Bicycle's side. She felt Bicycle's head and neck. Bicycle's pulse was rapid and her skin was dry. "Oh goodness, talk to me, Bicycle, say something," she murmured.

Dr. Alvarado was quite a bit farther behind. Sister Wanda called over her shoulder, "Doctor, it's time to stop messing around on that thing and *ride!*"

He stood up in the pedals and rode as fast as he could to the top, gasping when he arrived. He fell off his bike and tumbled like a gymnast in his hurry to get to them.

He checked Bicycle's vital signs, noting her pale, dry, hot skin. "She is experiencing the early signs of heat stroke. We have got to get her out of the sun." There wasn't a scrap of shade in sight. Dr. Alvarado turned to Bicycle's Fortune and anxiously tried to recall which button to push to get the tent out of the bike frame.

The Fortune 713-J flashed a question. Is she all right?

Dr. Alvarado answered, "In fact, no, she is not. Her body has gotten overheated and is unable to cool itself down. She needs to get into some shade and get some cool water on her skin to help lower her core temperature, right away."

Understood, the Fortune responded. Get her inside, I will do the rest.

"You'll do the rest of what?" Dr. Alvarado asked.

The Fortune didn't answer but immediately released and inflated the tent as Dr. Alvarado stepped back. He and Sister Wanda carefully scooped up Bicycle's unconscious form and carried her into the tent, kneeling on either side of her.

Stay inside, but zip the tent closed, the Fortune blinked.

Dr. Alvarado did so, and the temperature in the tent dropped ten degrees. A small jet started spraying a mist of cool water on Bicycle. The temperature kept going down until it was a very comfortable 72°F inside the shady tent, as opposed to the blistering 106°F it was outside.

"How did you learn to control the temperature inside the tent?" Dr. Alvarado asked, flabbergasted.

The Fortune blinked its own question. Is there more that she needs? Or just time to rest?

Dr. Alvarado stared at the screen for a moment. "Just . . . just time to rest, thank you," he managed to say.

The Fortune sat in silence for a moment, then started playing Stephen Foster songs.

Bicycle stirred a little and mumbled, "No more desert. No more brown hot dry yuck desert. Need *dessert* instead of *desert*." She opened her eyes a crack. "Ice cream sandwiches? Don't mind if I do." Then she passed out again.

Dr. Alvarado took her pulse.

Are ice cream sandwiches required for her optimal health? the Fortune blinked. I have no such capabilities. You have failed as an inventor for not having included ice cream sandwiches in my programming.

Dr. Alvarado looked flummoxed. He had no response.

Sister Wanda said, "Thank heavens, she's cooling off. I do believe we got her out of the heat in time." She sighed in relief. "We're most certainly done riding for today. Dr. Alvarado, why don't you go outside and see if you can flag down a car? Have them take you to the nearest store and get supplies for us, some cold water and real food."

And get the ice cream sandwiches. Go like the wind. Make her well. I will maintain her temperature until you return.

The Fortune started beeping, and when Dr. Alvarado didn't start moving fast enough, it started playing a military march at full volume until he vacated the tent.

He hitchhiked back a few hours later with juice, water, sandwiches, and a box of slightly melted ice cream sandwiches in an insulated bag. Bicycle had awakened and was feeling much more normal. She downed nearly a half gallon of water and three ice cream sandwiches before coming up for air. Dr. Alvarado's ice cream sandwich dripped on his tie, and the Fortune spit out a napkin for him.

He gave a little bark of laughter. "This is much more improbable than anything that has happened to me in years," he said as he wiped his tie. "Thank you. Thank you for reminding me why I should get out of the workshop more often."

"What happened?" Bicycle said. "I remember climbing a hill, and then feeling like I was in a nice cool shower for the first time in way too long."

Dr. Alvarado tried to explain. "You became ill, and what happened next is an unusual illumination of the Heisenberg uncertainty principle. As far as I can deduce, the Fortune 713-J appears to have generated its own system of machine learning . . ." When he saw Bicycle's baffled expression he stopped talking and stroked his chin. "Hmmm. How to explain it to a layperson? Bicycle, when you got sick, the Fortune 713-J did everything it could to make you better. I think it likes you and considers you its friend. Attracting metal friends . . . Clearly, you have a *magnetic* personality."

Sister Wanda looked amused at the bad pun and turned

her attention back to Bicycle, smoothing Bicycle's hair off her forehead. "You rest now. We're not going anywhere until you are one hundred percent yourself again."

Bicycle closed her eyes as Sister Wanda smoothed her hair back once more. She fell into a moist, cool, restful sleep.

When dawn lit the next day, Bicycle woke up and stretched. "How long was I sleeping?" she asked Sister Wanda, who was already awake and puttering around in the tent.

"A good long while. Dr. Alvarado and I turned in early ourselves, but spent some time talking first. I learned these bikes are miracles of engineering," Sister Wanda said. "Did you know they come equipped with board games? I beat the doctor in a spirited game of Battleship before bed."

Bicycle slipped on her shoes and they climbed out of the tent. The Fortune 713-K's tent was inflated a few feet away, and Bicycle could hear Dr. Alvarado rustling around inside.

"Please put the tent back in the seat post," Sister Wanda asked the Fortune, and after it did so, Sister Wanda gave it a pat. "Miracles, I tell you. Also, Doctor Alvarado remembered after his hitchhiking experience that there is a satellite phone located in each bicycle's left pedal, so I called the Calamity Cab Company last night and arranged for them to send us a taxi this morning. No more bicycling for you, young lady. I'm getting you out of this desert posthaste and checking you into your room at the Friendship Factory as soon as possible."

Bicycle felt it was much too early in the morning for such unspeakable words to be spoken. There hadn't even been a mention of breakfast yet.

"We're going *now*? Can't we talk about this at all?" Bicycle asked Sister Wanda, panic rising in her voice.

"I told you, there is nothing more to be said," the nun answered. "We'll bid farewell to Dr. Alvarado, pack our bikes in the trunk of the taxi, and get you to the Factory. As soon as you're settled there, the taxi can get our bikes and me to the nearest train station for my trip back to D.C. I'll ship my bike to the Nearly Silent Nunnery in Kentucky once I'm home." A small cloud of dust appeared on the horizon and began moving closer. Sister Wanda put her hand over her eyes and squinted at the dust cloud. "That must be the taxi now."

Bicycle pleaded, "Maybe there is nothing more to be said for you, but there is a lot more to be said for me! Won't you take a minute to listen?" The nun calmly bent down to tie her sneaker. Bicycle's voice rose. "Don't you remember how to *listen?*"

Sister Wanda straightened up and gave Bicycle a blazing blue stare.

Bicycle swallowed and very quietly added, "Please?"

Never taking her eyes off Bicycle's face, the nun sank slowly into a no-nonsense cross-legged position. "I am listening," she said.

Bicycle took a deep, deep breath. "I know you think you are doing the best thing for me, commanding me to make friends. I don't want to break your rules, believe me! That's why I took off biking—I was trying to do what *you* want but in the way that *I* want. I swear I made a friend already. Let me tell you about Griffin, the ghost. I know you think he's imaginary, but he isn't, and I don't know exactly how we became friends, but I'm sure we did. And Dr. Alvarado said yesterday that the Fortune was acting like a friend to me, too. I don't need to get changed or fixed by the Friendship Factory. I can do this. Can you give me just one more chance to make a regular human friend my way before you lock me up at the Factory? *Please?*" Her eyes wide, she put every ounce of agonized hope she had into the last word.

Dr. Alvarado emerged from his tent, rubbing his face. "Anyone thinking about breakfast yet?"

The Fortune beeped at him and he came over to read its display. Hush. My sensors indicate this is not the optimal time to interrupt.

Sister Wanda's face was unreadable. "Are you finished?" she asked.

Bicycle nodded.

Sister Wanda stood up. She took her own deep breath. She let it out in a noisy sigh so big it seemed to come up from her toes. "No."

Dr. Alvarado was watching the approaching dust cloud. "Is that the taxi you called coming our way?" he asked.

Bicycle could not believe her ears. "No?" She thought she'd come up with a pretty good speech, especially on an empty stomach.

The Fortune beeped. No?

"That doesn't look like a taxi," Dr. Alvarado said. "All black. But it is parking right over there. Looks like whoever is driving is coming to have a chat with us."

Sister Wanda picked up Bicycle's backpack and helmet and handed them to her. Bicycle took them automatically, noticing the figure getting out of the car behind Sister Wanda. She squeezed her backpack in shock and shouted, "No!"

Sister Wanda put her hands on her hips. "There's no need to start shouting, young lady."

"No, not no to you, no to *her*." Bicycle pointed at the bony woman striding menacingly toward them. "That's the lady in black from the auction! The one I thought you were when we hit you with the tomatoes. The bike thief!"

Two burly men in black T-shirts and slacks also emerged from the car, and the bony woman said something to the men over her shoulder, stabbing her finger toward Bicycle and the Fortune.

"And she brought more thieves to help her!" Any thoughts of Friendship Factories were now secondary.

Dr. Alvarado clapped his hands together. "Bike thieves

before breakfast? I really do need to get out of the lab more often. Can I be of some assistance?"

Sister Wanda faced the oncoming trio and squared her shoulders. "Oh, bike thieves, is it?" she asked. "We'll see about that."

The Calamity Cab Company taxi chose that moment to crest the hill and pull over.

Sister Wanda turned to Bicycle, putting a firm hand on her shoulder and propelling her toward the taxi. The nun opened the rear door and guided Bicycle and her backpack onto the seat. "Go on ahead now and wait for us at the Friendship Factory in Calamity. The doctor and I will take care of these *bike thieves*."

The way she said the last two words left Bicycle in no doubt that the bony lady in black had met her match.

She didn't hesitate to obey Sister Wanda this time. She shut the cab door while Sister Wanda handed the driver some bills and instructed him to leave her at the Calamity Friendship Factory. In moments she was watching Sister Wanda, Dr. Alvarado, and the group of menacing people in black grow smaller in the taxi's back window until she lost sight of them completely.

The taxi ate up the miles with no effort at all. Far too soon, they reached Calamity. Its cozy main street was lined with low brick buildings. The taxi cruised past an elementary school, a playground, an all-day-breakfast restaurant, and a neighborhood of small houses. The taxi driver slowed and stopped next to the sidewalk outside a windowless two-story concrete structure.

"Friendship Factory, here you go," the driver said.

Bicycle climbed out mechanically, dragging her backpack and helmet behind her. She stood stoop-shouldered in front of the glass door with the letters FF painted on it. It looked nothing like a camp. It looked like a factory. One where hard and unpleasant labor was done. Bicycle stared at the door and wasn't even surprised that the building looked practical and ugly and un-camp-like. Camps were supposed to be fun. Forced friendmaking was going to be work.

The taxi pulled away, and Bicycle wondered what the Friendship Factory did with you if you couldn't make the three guaranteed friendships. Would you have to stay forever? She was about to ask the Fortune what the odds were of her being imprisoned for the rest of her life at the Calamity Friendship Factory when she slapped her forehead.

"Wait! Sister Wanda forgot to put my bike in the trunk!" she yelled too late as the taxi turned a corner and was gone. Bicycle took another look at the concrete building and decided she wasn't going in there until Sister Wanda dragged her in.

Before anyone could come through the glass door and ask what she wanted, she hurried back toward the center of town.

She sat on a swing in the playground and wondered how the Fortune 713-J would get down the hill without her pedaling it. Did it have some autopilot feature that Dr. Alvarado could activate? Then she wondered what Sister Wanda was doing to Miss Monet-Grubbink. Sister Wanda could be both an irresistible force and an immovable object, but no matter how much that frustrated Bicycle, she had to admit the nun took her job as a guardian very seriously.

The road back to what she was thinking of as "The Lady in Black's Last Stand" stayed empty for quite some time. The sun moved upward in the sky until it shone right in Bicycle's eyes, so she went to sit in the shadow of the schoolhouse, where she still had a good view of the road. She nibbled a snack from her backpack and finally saw a cloud of dust moving along the road toward the town. She squinted to see better. And whimpered.

It wasn't Sister Wanda and Dr. Alvarado coasting down the hill with the Fortune 713-J in tow. It was the bike thieves' black sedan. As it came closer, she could see the front wheels of both of the Fortunes and Sister Wanda's pink cruiser poking out of the half-closed trunk.

"Holy spokes! They stole all three bikes?" Bicycle blurted out, and then immediately cast around for somewhere to hide. She squeezed into the playground's miniature wooden playhouse. She peeked out the little window as the car pulled up and parked in front of the all-day-breakfast restaurant.

Bicycle was confused when she saw Sister Wanda and Dr. Alvarado get out of the backseat, and became even more confused when the lady in black and the two hulking men emerged to walk at their side. They all looked . . . friendly with each other. Bicycle shrank back from the window and listened to them talking in the still morning air.

"I told the taxi to drop her off at the Friendship Factory," said Sister Wanda. "This town isn't big, so I'm sure it's close. I'll ask for directions from the folks in this restaurant. We haven't had a chance to eat yet. After I go over and get my girl settled, would you like to join us here for breakfast?"

The lady in black nodded. "Allow us to buy forrr you." She rolled her *r*'s so they sounded like a cat's purr. "It's the least we can do to seal the deal." She smiled a crocodilian smile. "We'll wait forrr you inside while you rrrun yourrr errrand."

She's inviting the bike thieves to breakfast? Seal what deal? Did Sister Wanda get brainwashed? Bicycle thought. *Drugged?* She narrowed her eyes as a nasty thought occurred to her. *Did Sister Wanda agree to give them the Fortune to teach me some kind of lesson? Did she decide that is what's "best" for me?* She watched them file into the restaurant.

Bicycle could not be separated from the Fortune like this. Directly disobeying Sister Wanda a second time was something Bicycle could hardly bear to do, but the thought of losing her freedom and another bike—another new friend!—at the same time was even more unbearable. She ran to the black sedan and wrestled the Fortune out of the trunk and onto the road.

"I'm stealing you back," she whispered. "We're going to get each other out of here."

SAY SOMETHING NICE IN CALIFORNIA

Bicycle ran with the Fortune across the sidewalk to the shady rear of the playground and strapped her backpack to its familiar spot on the rear rack. "Is there a way out of town that keeps us off the main road?" she asked.

We can head through the desert on an old cattle track. It will eventually join a road to the California border. Are we continuing on to California? Sister Wanda said no. The probability that she meant it is 100%.

"There's no time to talk about it now! Just tell me which way to go."

The Fortune promptly flashed directions to the old cattle track, and Bicycle clapped her helmet on her head and navigated across an alley behind the park. They soon left Calamity behind. She only stopped to forage in her backpack for food when they had reached a hard-packed dirt trail that didn't look like it was trod by anything but cattle hooves.

She unearthed an ancient granola bar from her back-pack and ate it while she rode. When the sun hit the top of the sky, Bicycle stopped and the Fortune set up the cool tent again, this time camouflaging the outside to match the yellow-brown landscape. They'd gone miles without the slightest indication of anyone following them. Bicycle had tried to keep her mind on her legs pushing the pedals, but the Fortune's statement Sister Wanda said no kept bubbling up in her mind. She took a drink of water and asked her bike, "If I keep going to San Francisco and make friends with Zbig like I planned, what are the odds that Sister Wanda will decide she was wrong and not send me to the Friendship Factory for the rest of my life?"

Odds of Sister Wanda deciding she was wrong: 3,720 to 1.

Whatever 3,720 to 1 was, it was not nothing. "So you think there is some possibility? Even a tiny one?" Bicycle knew she was grasping at straws. "How about this: What are the odds that you and I are going to make it to the Blessing of the Bicycles without getting caught again?"

94.6% in our favor. Those odds are better because I am very helpful, the Fortune blinked. But Sister Wanda knows where we are going. The chances she will find you at the Blessing and send you to the Factory are equally high.

"Let's stop talking about the odds, now, thanks," Bicy-cle said. Of course Sister Wanda knew where she was going. This escape was temporary. But it was her last chance to make friends with Zbig and prove the nun wrong. She pulled out her tiny spiral notebook and a pencil, determined to work out a foolproof friendship plan. Failure was not an option.

She thought as hard as she could about her trip so far. Why had she gotten along so well with Griffin? And could she call Jeremiah and Estrella friends, too? Why not Chef Marie? Or Bird Tattoo—Carlos—and his buddies? How long did you have to spend with someone before they were technically your friend? Did both people need to agree you were friends at the exact same time? And did it matter if your friends could talk? She thought she'd like to count The Cannibal as a friend as well—was that allowed? And why did Dr. Alvarado think the Fortune liked her? She wrote down every one of these questions and found herself absolutely stumped.

"Fortune, do you feel that you're my friend, like Doctor Alvarado said?" she asked the bike, desperate for some solid answers.

YES.

She thought about how her heart had felt when she saw the Fortune's wheel sticking out of the bike thieves' car trunk. "Yeah, me too. Exactly what made us become friends? Do you have some data on that?" she pressed.

The bike began scrolling down a complicated explanation that sounded exactly like Dr. Alvarado, blinking about an illumination of the Heisenberg uncertainty principle. Bicycle sighed.

"Sorry, I don't speak physics. Answers are no good if they're not in a language I understand," she said to the Fortune, and then stopped. *Language. Understanding someone's language.* She tapped her pencil on her notebook. When she'd begun her journey sixty-two days ago, she'd packed up the Polish-English dictionary because she knew being Mostly Silent around Zbig would get her nowhere. She'd always intended to learn to speak a little of Zbig's native language to impress him when they met, but that part of her plan had been pushed to the back of her mind until now.

She dug to the bottom of her backpack for the not-at-all-waterproof Polish dictionary The pages were now floofed apart, and the whole thing was twice as thick as it had been when she'd originally taken it. She thumbed to the *F* section and looked under "friendship" and groaned when she saw there were six different words for it in Polish depending on how friendly you wanted to be. She flipped through until she found a section on "greetings" and started learning to pronounce some words as quickly as she could.

"Hello. How are you? Hello," she said. *"Dzień dobry. Jak się masz? Dzień dobry!"* Her voice rose as she wrestled with the unfamiliar combinations of sounds.

The Fortune interrupted her. You may attract unwanted attention if you use your top volume level. I suggest you reduce by at least 10 decibels.

"Sorry, you're right. I just don't have a lot of time, and

I have to get this perfect. I should have started working on this earlier." She focused hard and tried to roll the language around her mouth more quietly, forming the sounds of the letter Ł and the letter Ń and the letter Ą. She flipped through the dictionary and wrote down every word she needed for the sentences she wanted to get down pat. After repeating the Polish for "I biked across the country to meet you! Do you think there's a chance we might be friends?" six dozen times, she started to yawn so hard she couldn't mouth the words any longer. She fell into a hazy midday nap mumbling in Polish.

The Fortune rang an alarm once the heat of the day had passed, and Bicycle awoke with the dictionary open on her chest. She packed everything up, still practicing her new sentences under her breath, and continued riding along the cattle track, determined to put in as many miles as possible before dark. A couple of hours farther along, the track joined a paved road. Bicycle squinted ahead and saw the strip of asphalt meandering through more unchanging desert.

Turn here.

"Are you sure we're headed the right way?" she asked the Fortune. "Your navigation can't let us down. We'd really be in trouble, because we're way off my maps now."

This alternate route will lead us to San Francisco. I will not let you down. Until it is time to sleep again, when I will let you down, since sleeping while sitting on a bike seat is impossible.

Bicycle smiled. Whatever else happened, she was glad she had made the choice to keep the Fortune by her side. Well, underneath her. "Imagine if I could bike in my sleep, though? It'd be awesome. We'd be in San Francisco with time to spare." She made the turn and continued practicing her Polish sentences in time to the rhythm of her revolving pedals.

They went on like this for more than a week. Then, after the Fortune deflated the camouflage tent one morning, Bicycle wondered how different things would look when they left Nevada and crossed into California. She expected it to be a land lush with lemon and avocado trees, filled with movie stars in red convertible cars and sweeping views of the ocean. But as far as she could see, dirt and lifeless gray shrubs lined the way ahead. In a history book, she'd read that some pioneers who couldn't afford covered wagons had loaded up their wheelbarrows with everything they possessed and walked from Missouri to the Great Basin Desert in Nevada to settle the Wild West. She'd wondered then why the pioneers hadn't kept going all the way to the ocean, but now she thought she understood. After you travel for a few thousand miles and see a lot of hot and brown and hopeless, maybe you give up wishing for oceans and lemon trees. The only thing you want to do is lie down and stop pushing your wheelbarrow.

She halted her Polish practice for the day when her mouth got too dry. She was nearly ready to lie down and stop pushing herself when she saw the Sierra Nevada range ahead. Despite the desert heat all around them, the serious, plum-shaded mountains were crowned by a white frosting of snow. The frosting seemed to whisper promises of deep lakes, rushing rivers, and green, ferny forests. Bicycle inhaled with her mouth open, imagining she could taste a faint breath of coolness.

Up ahead, she saw a state line sign. Her last one. The sign was nothing special, a run-of-the-mill green-and-white highway sign, but Bicycle solemnly read it out loud to the Fortune as they pedaled past. "Welcome to California."

Thank you, the Fortune wrote.

A round yellow moon was already high in the sky as the sun finished setting. Even as the sky grew darker and darker, the white frosting atop the mountains ahead still seemed to glow. Bicycle stuck her tongue out to see if she could catch another breeze from the Sierras. Then she sniffed the night air. "Do you smell that?" she asked the Fortune.

The bicycle made a fizzing sound. Nitrogen, oxygen, argon, carbon dioxide, and methane.

"Well, yeah, I guess." Bicycle said as she dismounted for

the night. "But it also smells like we've finally left the desert behind."

The next morning, Bicycle felt the pleasure in riding west that she'd lost on the way to Calamity getting restored pedal stroke by pedal stroke. The simple purpose of riding onward buoyed her slim sense of hope. *I still have my chance to do this my way,* she thought, *3,720 to 1 though it may be. It's one week until the Blessing of the Bicycles. That should be enough time to finish getting a handle on my Polish words and work out a step-by-step theory of How to Make Someone Your Friend. I already know the first step: Say Something Nice in a Language They Understand.*

A few short miles beyond the state-line sign, Bicycle saw a sapphire-colored lake on the side of the road. Evergreen trees rose ahead, and the white-capped mountains got closer with every rotation of her wheels. The brown of the desert was now behind them. "Those poor wheelbarrow pioneers," said Bicycle. "They gave up before things got really good." They were passing the sapphire lake and she could see that it was filled with birds splashing in the shallow water. Clouds of insects buzzed around the rocky shoreline. The birds chased after the insect clouds and clacked their beaks shut on tasty mouthfuls.

Soon the road passed under the shadow of the mountains. The Fortune directed them toward the entrance to

Yosemite National Park, recommending riding through the park as a way to throw Sister Wanda off their trail. The road into the park wound its way up the foothills and gradually took them right over a mountain pass. Families on their way into Yosemite waved at Bicycle from their car windows. She grinned back and chanted at them in Polish. *"Dzień dobry!* Hello! *Jak się masz?* How are you?" Her words echoed back to her off the mountainside. The Fortune played polka music.

Bicycle coasted down the park's long, twisting entry road, pedaled through a short tunnel, and found herself at the edge of a glacier-carved valley. Distant waterfalls shot down from towering granite monoliths in frothy white cascades toward the dense forest below. It was breathtaking.

She guided the Fortune into the lower part of the valley. It was like a miniature town down there, crisscrossed with campgrounds, restaurants, lodges, roads, and paths. Bicycle located an empty campsite, had the Fortune set up the tent, and considered doing some exploring before dinner. As she studied the park map and pondered where to go, a large motor home the next campsite over with GIRL EXPLORERS on the side wheezed open a pneumatic door. Girls wearing identical khaki uniforms and hats poured out.

The girls looked to be a little younger than Bicycle. A woman dressed in a spiffy khaki outfit with a red kerchief around her neck came out of the trailer and was trying to direct the girls into some kind of order, but they were talking over each other, ignoring the woman completely. Bicycle felt suddenly shy amid the bustle. She tried to look busy with her tent, which was, unfortunately, already set up.

One girl with two precise blond braids came over to her. "Hi! Are you a GIRL EXPLORER?" she asked. (She actually shouted the last two words like they were in capital letters.)

"Er, no, I'm . . . just a girl, I guess," Bicycle answered.

"Oh," the blond girl answered. She polished her red EXPLORER pin with one braid. "Well, I'm going to get *my* Camping Badge this week. Then I'll have *all* of my Junior Adventurer badges, so I'll be able to get my official Explorer belt. The one with the rhinestones. Have you ever camped before?"

"Yes," Bicycle answered, "lots and lots, actually."

Two more girls came over when they heard this. "Really? Is this your tent? It's so small! Where do you put your television set?"

"What?" asked Bicycle.

Another girl jumped in. "We have a big flat-screen. You can come over to our camper tonight to watch a movie about the great outdoors."

"A movie?" Bicycle was at a loss. "Don't you want to . . . just . . . *be* in the great outdoors?"

The blond girl tittered. "You've got to be kidding. Nature

is full of bugs and dirt and sticks and bugs shaped like dirt and sticks. Movies about nature are better. They won't chip your nail polish, you know."

"You don't even want to hike over to see the waterfalls?" Bicycle thought she'd like to see one of them up close.

"Maybe in the morning. What time do they turn them on? But come on over for now, we're going to microwave some s'mores and then practice giving each other facials. I already have my Facials Badge." She gestured for Bicycle to join her. Their trailer squatted on the campsite like a giant khaki toad, blocking out any view of the sky.

Bicycle hung back. She realized this was a golden opportunity for some friend-making practice, but she felt hesitant as she watched the troop leader and an older girl setting up a satellite dish. She tried to remember the steps she'd been planning in her theory of friendship. The first step was . . . What was it? The troop leader cranked up a noise-belching generator, and Bicycle found it even harder to think straight.

A short girl noticed her and ran up. She grabbed Bicycle's hand and starting painting the nails a repulsive shade of purple. "You'll look so much less ugly with your nails done in Midnight Eggplant," the girl said. Then her Explorers utility belt starting ringing. It was her cell phone. "Oh, hold on a minute—it's my boyfriend," she said, pinning the phone between her chin and ear while continuing to paint Bicycle's nails purple. "Hello? Hello? Hel-*looo*? Yeah. Oh, yeah. Yeah!

Totally. No, nothing here, just trapped in bor-ing nature, boring, boring, boring," she said in a singsong voice.

"No thanks," Bicycle said, gently trying to pull her hand away.

The girl's grip tightened.

"Hey, I really don't want my nails painted," Bicycle said, trying to pull her hand away again.

The girl gave no sign of having heard her, except to speed up her nail painting. Now four of Bicycle's nails were dark and glittering.

Bicycle couldn't take it. She kicked the cell-phone girl in the shin, and the girl released her with an "Ow!" of shock. Bicycle ran.

She ran through the crowds of cars and tents until she was some distance away from the campsites. She found a big rock and flopped on her back and let out a big groan.

"I like your shirt," said a nice voice.

Bicycle lifted her head and saw another Girl Explorer standing in front of her. This one had short brown hair and warm brown eyes and was holding two cheese sandwiches.

"Are you hungry?" the girl asked. "I was making these when I saw you escape from Brittany."

"Thanks," Bicycle said, taking the proffered sand-wich. She suddenly remembered the first step in her friend-making theory: Say Something Nice in a Language They Understand. "I'm sorry I kicked Brittany. I lost it. I couldn't seem to get her attention to tell her I didn't actually want my fingernails painted."

"Yeah," the girl answered. "Brittany is like a nail-painting demon. None of us can stop her without kicking her. Don't worry about it. She's used to it. Look what she did to me on the way here." She spread out both hands, showing that her nails had been painted five different mismatched shades. "I'm Sally, by the way."

"Bicycle," said Bicycle.

"Cool name."

They started eating.

"You must love to ride bicycles. Me too," Sally said with her mouth full. "My mom and I have a two-seater tandem that we ride at home together."

"Really? I've never ridden a tandem before. The bike I have now is pretty amazing, though . . ." Bicycle started to tell Sally about some of her travels. The girls chatted back and forth, and time sped by like a Tour de France race on a downhill stretch.

They walked back toward the campsite near dusk and found the Girl Explorers in a frenzy of activity.

Sally sprinted over. "What's going on?" she asked her troop leader.

"Wild animal attack!" yelled the leader. "We're leaving now! Forget the nail polish, girls, and go, go, go!"

Sally turned to Bicycle with a regretful wave before she

climbed into the camper. Bicycle waved back. With a burst of exhaust, the motor home started up and lumbered away, leaving nothing but tire tracks, food wrappers, and a few bottles of Midnight Eggplant in its wake.

"What kind of animal attacked?" she asked the campers in the next site over.

"Big black bear showed up," the man answered. "Pretty common here in the valley. This one smelled whatever those girls were microwaving and came after their dinner. I'd guess they didn't plan on exploring nature quite that up close."

Bicycle was sorry to see Sally go before she'd had a chance to ask her if she felt like they could be friends. She climbed into her tent and asked the Fortune, "What makes people act so different from one another?"

The Fortune replied, That question is beyond the ability of my programming to answer. People are complicated. Storing data on you alone keeps my central processing unit constantly occupied.

Listening to the velvety rumble of far-off waterfalls, Bicycle thought about why some people needed kicking while others shared sandwiches. She decided two people could get along only if they had the ability to talk, listen, and actually hear each other. So she formed the second step in her friend-making theory: Listen Well to What They Say Back. Then she pulled out her Polish dictionary and kept practicing.

The next morning when leaving the valley, Bicycle caught a glimpse through the trees of a black bear lumbering by. Thinking it might be the one that had so conveniently scared away the obnoxious girls, she waved at it and shouted, "Hey, thanks, Mister Bear!" It stopped lumbering and turned toward her. Then it stood on its hind legs and pointed its nose right at her, sniffing with great interest. It started to walk toward the road. "Um, no need to come over here, really!" she called out. It started walking faster. "Whoops," said Bicycle.

Avoid eye contact, the Fortune advised. Wild animals generally prefer not to seek trouble with humans.

Contrary to this assurance, the large bear was coming closer and closer, making a low, inquisitive whuffling noise. It looked ready for all kinds of trouble. Bicycle tried to stay calm, but when she could see that the bear on four legs was taller than she was on two wheels, she poked the Fortune's on-screen buttons and squeaked, "Do something!"

The Fortune responded by blaring the blattiest bars of that ancient music Bicycle didn't enjoy—this time it sounded like the tubas were attempting to swallow one another as well as the goats. The bear immediately stopped and sat back on its haunches, bringing up a paw to rub its ears. It had a look on its face that said *I'm not ready for this.* After a moment, it stood up and shambled away into the underbrush.

Bicycle said, "Who needs missiles? I guess that 'upbeat' music has its uses after all." She gave the Fortune a relieved pat.

Even without movie stars in red convertibles, the next three days in California did not disappoint. Bicycle stayed up well past her bedtime on the Fourth of July to watch a short but effervescent fireworks display light up a corner of the night. She pedaled past farm after farm with neatly planted rows of trees heavy with lemons, avocados, nectarines, and plums. Between the fruit farms, they saw wind farms. Huge windmills stood on hilltops, twirling in the air currents like tall aliens waving hello with many arms. She envisioned buying little boxes of wind to carry with her so she could unwrap a tailwind whenever she wanted.

They made their way without any sign of Sister Wanda or the bike thieves. The night before she expected to arrive in San Francisco and attend the Blessing of the Bicycles, Bicycle told the Fortune, "It looks like you picked a good route to keep us out of trouble."

Of course. If you wish to continue to avoid trouble, I can plan us a route to Portland, Oregon, or to Canada's Yukon Territory instead of San Francisco.

"Thanks anyway," Bicycle answered. "I knew when we took off in Calamity that I'd have a showdown with Sister Wanda eventually. I've done everything I can to get ready for meeting Zbig tomorrow. I think I'm practically snoring in Polish at this point." Four hundred miles of practicing her greetings and friendship questions had drilled the new language into her brain. "I've paddled as hard as I can in the river of luck."

Poking through her backpack later that night, Bicycle found a few unused postcards. She lay on her stomach and wrote to Griffin, explaining that her doom had been at least temporarily postponed, to Brother Otto saying she didn't know if Sister Wanda would ever let her come back to the Mostly Silent Monastery but that she hoped he was enjoying being Mostly Talkative now, and to the Cookie Lady. This last one said:

Almost to San Francisco, CA

Dear Cookie Lady,

Here's one more postcard for your wall from someone who wasn't sure she'd make it all the way. I hope some other tired person comes to your house, sees this note hung above the cookie table, and realizes they can do more than they think they can.

Sincerely,
Bicycle (A Girl You
Rescued with Cookies
and Lemonade)

THE BLESSING OF THE BICYCLES

Bicycle woke the next morning to a sort of a whizzing, whirring noise outside the tent, like a thousand dragonflies buzzing down the road. Then she heard laughing voices and identified that *whiz-whir* sound: bicycles rushing by, and a lot of them.

She poked her head out of the tent and saw a crowd of bicyclists coasting along together. They were all ages and ethnicities and dressed in a wide variety of clothes. Some were in expensive team jerseys, some were in T-shirts and shorts, and others wore rags held together with duct tape. One guy was dressed like a rooster. One woman was dressed like a pirate. There were lots of cyclists on elegant racing bikes, plenty of cyclists on knobby-tired mountain bikes, as well as people riding two-person tandems, beach cruisers with baby trailers, unicycles, three-wheeled recumbent bicycles, and tall, old-fashioned high-wheeler bicycles. All of them were headed in the same direction.

"What's going on?" Bicycle called out in a sleepy voice.

A dark-skinned man with dreadlocks flashed her a grin. "It's a celebration! We're headed to the Blessing of the Bicycles!" He pedaled past and was swallowed up in the crowd.

Bicycle ducked back in the tent and started pulling on her socks and shoes. "Fortune, get ready for a party! You're going to get blessed today!"

The Fortune beeped and blinked, If they plan to bless every bicycle that arrives there, then you, Bicycle, shall get blessed, too.

"Hey, that was funny! Did you mean it to be? Have you learned how to make jokes now?" Bicycle asked, tying her sneaker.

The Fortune didn't bother to answer that, instead blinking Let us go.

Bicycle had to pick apart a knot in her shoelaces, and the Fortune made an impatient humming noise, repeating Let us go.

Bicycle and her blue-and-yellow flame-embossed bike joined the colorful throng of cyclists whizzing and whirring toward San Francisco. Everyone was riding at a comfortable pace, giving room to the other riders around them. Most people were laughing or joking. Bicycle soaked up that wonderful feeling she'd discovered early on her trip—she was an automatically welcome member of a community with whom she didn't have to share one word.

In a few short miles, she saw a flash of shimmering water up ahead and knew it must be the San Francisco Bay.

The Fortune started buzzing and blinked: According to my calculations, you have traveled precisely 4,000 miles (rounded to the nearest ten-thousandth of a mile) from your home to this place. It blinked a bit more, as if considering what to say next. Congratulations.

"Thanks," Bicycle said. She felt a mix of excitement and worry, with a tangled thread of loss thrown in. Even if she succeeded in her goal of befriending Zbig and dodged the wrath of Sister Wanda, it was hard to imagine giving this up and returning to a life that stayed in one place instead of pedaling headfirst into each day.

The big group of cyclists came around a corner and charged up a steep hill. At the top, Bicycle gasped to see a magnificent red bridge soaring over the bay from the mainland to the city. It seemed too delicate and pretty to ride across. Nonetheless, the group did just that, snaking into a neat line on the bridge's sidewalk, a bicycle train funneling over the big blue bay.

On the other side, she followed the group of cyclists through city streets until they came to an archway marking the entrance to Golden Gate Park. Underneath the archway, someone had hung a banner declaring BLESSING OF THE BICYCLES TODAY—ALL ARE WELCOME!

When they passed under the archway, a volunteer handed each person a raffle ticket and stamped his or her hand with a bicycle-wheel-shaped stamp. People and bicycles filled the meadow where the blessing was taking place. Vendors were selling sweet cakes, crispy chips, and bubbly drinks. Others sold bike parts and bright cycling clothes. There was a booth where you and your bike could get your picture taken. Bicycle was pretty sure she saw the neon-yellow uniforms of the King Tutter's Butter Popcorn Team near a giant popcorn popper. One stand sold bicycle-shaped hot dogs. Another right next to it sold hot-dog-shaped bicycles. The local Mostly Silent Monastery had put a Mostly Silent Monk under a pop-up tent on a comfy pillow, ready to listen. A table covered in postcards advertised WRITE TO THE COOKIE LADY.

Bicycle dismounted. "Where to first?" she asked her bike, but for once, the Fortune didn't have a ready answer. She had just decided to walk to the photo booth when one crispy chip vendor waved at Bicycle and called out, "Yoo-hoo!" It was Chef Marie.

Bicycle headed straight over and received a hug of welcome. "Chef Marie! Chips? Aren't those like fast food?"

Chef Marie clucked her tongue. "Don't tease, *ma chérie*! When we received the invitation from the Blessing of the

Bicycles Committee to be part of this event, I could not say no, *non*? They ask me to make something people can eat with one hand while walking around with their *bicyclettes*, so I made chips from local kale and avocados."

Bicycle accepted Chef Marie's offer of a salty green morsel. "How is Truffle doing?" she asked.

"That fatty! He is still at my café in Illinois, happy as a clam in clover! But *allons-y*, let's go, I have been waiting for a break to visit the booth over there that everyone keeps talking about."

Chef Marie linked arms with Bicycle and led her and the Fortune over to a crowded corner of the park where people were milling around eating little food pockets and *mmmmmmm*ing with delight. They found a table laden with plates of hot fried pies and two voices singing in harmony, "I come from Al-a-bama with a banjo on my knee . . ."

"You?" yelled Bicycle.

"Me?" yelled Griffin.

"Eh?" yelled Jeremiah.

"You, too!" yelled Bicycle

"Yoo-hoo!" yelled Chef Marie, not to be left out.

The crowd parted to let Bicycle through to hug Clunk (and Griffin) and Jeremiah under the sign PARADISE PIES SAYS BLESS YOU. She introduced the Fortune, who beeped politely, and Chef Marie, who immediately pulled out a recipe notepad and began conferring with Jeremiah.

Griffin started talking at top speed. "We did it, Bicycle, we did it, we got ourselves world famous! People even know about our shop in *Canada*! A newspaper reporter came and tried our newest thing, sandwich fried pies, and they spread the word and then the Blessing of the Bicycles invited us to come run a booth, and we had to come, you know we did, and here we are. And here you are! Aren't we a great surprise? Hey, you gotta try a sandwich fried pie! We got turkey-'n'-lettuce and ham-'n'-cheese and kielbasa-'n'-mustard that Estrella helped us come up with. She said to say hi and to come visit soon, by the way. Oh, try this one, it's our bestseller, the peanut-butter-and-jelly fried pie!" Griffin repeated Jeremiah's name over and over again until Jeremiah interrupted his discussion with Chef Marie and handed a fried pie wrapped in wax paper smelling of roasted peanuts and grape jelly to Bicycle.

Jeremiah said with a grin, "We decided whatever we sell the most of today, we're gonna name it the Piecycle in your honor. Get it? Pie-Bicycle? Piecycle?"

Bicycle took a big bite of the peanutty fried pie and hugged Clunk again with her free arm. "I get it," she said with her mouth full. "You have no idea how happy I am to see you all. I also need you to help keep a lookout for—" Bicycle began, but was interrupted by a voice booming over a loudspeaker.

"PLEASE WELCOME OUR SPECIAL GUEST OF HONOR, THE GREAT ZBIGNEE SHENKEEWEE . . .

ER, ZBIGNOO SEVENKEVYWIK . . . THAT IS, ZBIG!"

Everyone turned toward a large stage set up near a grove of redwood trees and broke into wild applause as Zbig walked out, all smiles, waving his trademark wave. He took the microphone and said a few words, but he couldn't be heard over the din of his adoring fans. He gave the microphone back to the announcer, shrugging. The announcer made exaggerated shushing noises with one finger to his lips until the crowd calmed down enough for him to talk.

"AFTER THE BLESSING, WE WILL BE CHOOSING THE WINNER OF THE RAFFLE. ONE LUCKY PERSON HERE TODAY WILL WIN THE CHANCE TO RIDE ACROSS OUR GREAT COUNTRY WITH ZBIG!"

The crowd roared its approval.

"MR. ZBIG WILL ALSO GREET FANS AND SIGN AUTOGRAPHS AT THE MAIN STAGE AFTER THE BLESSING. BUT NOW, PLEASE TURN YOUR WHEELS AND YOUR ATTENTION TOWARD OUR BICYCLE BLESSERS WHO ARE READY TO BLESS YOUR TWO-WHEELED CONTRAPTIONS FOR SAFE RIDING AND FAST RACING!"

A few of the unicyclists and recumbent tricyclists booed the speech.

The announcer hastily added, "THAT IS, THEY WILL BLESS YOUR TWO-WHEELED CONTRAPTIONS, YOUR ONE-WHEELED CONTRIVANCES, AND YOUR THREE-WHEELED CONFABULATIONS. ANY NUMBER OF WHEELS YOU WANT THEM TO BLESS, THEY'LL BLESS. WE'RE READY TO BEGIN NOW."

The announcer directed the crowd's attention to a dozen smaller stages set up in a circle surrounding the meadow. Bicycle and the other folks at the fried-pie booth turned to look.

There were bicycle blessers of various faiths and religions gathered on the smaller stages: priests, pastors, rabbis, mullahs, shamans, lamas, fakirs, medicine men, and pagan priestesses. An orange-robed lama hit a big gong with a mallet and it rang out with a sonorous *bong*. The crowd went, "*Ooooh*." Many of the bicycles picked up the vibrations of the reverberating gong and started to hum. Bicycle remembered Estrella tapping Clunk with a wrench and listening to its frame to tell if it was safe to ride. These bikes sounded not only safe to ride but also happy, as if they were humming with contentment.

When the gong's sound died out, the blessers began reciting their prayers over the bicycles. Though there were many different languages echoing through the air, they said the same thing: *May you ride safely all of your days on this earth. May your wheels spin around as fast as you could wish, and may your brakes always stop you with ease. Lo, though you may pedal through the shadow of the Valley of Potholes, you shall fear no flat tires, nor shall rust ever darken your frame. Since you are bicyclists, you are already blessed: the joy of bicycling brightens your life. Go forth, and spread that joy wherever you may roam.*

It went on for some time. The crowd had become quiet and serene, people swaying gently, nodding as one. Griffin was humming a soft song. The Fortune's handlebars vibrated under Bicycle's fingers, and she swayed herself, listening to the words of the blessings, caught up in the peacefulness of it all. She caught sight of Zbig Sienkiewicz standing on the stage, his hands clasped and his head bowed.

At the end of the blessing, the lama bonged the big gong one more time. The crowd let out a big contented *"Ahhhhhh."*

"THANK YOU AGAIN FOR COMING," the announcer began. "NOW, PULL OUT THOSE RAF-FLE TICKETS!"

Bicycle clutched hers.

The announcer turned the handle on a big drum filled with numbers, then opened up the top and let Zbig pull one out. Zbig handed it to the announcer, who read out loud, "NUMBER FOUR-SIX-ZERO-EIGHT! THAT'S FOUR-SIX-OH-EIGHT! YOU'VE WON! COME UP TO THE STAGE AND SHOW US YOUR TICKET!"

Bicycle quickly checked her number. Nope—7642. Darn. Not even close. This didn't bode well for the river of luck flowing her way.

You are making a face indicating disappointment and disquietude. Shall I print a raffle ticket number 4608 for you? the Fortune blinked.

"It looks like someone else already won," she said. The man in the rooster suit started crowing and jumping up and down, waving his ticket. He pushed his way to the stage, where the announcer checked his ticket.

"UM . . . YES . . . WELL, IT APPEARS WE HAVE A WINNER. YOUR NAME, SIR?"

The rooster crowed.

"UH . . . ALL RIGHT, THEN," the announcer said.

Zbig was grimacing at the rooster-suited man, backing away from the giant flapping wings.

"OKAY . . . LET'S MOVE ON TO THE PORTION OF THE DAY WHERE YOU FINE FOLKS COME TO THE STAGE FOR A HANDSHAKE AND A WORD OR TWO WITH ZBIG."

Griffin said, "So you didn't win, but Zbig is standing right over there—nothing says you can't go meet him right now. Can I come with you? I'm coming with you. We should all come with you. Let's go!"

It did seem like the only thing to do. "Okay," Bicycle said, scanning the crowd to see if she could spot Sister Wanda anywhere. No sign of her. "Here goes nothing."

Jeremiah put a BE RIGHT BACK sign up on their booth. Then he pushed Clunk along while Chef Marie helped Bicycle maneuver the Fortune through the crowd gathering near the main stage. Jeremiah politely repeated, "Excuse us, pardon us," over and over again until they secured themselves a spot right in front, Jeremiah and Clunk standing on one side of Bicycle, and the Fortune and Chef Marie on the other.

Bicycle looked up to see where Zbig was standing now. He was to their left, working his way through the mob of people clustered around the stage. "*Dziękuję! Dziękuję!* Thank you, thank you! Thank you for coming, everyone!" He was waving and smiling and shaking hands, moving quickly. Very quickly. He seemed to want to get as far away as possible from the rooster man, who was still waving his ticket and crowing at the top of his lungs.

Zbig was twenty people away, then ten people away, then five. Bicycle really hadn't planned on being in a crowd of this many people when she met him. She thought she'd be able to talk to him one-on-one. Who knew there were this many bicyclists in San Francisco, or even the whole country? It looked like Zbig was going to walk right by her with a "*Dziękuję*" and a wave and never even know she was there.

A voice murmured in her ear, "So here you are."

She turned to see Sister Wanda at her side.

"I . . . I . . . I . . ." Bicycle was at a loss. Should she apologize? Try to explain? Ask Sister Wanda to wait five more minutes before lecturing her so she could demonstrate that she could befriend Zbig?

Sister Wanda reached out to her. Bicycle felt relieved that she was going to get a hug before any reprimand. Instead, Sister Wanda put both hands around Bicycle's waist and hoisted her up. She set Bicycle's feet on top of the Fortune's seat and her backpack on the rear rack, then steadied her as Bicycle found her balance. Now Bicycle was taller than anyone else in the crowd, standing out like a sore thumb. "You know what the Top Monk always says!" Sister Wanda called up to her. As Zbig approached them, the volume on the crowd around them rose.

"Sandwich?" Bicycle yelled back, starting to panic. Zbig was coming her way.

"Yes!" Sister Wanda called up again. This time Bicycle could barely hear her over the noise. "But you know what he sometimes means: always finish what you start!"

Then Zbig was there. He'd straightened up after crouching down to shake the hand of the person next to Bicycle, and tilted his head to look right into Bicycle's eyes.

This was it. If there was a friendship-making power inside her, she would activate it now. First step: Say

Something Nice in a Language They Understand. This time, in Polish. *"Dzień dobry! Jak się masz? Czy nie chciałbyś włożyć zebrę do nosa?"*

Zbig frowned and cupped a hand to his ear. He leaned in a little closer and said in English, "Excuse me?"

Bicycle spoke more loudly. "My name is Bicycle and I'm a big fan. I came a long way to meet you," she said in English. Then she repeated slowly, with an excellent Polish accent, *"Czy nie . . . chciałbyś . . . włożyć . . . zebrę . . . do . . . nosa?"*

Second step: Listen Well to What They Say Back.

Zbig looked at Bicycle, who was smiling expectantly at him. He furrowed his brow. "No, not at all," he answered, shaking his head emphatically. He pulled something out of his back pocket, scrawled a message on it with a big black pen, and handed it to Bicycle. "Um . . . thank you for coming. Good-bye now," he said. His manager took his arm, whispered in his ear, and started moving him off the stage and toward a waiting limousine. Zbig waved good-bye to the crowd, blowing them kisses as they roared his name. "Take care of your bicycles, so long!" he yelled. And he was gone.

Sister Wanda helped Bicycle down to the ground between the Fortune and Clunk. Griffin asked, "What did he say to you? What did he give you?"

Bicycle looked down at the crumpled paper she was

clenching in her hand. It was the same publicity photo of Zbig that she'd gotten in the mail eighty-seven days ago. He had written at the top, *Keep riding!* and he'd autographed it at the bottom with the same words that had inspired her whole trip: *Your Friend, Zbig Sienkiewicz.*

She dropped it and drooped to kneel on the ground in defeat. She'd come four thousand miles. She'd climbed dozens of mountains, braved animal attacks and broken bicycles and thieves and heat stroke and was probably going to spend the rest of her life locked up in a Friendship Factory, and she'd gotten . . . another autograph. She closed her eyes.

NO ZEBRAS, NO NOSES

The Blessing of the Bicycles crowd was dispersing. City workers were starting to clean the grass with rakes and garbage bags, picking up discarded popcorn cartons and hot-dog wrappers. Bicycle kept her eyes closed but could still feel the presence of Sister Wanda, Chef Marie, Jeremiah, Griffin, Clunk, and the Fortune hovering around her.

"Isn't it wonderful?" announced a man's voice. It was familiar, but Bicycle couldn't place it. She opened her eyes.

Dr. Alvarado was bouncing up and down on his heels. Next to him, the lady in black and her two henchmen were standing near Sister Wanda.

"Are you taking away the Fortune now?" Bicycle asked tonelessly. "Is this how it ends?"

Sister Wanda frowned, but Dr. Alvarado began talking first. "This is how it *begins*! Don't you see? Hasn't anyone told her?" Dr. Alvarado looked around. "I thought it was the main thing everyone would be talking about. Luck research is never going to be the same! The Monet-Grubbinks and I will be leaving late tonight for Molrania."

"Wha—" Bicycle began, but the lady in black interrupted by awkwardly patting her on the head.

"Young girrl, I underrstand I frrightened you, I'm sorrry," Miss Monet-Grubbink purred.

Dr. Alvarado said, "Bicycle, this is Mona Monet-Grubbink and her brothers, Marku and Mittuk. They are representatives from the country of Molrania, the unluckiest country in the world. No one who lives there ever, *ever* has good luck. Their supply of four-leaf clovers was wiped out by tornadoes. When their children play Chutes and Ladders, all they do is chute without a chance to ladder. They've even had a national lottery for twenty-seven years, and not a single person has won it."

Miss Monet-Grubbink nodded solemnly. "And it is only thrrree numberrrs." The nodding dislodged her sunglasses, which slid off her nose and got crushed by a passing unicyclist. The three Molranians shrugged—they looked like they'd had lots of practice at it—and one of the brothers handed Mona a new pair of black glasses out of his trench coat.

Dr. Alvarado continued, oblivious to the fact that he was the only one in a happy mood. "They came to the United States to find some help. While her brothers visited casino operators in Nevada to learn why gamblers win or lose, Mona attended that Alvarado Estate auction in hopes of purchasing any scrap of my luck research. But, quite unluckily"— he winked—"she didn't bid on the one item that may have helped them, the Wheels of Fortune 713-J."

The brothers waved their hands in the air, as if to say "What do you expect from Molranians?"

"When Mona realized her mistake, she tried following you to see if you'd be willing to part with the Fortune. She kept losing your trail and eventually gave up and came to Nevada to meet her brothers. A wrong turn led them to Highway 50 and to us—perhaps the first good luck they've ever experienced. They explained the whole situation, and ended up with something better than they could have dreamed—me!" He hugged himself, then went on. "We made a plan and went back to my house to pick up my luggage and a cargo case for the Fortune 713-K. I am flying with them to Molrania to continue my studies there. The whole nation has to be some sort of luck vortex. So much data to gather!" He glowed with glee. "We gave Sister Wanda a ride here, and I wanted to come tell you the news in person."

Sister Wanda nudged him gently with her elbow. "I know you are excited, Dr. Alvarado, but perhaps you can tell her more later," she said. "Bicycle and I have some things to discuss."

"Oh, certainly, certainly. We'll go see if there are any of

those bicycle-shaped hot dogs left." Dr. Alvarado waved for the Monet-Grubbinks to follow him.

Bicycle climbed slowly to her feet and said, "You were right in Nevada, Sister Wanda. There's nothing more to discuss. I blew it."

"Hush, child, and let me speak. I got here well before you did and had a chance to meet Chef Marie, Jeremiah Branch, and Griffin G. Griffin. While I tried a lovely kielbasa fried pie, I got an earful of stories about your travels."

Bicycle looked at Jeremiah and Chef Marie in surprise and they nodded.

Sister Wanda cleared her throat and fiddled with her fingers for a moment. "I thought the Friendship Factory would be what was best for you. Life without friends is not a nice thing, not a nice thing at all. I know this for a fact because I've gone through it myself. I took my Nearly Silent vows earlier than I should have, and as a result, I was very lonely for a long time. I simply didn't want you to endure the same experience, especially at your age," she said. She heaved a sigh and waved the past away. "After sharing this journey with you, I must admit that you could teach me a few things about making friends."

Tears welled up in Bicycle's eyes and she hung her head. "I can't teach anyone anything. I couldn't make the one friend I set out to make! Did you see the horrified look on Zbig's face when I asked him if he wanted to be friends? Why did I think I knew anything about making friends? I'm a failure."

"Oh, sweetie," said Jeremiah, "that's not one bit true."

Griffin said, "Don't cry, Bicycle. Do you think it would help if we got you a ham-'n'-cheese fried pie?"

Bicycle continued to hang her head. A tear dripped down her nose and fell on the grass.

The Fortune 713-J buzzed to get Bicycle's attention. My calculations indicate you are 100% better off without that unhelpful mustache-faced human. I make a much better companion than he ever could. I even come equipped with a tent, which most humans do not.

Sister Wanda gave the bike a spicy look, but she granted, "Mr. Fancy Bike here does have a point. Forget about that mustache-faced bike racer. Some famous people have heads so big they can't see beyond their own noses, even to see a potential friend in front them as wonderful as you." She put one arm around Bicycle's shoulders and spread her other arm. "Darling girl, lift your eyes. This is *not* what failing to make friends looks like."

Bicycle looked up and saw a former Nearly Silent Nun, a French chef, a fried-pie baker, a ghost inside her first bicycle; and the perfect long-distance traveling machine. She sniffled and wiped her face with the back of her hand. "So," she asked the group, "you all think of me as your friend?"

"Yeah!" said Griffin, and Clunk dropped a screw on the ground.

"O' course," said Jeremiah.

"Mais oui," said Chef Marie.

I already thoroughly explained the Heisenberg uncertainty principle, blinked the Fortune. We will always be friends.

"Count me in, too," added Dr. Alvarado, walking up with a bit of mustard on his lip and the Monet-Grubbinks right behind him.

"Then you aren't going to lock me up in the Friendship Factory?" Bicycle asked Sister Wanda.

"You said it yourself on that hill outside Calamity: you don't need to get changed or fixed by the Friendship Factory," Sister Wanda said, echoing Bicycle's own words back to her. "You thought I didn't listen, but I did. It just took a while to properly sink in. Besides, after some serious thinking, I doubt anyone can guarantee a friendship. I'm beginning to see that the whole process of making friends involves a lot of luck. Anyway, the Factory gave us a refund. We can use the money to buy plane tickets back home. Plus we can stay tonight in a nice hotel. And treat ourselves to a feast!"

At the word "feast," the Fortune 713-J ejected a napkin-wrapped Complete Nutrition pellet. Dr. Alvarado discreetly picked it up and threw it away.

Bicycle gave Sister Wanda a big hug and said, "We could treat everybody to a feast! The Monet-Grubbinks, too." Bicycle turned to Chef Marie. "Where's the nearest Slow-Down Café? You think they'll be able to make room for us?"

"I'll lead the way," Chef Marie said.

The local SlowDown Café had a nice view of the bay below. The café's long bike rack was almost full, but Bicycle wedged the Fortune into the last available slot. Chef Marie told them to save her a seat and she pushed her way into the kitchen, insisting she would help cook the evening's meal for her honored guests. The others waited for a few minutes in line inside the warm, good-smelling café until a waiter came up and informed them that if they didn't mind sharing a table with another customer, he could seat them right away.

"We don't mind a bit," Sister Wanda said. The waiter showed the group to eight empty seats at a table in the back, where an unhappy-looking young man hunched, apparently drowning his sorrows in a huge bowl of chili. Jeremiah lowered Clunk's kickstand and everyone sat down before Bicycle recognized the blond mustache of Zbig Sienkiewicz behind his chili spoon.

"You!" she exclaimed.

"You!" replied Zbig, seeming equally surprised. Surprised or not, though, he displayed fine manners. He stood up from his chair, clicked his heels together, and bowed to the group. "Gentlemen, ladies. A pleasure to have you at my table. My name is Zbigniew Sienkiewicz."

"Hi!" said Griffin.

Zbig bowed again. "And welcome to your talking bicycle as well."

Sister Wanda was impressed in spite of herself. She'd made up her mind that afternoon that Zbig was a bigheaded celebrity who didn't know how to behave well, yet here he was, bowing like a well-mannered schoolboy. "Charmed, I'm sure," she said guardedly. "I am Sister Wanda, and you already know Bicycle."

He nodded at Bicycle and took his seat again. "Bicycle," he repeated. "That is really your name?"

She nodded.

He said, "I think that is a tremendously good name. Perhaps the best name I have ever heard." He spoke English with a thick accent, like he had peanut butter on the back of his throat.

Bicycle couldn't help smiling. Then she frowned. She was hurt and embarrassed by Zbig's immediate rejection of her offer of friendship, and couldn't understand why he was being so nice. Sister Wanda saw her discomfort and jumped in.

"All right, Mister Mustache," Sister Wanda said. "You were rather rude to my girl here at the Blessing of the Bicycles. Now you're pretending nothing happened and we're going to get along, just like that? You ought to explain yourself."

Zbig took another mouthful of chili, giving himself a moment to think. He chewed, swallowed, and shook his head. "I am sorry. I didn't know I was being rude. All I remember is Bicycle here asking me if I wished to stick a zebra up my nose, and then—"

Bicycle interrupted him. "I never!"

Sister Wanda interrupted her. "You what?"

Bicycle defended herself. "All I did was ask if he thought we might have a chance to be friends. I asked him in Polish. I've been practicing that question from my Polish-English dictionary since Nevada."

Sister Wanda raised an eyebrow. "Let's hear it," she invited.

Clearly and distinctly, Bicycle said, *"Czy nie chciałbyś włożyć zebrę do nosa?"* (Or, for those of you who do not speak Polish, "Do you want to put a zebra up your nose?")

Sister Wanda covered her mouth with one hand, choking back laughter. Naturally, Sister Wanda, who knew nearly everything, spoke Polish.

"What?" Bicycle asked defiantly.

Sister Wanda gasped. "That . . . that was what you asked Mr. Sienkiewicz at the Blessing of the Bicycles?"

Bicycle nodded.

"Oh my, oh my." Sister Wanda tried hard to remain serious. "Do you have your dictionary here? I need to see it right now."

Bicycle pulled her dictionary out of the pack at her feet and handed it over to Sister Wanda, pointing over her shoulder at the words she had looked up and practiced so carefully.

Sister Wanda read and shook her head in disbelief. She used one fingernail to scratch at the word *zebrę* and a dried bit of paper flaked off, revealing the word *przyjaciel* underneath, which indeed means "friend" in Polish. "Was this dictionary soaked in a bathtub? These words are all stuck together. I'm surprised you didn't end up saying something much more disturbing to Mr. Sienkiewicz than asking him to stick a large animal up his nose."

Bicycle took the dictionary and started scratching off more fragments of paper. "All my stuff got seriously rained on in Colorado. So *jabłko* means 'apple,' not 'hairbrush'? And a *kurczak* is a chicken, not a kitten?"

Sister Wanda said, "Mr. Sienkiewicz, it appears there was a major misunderstanding."

Zbig was looking at Bicycle. "So you were trying to ask if we could be friends, eh? No zebras? No noses?"

Bicycle wanted to sink into her seat and disappear under the gaze of her hero. She dropped the dictionary into her lap. Luckily, Chef Marie brought over bowls of chili and plates of sourdough toast, which gave her something to stare at. She wished she hadn't tried to speak to Zbig at all. *Polish*, she thought, *might be one of those languages in which it is safer to be Mostly Silent, unless you are Polish.* "Yes, sir," she managed to mumble. "No zebras, no noses."

He roared with laughter, slapping his knee with one hand. Once he started, Sister Wanda couldn't keep it in anymore and began to laugh as well. Jeremiah, Griffin, and Dr. Alvarado joined in, and even the Monet-Grubbinks smiled a bit. Bicycle wanted to disappear for a moment longer, but the laughter was contagious. She imagined what she would think if someone accidentally offered to put a zebra up her own nose, and then she started to laugh along with them.

Sister Wanda controlled herself for a moment and inquired, "I'm almost afraid to ask, but what other Polish words have you been practicing?"

"Oh," Bicycle giggled, "Ordinary stuff, like 'yes,' 'no,' 'maybe,' 'help,' 'now,' 'later,' 'sleep,' and 'sandwich.' I also learned 'Hello, how are you?' and . . ." Here she said a complicated sentence in Polish that meant "There are no pickles at the egg library."

Zbig and Sister Wanda went off into another gale of laughter.

Sister Wanda spluttered out, "That dictionary is a hazardous muddle of incomprehensibility. Unless you really wanted to talk to Mister Sienkiewicz about pickles and egg libraries."

Zbig wiped his eyes with a napkin. "Oh, this is what I

love about Americans—you always make me laugh. And please, call me Zbig." He signaled the waiter to bring more sourdough toast and some chocolate pudding to the table. "This cheers me up a lot. I was sitting here thinking about the eight-week ride I am about to take with a man in a rooster suit, and I was getting very depressed."

"You're really gonna go on the ride with that rooster fella?" Jeremiah asked.

Zbig gave a regretful shrug. "I called my manager, and it seems the rooster man is very excited about winning. At least, we think he is—he hasn't said anything anyone understands yet except 'cock-a-doodle-doo!' Nonetheless, I said I would ride across the United States with the contest winner, and that is what I will do. I always keep my word." He reached gloomily for a piece of toast. "I guess we should have put a clause in the contract forbidding anyone dressed like a barnyard animal to enter." He chewed contemplatively for a while, then asked, "You know what the saddest part is?"

"What?" asked Griffin.

"We made up this contest so I could get to know the United States and learn about American bicycling. I was thinking of starting a bike-racing school somewhere out here, but I wanted to tour your country with a native, someone who knew the best, loveliest places for bicycling, before I made up my mind. Now I am going to spend eight weeks in an unfamiliar country with a rooster man. I don't even know if he's going to talk to me or crow and cackle the whole time." He whuffed a sad puff of air through his blond mustache. "What bad luck."

What good luck! thought Bicycle. "I've just biked across the whole United States!" she exclaimed. "I can tell you about some great places to start up a bike-racing school. There's the Continental Divide in Colorado, and fields of sunflowers in Kansas as far as the eye can see."

Zbig said, "Oh, sunflowers. That sounds marvelous. Maybe you can draw me a map and I can try to go visit the sunflower fields on my ride with the rooster man." He looked as though it physically pained him to say that. He took another bite of sourdough. "Maybe it will not be all bad. Only mostly bad."

Bicycle immediately started riffling through her pack for her collection of maps. She got out her pencil to circle the best places to see. Griffin made her mark a big X on the town of Green Marsh. Chef Marie asked the waiter to bring over an oversized postcard of all the SlowDown Café locations. Sister Wanda assured Zbig, "You won't regret taking this trip. Our country really is lovely. Across every state line, a new experience. Big cities, tiny towns. Rivers. Mountains."

"Fields," said Miss Monet-Grubbink, spilling hot chili on her lap.

"Deserts," said Dr. Alvarado.

"Farms," said Chef Marie.

"Kind people," said Bicycle.

"And fried pies," said Jeremiah.

The whole group chatted about beautiful places and bicycle adventures until the night grew long and they were yawning more than talking. Dr. Alvarado and the Monet-Grubbinks left for the airport to catch their red-eye flight to Molrania, and Chef Marie bid the rest of them a fond *au revoir*, recommending they get in touch to plan another slow feast soon. Zbig's manager eventually came in to lead him to his hotel, reminding the famous racer that he had to be at the Golden Gate Bridge to begin his historic ride at seven in the morning.

Zbig folded up the maps and the oversized postcard, tucked them into his pocket, clicked his heels together, and bowed once more to each person at the table. "Such a pleasure to have met you all. You have given me hope for my journey. *Dobranoc*. Good night." He waved and left them to last of the pudding.

After he had gone, Bicycle gazed around the table at Sister Wanda, Jeremiah, and Clunk (and Griffin). As she did, an idea began to form. Once the idea formed, it grew wheels and started rolling along fast in her mind.

Bicycle arrived by herself at the Golden Gate Bridge bright and early the next day. Sister Wanda was taking her time and admiring the scenery. While Bicycle waited for her, the rooster man pedaled up. He had taken off his rooster mask and replaced it with an aerodynamic helmet that fit over his face with a shiny yellow beak and a red cock's comb on top. He pulled up next to Bicycle, clucking to himself, bouncing up and down with excitement. Bicycle tried to avoid making eye contact, but she couldn't help but stare. Even his very expensive, skinny racing bike had rooster feathers glued to it. She looked a little more closely at the racing bike. It seemed oddly familiar. Then she noticed that the feathers glued to it were actually crafted from small sponges, and she recognized the rider.

"Mr. Spim!" she said.

The flabby president of Spim's Splendid Sponges was the man tucked tightly inside the rooster suit.

"What are you doing here? And why on earth are you dressed as a rooster?"

Mr. Spim said, "Hush now, mum's the word, my intrepid young colleague! I'm here to set a new world's record!" He glanced around and saw they were alone for the moment. "You see, when I met you on the path that fine spring day, you stirred my inspiration. My adventuring spirit reawakened as I pictured you biking to California. I said to myself, 'Horatio Spim, what are you doing with your life? Selling sponges, is that all there is left for you?' And I had a flash of insight. I may have set some records as an adventurer in my well-funded youth, but neither I nor anyone else has ever set a single record while dressed like a rooster!" He looked very pleased with himself and fluffed his feathers. "I got sponsorship money from the International Chicken Council."

Bicycle tried to understand. "So you're going to bike across the country dressed like a rooster to set a new world's record for biking across the country while dressed like a rooster?"

He tapped his beak with a wing tip. "On the nose, my little egg. Quite right. But please, don't tell anyone yet—if word gets out now, other people will start doing the same thing, swimming the English Channel dressed like a rooster, climbing Mount Everest dressed like a rooster, and so on. There won't be quite so much sponsorship money to go around." He clucked again.

Bicycle was at a loss for words. Happily, she was relieved of the responsibility of saying anything when Sister Wanda rolled up, followed by Jeremiah's van, followed by Zbig.

"*Dzień dobry!* Good morning!" Zbig greeted them with a wide grin. "It is so nice to run into you once more. Are you leaving today on your next adventure, too?"

"We certainly are, if you'll have us," said Bicycle.

"Have you what?" Zbig cocked his head, not understanding.

"I asked Sister Wanda last night if we have to get back to the Mostly Silent Monastery right away, but since Brother Otto's in charge for now, we don't have to get to D.C. until September," Bicycle started to explain.

Sister Wanda chimed in, "The Silence and Shushing Festival doesn't begin until the end of the summer, so we are free to cycle home."

Jeremiah said, "Bicycle talked to me 'n' Griffin about her idea last night, too, and we figgered we gotta get back to Green Marsh one way or another. I tell you what—this ol' van ain't much faster than a bicycle."

Clunk's handlebars stuck out of the passenger-seat window and Griffin added, "This ol' van might not even be as fast as a bicycle."

"So," Bicycle said, "like I said, if you'll have us . . ."

"Oh!" Zbig's face lit up like a lighthouse as he understood their offer. "You mean . . . you would . . . come with me? Show me the sights? Ride by my side? I would be honored and happy if you would join me." He eyed the clucking man in the rooster suit. "Join, that is, us. You have no idea how much your company would mean. Shall we start?"

Jeremiah carefully shifted his van into drive while the four cyclists started pedaling together across the soaring red bridge. Mr. Spim, despite his costume, rode rather well. Bicycle was happy for him. He had clearly been training since the last time she had seen him on the other side of the country. She thought he might actually have a chance to bike across the United States without turning into a puddle of sweat first.

Zbig turned to Bicycle and said, "You know, I never did answer your question about whether we have a chance to be friends. Let me tell you about myself and maybe you can judge. I like biking, of course, and I prefer to be around relatively silent people who are good at listening. I love to eat pretty much everything. Also, I'll tell you this: every friend I've ever made in my life, I made while we spent time together on the seats of our bicycles. Maybe it's strange, but to be honest with you, I don't know how to make friends any other way."

The Fortune blinked at Bicycle. Probability that Sister Wanda was right about the whole process of making friends involving a lot of luck: 99.973%.

Sister Wanda rode up behind them, leaned over, and poked Zbig in the ribs. "First thing you should do, you should start teaching the girl how to speak proper Polish. Maybe you can start with some correct questions about friends or friendship. No more zebras going up anyone's noses."

Zbig nodded seriously. He turned to Bicycle and

whispered loudly, "Want to learn how to say in Polish, 'Let's stick a zebra up the rooster's nose'?"

Bicycle laughed. Sister Wanda sighed. The rooster cackled. The Fortune blinked. Jeremiah and Griffin started to sing. And the little band started east.

AUTHOR'S NOTE

Bicycle's adventure includes many true-to-life details from my own 1996 bicycle trip from Washington, D.C., to San Francisco. I've done my best to faithfully describe the landscapes and state-line signs, and the way it feels to ride a bike across the United States. Some other details—like the ability of a girl with a bike to wander into Churchill Downs on the day of the Kentucky Derby without a ticket—well, I only wish those were true.

ACKNOWLEDGMENTS

Writing a novel has much in common with cross-country bicycling. Both can be long, lonely slogs that leave you tremendously grateful for the kind people you meet along the way. (And both require lots and lots and lots of candy bars, cookies, and pie.)

I'm so lucky to have been welcomed as a novelist by my editor, Margaret Ferguson, and my literary agent, Ammi-Joan Paquette. Thanks also to the entire Erin Murphy Literary Agency gang and the Emu's Debuts team—too bad there's not a word yet for old friends who've just met. A big hug to just about the whole town of East Longmeadow, especially the ELPL librarians and my MOMS Club, for sharing my excitement on this book-publishing journey.

And I don't know where I'd be without the support and love of my family and friends—lost in Kentucky?